No Direction Home

# No Direction Home

## Marisa Silver

W. W. Norton & Company | New York London

"Shooting Star," by Paul Bernard Rodgers, © 1974 (Renewed)
WB MUSIC CORP. and BADCO MUSIC INC. All Rights
Administered by WB MUSIC CORP. All Rights Reserved.
Used by Permission Warner Bros. Publications U.S. Inc.,
Miami, FL. 33014.

For information about permission to reproduce selections from
this book, write to Permissions, W. W. Norton & Company,
Inc., 500 Fifth Avenue, New York, NY 10110

Manufacturing by The Courier Companies, Inc.
Book design by Barbara M. Bachman
Production manager: Amanda Morrison

Library of Congress Cataloging-in-Publication Data

Silver, Marisa.
   No direction home / Marisa Silver.—1st ed.
      p. cm.
   ISBN 0-393-05823-9 (hardcover)
   1. Boys—Fiction. 2. Teenage girls—Fiction. 3. Illegal
aliens—Fiction. 4. Loss (Psychology)—Fiction. 5. Fatherless
families—Fiction. 6. Paternal deprivation—Fiction. 7. Los
Angeles (Calif.)—Fiction. I. Title.
   PS3619.I55N6 2005
   813'.54—dc22
                                        2005000933

W. W. Norton & Company, Inc.
500 Fifth Avenue, New York, N.Y. 10110
www.wwnorton.com

W. W. Norton & Company, Ltd.
Castle House, 75/76 Wells Street, London W1T 3QT


1 2 3 4 5 6 7 8 9 0

*For Ken*

With thanks to Henry Dunow and Jill Bialosky

for their wisdom and support.

No Direction Home

1.

*Blindness will be like this.* Will closes his eyes. He breathes deeply and settles into the darkness, testing it out. It isn't blackness. There is gray and red and brown. And there is texture to the darkness, too; it is a nubby plain, an ant's landscape of small rises and dips. But maybe he is seeing a sighted person's darkness, a darkness still shot through with traces of light and color and images of what he has seen moments before, when his eyes were open. He squeezes his eyes tighter, tensing all his face muscles so that the hues and textures disappear into a blacker blackness.

"What are you doing with your eyes?"

It is Ethan, Will's ten-year-old twin. Not wearing his glasses, never wearing his glasses, although how he gets along without them Will doesn't know and can only jealously imagine.

"Nothing," Will says.

"It's weird," Ethan says.

Will sits on the floor of their bedroom, a book on his lap. He pushes his heavy glasses up the bridge of his nose. Ethan sits on one of the twin beds, staring out of the window as the wind whips the dried leaves on the ground into exhausted circles. His body stiffens for a moment as he leans expectantly toward the window, then slides off the bed.

"Where are you going?" Will says. His skin prickles with uncertainty. Ethan's decisions are sudden and impulsive, and Will carries with him the constant worry of being left behind. Ethan doesn't answer. It is his habit to ignore direct questions, as though he finds it irritating to be pinned down by anything so tedious as an answer. He is like their father in this way—sealed up. The two seem as if they've rejected the set of rules that Will and his mother have accepted, the one that requires you to answer to your name or move out of the way when someone passes by you. Will often feels that his brother and father are hiding things, but he can never figure out what those things might be. He imagines that his father's secrets are about work or money or something having to do with the whispered talks he and Will's mother have in their bedroom at night, their voices rising occasionally to penetrate the wall to Will and Ethan's bedroom before he hears one of them hush the other, or a door open and slam shut, or the worst and most scary sound: silence. But what could his brother's secrets be? Don't Ethan and

Will live virtually the same life? Go to the same school? Play with the same fourth-graders? Make quarterly visits to the same eye specialist? It maddens him that Ethan has managed to integrate mystery into his life when Will feels as obvious as a blank sheet of paper.

Ethan kneels down and reaches for a sweater that lies curled in an inside-out ball halfway underneath the bed.

"Where are you going?" Will repeats.

"Nowhere," Ethan says, pulling the sweater over his head without bothering to shake off the dust balls that have collected on it.

"C'mon, Ethan," Will says, frustrated by the needy whine in his own voice. He wishes he did not care so much about Ethan, but he needs his brother to see what he cannot.

"The dog," Ethan says, sighing, as though finally giving in to a toddler's demands. The heat of shame spreads through Will's chest. Why is he always the last one to understand?

During the previous weeks Nelsie, their burled mutt, lumbered through the house, bloated and slow. She was unwilling to come to Will or Ethan, even for clandestine treats of hamburger or chicken skin dangled below the kitchen table. Will found a cardboard box that contained his and Ethan's tenth-birthday present from his grandparents (matchbox cars and plastic track, which they are too old for, but their grandmother is sick, and they've barely ever met their grandfather, who signed the card Vincent, turning himself into a stranger). Will lined the box with old baby blankets he found in a plastic storage container in the garage, then put the box in the basement by the furnace. He led Nelsie down the wooden stairs again and again, regardless of the dog's rotund reluctance. "Look," he whispered into her velvet ear. "Here's the place for your babies." He pushed on her head so that her wet nose rubbed against the blankets. He wanted her to remember so that when it was her time, some instinct would send her in search of the scent of tiny boys and baby detergent, drawing her down to this cradle.

But now she's made another choice.

It is late March, and the air still snaps with the leftover Missouri winter. Will sucks in the tangled smells of damp ground and decaying leaves that lie uncovered since the snowmelt, and he follows his brother from the house toward the woods behind it. The trees stand like a dark army, their branches crisscrossed lances that forbid entrance. The boys each wear their new binoculars. "For seeing what's hard to see," their father had said when they opened their individual gift boxes. Will, pushing his heavy, necessary glasses up the bridge of his nose as he runs after Ethan, wonders whether the gift was a reprimand. His father is an astronomer and has spent a lifetime peering into the dark corners of the universe waiting to discover bodies that have not yet been seen. Will knows that his father is uncomfortable about his and his brother's impairment, knows that somehow the difference between the distant life his father can see with a high-powered telescope and the ordinary, earthbound objects Will and Ethan cannot see even with their naked eyes separates father and sons in some way he cannot name.

Today the forest is thick with the tangy smells of wet

leaves and moss. Fallen trees lie across the foot-worn trails like pickup sticks. Their trunks are rotten and soft. Ethan runs gracefully through the thicket. He negotiates the snags and snarls of undergrowth as if the geography beneath his feet is imprinted in his bones. But when Will, running to keep up, misjudges a tree stump, he capsizes, belly flopping on top of the knobby outcropping before rolling to the ground. He loses his wind and, for a moment, feels what it must be like to be dead: time hurtling forward while he remains suspended in one instantaneously historical second. When he finally regains his breath, he looks up, hoping Ethan has not seen his mistake. But worse, his brother has disappeared.

Will pulls his hands out of the muck on the ground. Two paws emerge, covered with mud and twigs. Is that a worm crawling across his knuckles—that soft, white, stringy thing? His glasses have fallen off and everything looks filmy, as though he is seeing through a dirty window. The outlines of one object bleed into another. He rubs his hands on his jeans, then raises them to his face and inhales. Pitch, loam, the smell of . . . rosemary? Or maybe the smell is of a wild onion, blooming like a tart secret inside the earth. His nose is his keen guide. He can tell which of his family members is home the moment he enters the kitchen door just by the fugue of smells that meet him: his mother's rosewater perfume, his brother's briny sweat. Only his father has no remarkable odor, but his presence fills the house with an awkward uncertainty that Will can sense on his skin.

Will squints and sees the feathery shapes of bare branches in the near distance. And then—there! Movement in the trees. He pats the earth around him wildly until his hands feel the cold plastic of his glasses. He rubs the lenses against his shirt, then pushes the frames onto his face. The world falls together, a shaken kaleidoscope coalescing into a pattern. Now he can see the narrow ravine worn down by years of spy games. And there are Ethan's fresh footprints stamped in the mud.

By the time Will catches up with his brother, Ethan is crouched by the opening of the old stove. Will drops to his knees. The seat of his pants is already damp from the fall, and now wetness soaks through to his legs. The combination of cold and humiliation makes him shiver.

"What is it?" he asks.

"Shhh," Ethan hisses. His thinner-lensed glasses are streaked with dirt. This would make Will's already downy vision completely useless. But dirt, like the boys' shared disability, is only a minor irritation to Ethan.

Will pulls back a clump of tall weeds to see more clearly into the mouth of the old stove, a four-foot-high brick cube. Sloppily applied mortar runs in thick, uneven rivulets between the rectangles of dark rust. One side of the cube is open, and the cavity is charred and peeling. The brothers have invented countless tales to explain the stove's displacement. Sometimes the stove is the only surviving artifact of a pioneer home that burned down. Other times they are convinced that a mountain man camped out on this very spot year after year and built the stove to dry his beaver pelts. And now it has a use that none of their fantasies have assigned it: There, where there might have been loaves of crude bread puffing up, sending out a sweet, doughy smell, squirm six miniscule, verminous puppies.

They are terrible-looking things—hairless and slick with viscous wetness. Their tails are as thin and pink as rat tails. They lie piled on top of one another like balled-up socks, translucent lids closed over their eyes. Will can almost taste the iron in the blood that still speckles their bald bodies.

"Sick," Ethan drawls appreciatively. "She had them so fast. They must have just dropped out of her like turds."

The boys giggle nervously, then fall silent as they stare at the puppies. Will stands and looks beyond the stove, deeper into the woods. "Nelsie?" he calls, cupping his hands around his mouth. "Nel-*seeee!*"

She does not return. And though the boys wait for nearly an hour, they see no sign of her. The sun, which has brought intermittent warmth through the shifting leaves, now disappears entirely. Will is hungry and cramped with cold. The puppies begin to squirm furiously. Their heads poke up, their rheumy eyes scanning their close horizon, opaque noses twitching for a clue.

"They're blind, you know," Ethan says. "At birth. They can't see a thing. They probably don't even know their mother's gone."

"They're hungry," Will says.

"Let's take them home."

"What about Nelsie?"

"She left them here," Ethan says.

"Maybe she'll come back."

"She *left* them here," Ethan repeats witheringly. "She doesn't want them anymore."

Knowing how much more his brother grasps of the world, Will can do nothing but accept Ethan's blunt view. Although what he wants to say is that if they wait just a little bit longer, Nelsie will return. It is unnatural for a mother to leave her babies, isn't it?

Ethan removes his sweater and lays it on the ground. Carefully he reaches into the stove's opening and picks up a puppy, placing it on the material. Will removes his own jacket and follows his brother's example. The puppies feel like half-filled water balloons in his hands. Their rubbery skin and soft bones slip and slide between his fingers. Ethan walks back toward the house, carrying his bundle. The light is low. Will follows, struggling to differentiate between rock and ground. But he can see the fluorescent stripes of Ethan's sneakers and carefully matches his brother step for step.

Later that night the six palm-size, nearly pellucid dogs lie tangled in a box next to the basement furnace. In the kitchen the boys' mother demonstrates how to heat milk to lukewarm on the stove, then how to siphon the liquid into medicine droppers. Caroline says the nurses taught her how to do this when the boys' premature suck was too weak to pull milk from a bottle.

"I pumped the milk out of my breast and used the droppers, just like this," she says, holding the glass tube by the black rubber handle and letting loose a wobbly tear of liquid into the pan.

"Oh, vomit," Ethan says, screwing up his face.

"You're alive, aren't you?" Caroline says, brushing her

mass of dark curly hair from her eyes with a forearm. She smiles wanly at some memory Will cannot fathom. Their birth? Or maybe the moment she was told that they could barely see.

The boys decide to sleep in the cellar with the dogs. They bring down sleeping bags and extra blankets to ward off the chill of the concrete floor. Caroline stays with them as they lie on their bellies, heads resting in their hands. All three are mesmerized by the puppies' soft breath, the intermittent twitches of their dog dreams.

The phone rings.

"Daddy," Caroline says, getting up, sighing heavily.

"Tell him about the dogs," Ethan says.

"I will."

His father will be interested in the dogs, Will thinks excitedly. He will tell them curious facts about puppies or biology. He might even compliment Will on his box-and-blanket cradle. But he will not want to hold the dogs. No, his father won't want to do that, and Will must remember not to ask him to and risk the discomfort of his father's mute rejection. Because that is what his father is like, not really angry ever, just silent, and always disappearing even when he is there. He is a subtraction. Zero take away one. "Tell him to come home soon," Will calls out anxiously as his mother climbs the stairs.


*The boys do not hear* Caroline's return. She watches them as they lie motionless, transfixed by the dogs. She wonders if it is possible not to tell them the news. Is there some way to skip beyond this moment and arrive at a place where it has already happened and a time when pain and confusion are softened into a stew of bearable sadness?

"Listen," she says. "There's something I need to tell you."

The boys crane their necks towards her. She can tell they are impatient, eager to get back to their vigil. Neither wears his glasses. She imagines how indistinct she must look to them, her voice and her raft of hair the only characteristics that confirm her identity as their mother. They both have learned to trust a world they can barely see.

"Dad's not coming back," she says.

The boys' faces register nothing. She realizes she has missed the point. Her words don't convey the message that Frank is not simply late, delayed at the observatory, or staying for one of his increasingly frequent overnights, but that he is finally, fully, gone. His passivity, his unbearable silence in the face of her relentless campaign to pull him out of the vortex of himself into the messy, banal life of his family has finally, after all these long years, resulted in an act.

He said "Carrie, I have to not come back," as if coming back had been something he needed to make a concerted decision to do each and every night of their married life. And then he thanked her.

"Thank you?" she said, incredulous.

"I don't know what the right thing is to say in a situation like this," he said.

"Situation," she repeated, her mind still trying to draw the fuzzy facts of the conversation into focus.

"I'm no good to any of you," he said.

"Fuck you," she said. But her vehemence was mitigated

by tears, which had sprung forth at the sound of his voice as if they had been standing at attention these past months like eager volunteers ready to be called into action. She knew he was right. His unhappiness was deep, pervasive. The palliatives of wife and children made his discomfort all the more pronounced. The crowd and need of them only added to his feeling that he would forever fail at the fundamental task of relating. *She should have known*, is what she said to herself as they both listened to one another breathe. And of course she knew from the very first that he was a man for whom the effort to *be* among people was painful at best. When she was an undergraduate, it had felt like such victory to draw the handsome, antisocial scientist away from his telescopes and into her bed. She had blithely, stupidly ignored the fact that every conversation was not a conversation at all but her voice filling silences as she tried to infuse him with her life. And when she did ask him about himself—*Do you like your father? Do you love me?*—Frank would wince and the words would come out as if dredged up from some thick, sticky tar in his soul. *Carrie, why do I have to . . . say things? I don't know what to say.*

She knew no words for it then, but over the years she bought him books on depression, found names of university psychologists who would help him at a discount. But Frank does not understand himself as a disease. He has lived with his particular heaviness all his life. It is a fact of him no more mutable than the arrangement of the stars.

Facing her boys now, Caroline begins to shake. She tries to hide the rack of her body, rubbing her arms to make it appear she is cold.

"He's gone," she says. "He's not going to live with us anymore."

"Why?" Will says.

"You shouldn't fight with him anymore," Ethan says accusingly.

Of course they've heard, she thinks. The house is tiny, the cheap walls no thicker than a few sheets of paper. They have heard her begging him. *What's wrong with you? Where are you? Why don't you talk?*—her questions frantic and increasingly angry attempts to fix him.

*I can't.*

*Can't what?*

*I just can't.*

They had argued their life down to these essentials. Can and cannot. And he couldn't. Do it. Handle the incessant needs of children. Respond to the yearnings of an injured wife. Be present to earthly things. And she is an idiot to imagine that her marriage could have been improved through sheer will—the way, sitting in the bleachers on game day of Little League, she believes that it is only a failure of her silent urging that stands in the way of Will, for once, catching a ball.

How much have her boys hidden from her this last year as they continued to go to school, get into arguments about who was touching whom in the backseat of the car, as they persisted in annoying her with penis jokes? Has it been her folly to think their near-blindness renders them without any other senses? Is she no better than those strangers who yell in their presence as though their ears can somehow make up for their disastrous eyes?

"He'll come back, right?" Will asks. He palms the floor for his glasses, as though their correction will allow him to understand better.

Ethan stands, letting the sleeping bag fall to his feet. He wears boxer shorts. Suddenly his choice of boxers over briefs seems dangerously assertive to her. She wants him back in his Superman underpants. She wants that gently swelling tummy instead of this flat belly, these prematurely appearing muscles. She wants everything to go back.

Her legs give out, and she sinks down to the bottom stair. She should go to her sons and take them in her arms. But her gesture will cement this new truth of their lives, and she isn't ready for that.

"I don't miss him," Ethan says.

"It's too soon to miss him," she says.

"Are you sad?" Will says.

"Of course I'm sad."

"Then why don't you cry?"

In the hours afterward the boys ask her many questions that are ultimately the same question: Why did he go? She gives them patient answers, knowing she will forever fail at the task of making sense of what has happened. Finally the boys fall asleep, choosing the reassuring familiarity of their beds rather than the sleeping bags and the cold basement. She feeds the puppies one more time, then climbs the stairs to the kitchen. The house's stillness frightens her. She puts on a coat and a pair of fleece slippers and walks out the front door. The yard smells ripe and wet. Another month and she will wake to the scritch of squirrels and chipmunks digging for seeds. Soon, too, there will be a population of daffodils enlivening the small, uninspiring yard with their butter and froth. She planted the bulbs that first year of her marriage. Frank objected to planting flowers in land they did not own, but Caroline felt this was exactly the reason *to* plant the flowers—because it showed a faith in whimsy and unpredictability. *Fuck rational!* she'd said, gleefully roasting the very foundation of her new husband's ordered world. Frank twisted his face as if freshly reminded that he had performed the one inexplicable act of his life by marrying Caroline Rafallo, an Italian girl from a valley east of Los Angeles, who laughed and cried and exclaimed at the beauty of any normal day in a way he found perplexing.

She had fled California for the Midwest, misunderstanding the place to be a benign, deliriously empty slate on which she could rewrite herself and be rid of her own broken family. But of course, she thinks now, sighing and watching a cloud of steam from her mouth evaporate in the night, this was a ridiculous assumption. Look! Here is her past showing up again for a repeat performance. She laughs softly and gazes past her front yard, across the road. It is too late for traffic, too late for the comforting glow of television blue to light up the windows across the street. She is alone.

The strangest thing about Frank's departure is its familiarity. How easily she feels the self-hatred that comes hand in hand with yearning, the confusion of missing someone who has wounded you. Her body settles into these feelings as though they are old clothes not worn for years that she has dug out of the back of her closet, clothes that have waited patiently, knees and elbows formed to her body's particular curves. She remembers herself at twelve and thirteen, when her father would park at the curb and honk the horn of his Oldsmobile station wagon too loudly for the drowsy street. Her chest would pound and her soul grow numb at the same time, a paradox of that loathsome wanting. And her mother would poke her head into the bedroom and tell Caroline to go to him. *He's your father, after all.* Biology superseding injury.

She remembers, too, her mother's unnatural calm in the face of her own marital disaster. Eleanor Rafallo did not adhere to the rules of bad novels and women's magazine articles—she never fell apart, never spent days in a bathrobe or nights with a drink. Instead she continued to tend her cuticles weekly with her orange stick and wear stockings in summer, offering her only daughter no adequate role model for rage. Will Caroline be seemly, too, in the face of this new abandonment? Or will she demonstrate for her sons how easily and utterly a person can collapse from the inside out so that, when they feel their own souls shrivel under the weight of enduring sadness, they will know how to behave? It will be painful to watch the boys begin to fashion the carapace around their hearts, awful to watch them take to loss. Well, she supposes they know how to fold deficit into their lives better than she did as a child, better than she does now.

*They were born* eight weeks early, each no bigger than a Cornish game hen. At first there was concern about whether they would survive—their lungs were not fully formed and they were immediately placed on ventilators and pumped with drugs. Later, when their durability was reasonably assured, the aperture of worry narrowed down to the details. Days were full of crises: Ethan's collapsed lung, Will's fever, a murmur detected in one of their walnut-size hearts. Frank approached the touch-and-go ambiguity of those early days with scientific rigor. He devised two progress charts. Each day, after conferring with doctors and nurses, he would plot points on the individual graphs corresponding to each baby, then draw a line connecting the dots. Some days the boys were ascending in health. Other days they leveled off in uncertain plateaus. There were dips—an infection in Ethan's hand at the site of the IV, Will's spiking blood pressure—but these were short-lived and resolved into optimistic rising trajectories. Caroline was unconsoled by the logic of these diagrams. She imagined her babies' deaths continually those first weeks. She felt the sense of loss and subsequent desolation so completely that she would break down in tears. Frank, mystified by her illogical grief, tried to comfort her with his charts. She nodded dutifully, trying to form the connection between the two lines and the two small bodies sleeping restively under plastic domes.

At three months the babies were released from the hospital. Once back home, Ethan and Will proved surprisingly strong. They ate and grew, turned over and grasped objects at the appropriate times, adjusted for their prematurity. Ethan was the heartier-looking twin, with doughy folds of fat quickly appearing at his wrists and underarms. Will remained thin. His bones poked at his skin like caged animals. His veins were visible canals. Caroline worried for him especially; he seemed so fragile, so nearly not present. But the doctors assured her that he was just as healthy as his ruddy brother.

And they *are* healthy, she reminds herself now, as she bends down to push a daffodil bulb more deeply into the earth. Except for the eyes. Both boys were struck by a virus in utero. The diminution of vision will progress at an indeterminate rate, according to the doctors. The boys might become blind in adulthood, or they might not. There is no way to predict what they will or will not see in their lives.

Ethan, a confident child, is unperturbed by the defect of his eyes. There are times when he rips off his glasses in frustration and bounds into the next game or adventure with faultless assurance, as though the glasses, not his eyes, are the impediment. But not Will. Will is an agglomeration of angles and bones. Caroline can still wrap her hand around his upper arm, thumb overlapping forefinger. The coordination of his separate parts seems to require thought. When he runs, his lower half works to keep up with his torso. He negotiates his days with edgy watchfulness. Caroline always has the uncomfortable impression that when he listens to her, he can see inside her brain. She scrolls hungrily through her sons' characteristics, wondering which traits will protect them now.

She is terribly cold. The thought strikes her well after the fact, and she is suddenly shivering uncontrollably. She remembers this too—how, when her own father left, her emotions seemed to lag behind her like a slow dog. She walks around to the back of the house, trying to stay warm.

In all the years she's lived here she has never gone into the woods alone. Occasionally she agrees to accompany the boys on their adventures. Holding her hands, they proudly show her the fixed geography of the forest: the grand doorway to their arboreal palace is located where two pines bend toward each other, their Indian hideout is beneath an ash tree that has fallen across two rocks, creating a dark cave that fits two crouching boys. They respect these spaces and criticize her when she absentmindedly walks through a "wall" or breaks down a "door." They are drunk with her presence, old enough to be wary of holding her hand in public but still young enough to be uncertain about holding their secrets from her. They yearn for validation in her gaze. *Mom, look over here! Mom, look at me!* But the moment they hear Frank's pickup scratch up the gravel driveway, they tear out from the brambles, forgetting their imaginary boundaries and their mother entirely, running headlong toward a man who greets them with customary surprise, as if, during his day, they've slipped his mind. "Okay now," Frank says, peeling the boys off him like wet clothing, looking past their heads at some indeterminate place where he would be safer.

Now Caroline steps carefully between two trees. A foot lands on a root and her ankle twists slightly as she rights herself. She takes another step, then another. The twigs snap under her. She imagines herself moving farther and farther into the forest, losing all sense of direction, not caring where she is or where she is going. But when she thinks of her boys waking up and finding her bed empty, her breath catches in her chest. She turns and quickly retraces her steps until she is safe on the small lawn. It is awful to be all they have left. She has to be careful now. She cannot go missing, too.

*Will lies awake.* He hears his mother's steps crunch-crunching toward the house and then the squeal and bang of the screen door. He cannot sleep, cannot stop his heart from racing or his mind from spinning with this terrible truth: He knows why his father has left. He knows it is all his fault.

Two nights earlier a comet crossed the sky. During the weeks leading up to the event, his father was as excited as Will had ever seen him. He brought home maps and showed the boys the route the comet would take. He told them how close the comet would come to certain planets, and of cataclysms that would occur if the course was altered by a fraction. Will was excited, dizzy with his father's attention, with the way he looked right at Will when he spoke. He had always felt as though his father was elsewhere, but now his father was talking to him! Asking him questions! Will, what do you think of . . . Will, what do you imagine would happen if . . . ?

The night of the event, the three lay under blankets on the back lawn. The boys wore jackets and hats. Caroline had made them a thermos of hot chocolate.

"Show me Polaris," Frank said.

Ethan raised his arm and pointed to the obvious star, drawing his father's approval.

"Ursa Major."

"Easy," Will said, counting off the stars. "Give me something harder."

"I'm working up to it," Frank teased. "Virgo," he said.

The boys were silent as they scanned the sky, then Ethan's arm shot up. "There!" he said.

"Good boy," Frank said.

"My turn!" Will cried eagerly.

"Ursa Minor," Frank said.

Will searched for it.

"It's obvious," Ethan said witheringly.

"Shhh," Frank warned.

Will began to see less and less. The brightness at the sides of his vision was fogged and the darkness seemed too dark, as if someone were sliding black construction paper over his eyes.

"Come on," Ethan said, impatiently. "Let me do it."

"It's not a particularly hard one, Will," Frank said.

"I know, I know," Will muttered. His heart pounded. He tried to remember the night sky at this time of the year, tried to pull up all the information he'd learned on his own in order to please his father. But he couldn't remember, and his eyes betrayed him.

"I can't see it," he admitted finally, defeated.

Frank sat up. "You mean you don't know where it is?" he said, his voice tightening.

"It's just . . . it's too dark," Will said.

"What do you see?" Frank said.

"Clouds," Will said. "Black. Or gray," he corrected, trying to better the situation.

"Clouds," Frank repeated.

"It's a cloudy night."

"No," Frank said. "It's relatively clear."

Will could hear his father's voice deflate and knew it was over, this strange day when he felt like the right kind of boy in a world that was somehow *righter* than it had ever been before.

And now, not even a week later, his father is gone.

2.

*Eleanor Rafallo is missing.* Vincent wakes up from a burdened, dreamless sleep to find his wife's side of the bed empty, the blanket pulled back neatly and the sheets smoothed as if by a hotel maid bent on obscuring the bed's history. His search of the small house in North Hollywood takes only a minute. She has not gotten up to use the bathroom herself (it's been months since he trusted her forgetful mind with this task). She is not in the kitchen or the living room. Finally he notices that the front door is ajar. His heart races as he imagines her dead in the middle of the street, mowed down by some speeding car. When he swings the door open, he is relieved to find her sitting on the cracked slate steps of the low porch.

"Eleanor?" he says, too loudly, but his heart is racing, spurred on by a cocktail of fear and guilt and bourbon.

Her nightgown stretches tautly over her knees. Light from the porch shines through the pyramid of cloth, outlining her legs, once slender, now flaccid from lack of exercise. Skin falls away from her bones like sails. The night-blooming jasmine she planted like a lace collar around the front of the house forty years ago cloaks her with its mesmerizing scent.

At first, he thinks she's simply followed a restless urge to take in the night air, the distant sounds of traffic, the steady hum of the resting Valley. He is heartened to think that such reality still compels her.

"Eleanor?" he repeats, softly this time.

But she doesn't turn to him. Instead, he hears the thread of her flutelike hum wind its way into the night. He sits next to her, remembering the way her voice used to meander up and down an unpredictable melody when she sat on the edge of their bed, braiding their daughter's hair. He'd been awed by the efficiency with which she reined Caroline's scrambled tresses into neat plaits, by how their otherwise willful and unruly child stood in front of her mother dutifully, hands at her sides, conforming to Eleanor's religion of order.

But he realizes Eleanor is not humming now. She is having a conversation.

"Did you send my letter to Santa?" she asks, her voice full of childish worry and expectation. She nods at the silent reply, then cranes her neck to look upward, as though following the invisible trail of her wishes.

He takes her hand in his but does not have the energy yet to bear her back into the house. The two sit quietly on the steps, lost to the sounds of the night.

*A month later* she escapes again. This time he has gone to bed drunk and has slept through the noise of her flight. He wakes to a phone call from the fire station two blocks away.

"We have your wife here," says a man who identifies himself as Sergeant Lopez.

"What?" Barely awake, Vincent's insides buzz with adrenalized confusion. Sergeant? Has she committed a crime? Is she dead? But when the noise in his head subsides he hears the man's gentle chuckle.

"Yeah. One of our guys was getting groceries at Vons and saw her walking down the street. She remembered her phone number right off the bat." Lopez chuckles as if praising the prodigious accomplishments of his own child. "My mother did the times tables when her mind started to go. Couldn't balance a checkbook all her life and then she starts doing the twelves without missing a beat. In English, too!"

When Vincent arrives at the station, Eleanor is wearing an oversize fireman's jacket over her thin nightgown. The tendons in her feet rise and fall like plucked harp strings as she spins in a circle, showing off her dress-up treasure. The blanket of her long gray hair lifts off her back in the wind of her twirl. The firemen clap, and she smiles a child's proud and shy smile. Vincent feels ashamed in front of these men. They must think he's a fool to have misplaced his own wife.

"Where were you going?" he asks, as they drive the short distance home.

"To the river."

"There is no river anymore," he says. "You know that."

The next day Vincent attaches alarms to the doors and windows. He places a deadbolt at the top of the front door, higher than Eleanor's reach. But three weeks later he is rocked out of his sleep by a drunk-tangled dream, only to find her half of the bed empty. The deadbolt lies open. The kitchen chair sits neatly by the side of the door. He can still see the faint imprint of her flip-flops on the yellow plastic cushion.

Home nursing is not covered by his insurance plan, and there is hardly any chance of making serious money as an actor at this point in his life. He is no longer on the radar of casting directors, and the effort to reengage with his agent would be humiliating and fruitless. On the strength of some old television credits on a show that is inexplicably popular in cable reruns, he manages to get work teaching nights at an acting school on Magnolia. The pay is laughable—he did better on his worst days as a commercial extra—but it is enough to cover a nurse and relieve himself of his evening custodial duties.

He cannot afford the fees charged by the employment agencies, so he places an ad in the *LA Times*. He receives eighty-two calls in a single day. Most applicants cannot speak English. Vincent's Spanish is limited to the few lines he learned playing a Central American dictator in a movie-of-the-week. He can order someone to be killed. He can order someone to light his cigar.

He meets a few of the more likely prospects. They are all female, all pleasant, hopeful women from one or another Latin American country; he can never keep them straight. He tries out two women. One does not last beyond the first night, and the other he sends home a barely respectful hour after she arrives. There is nothing inherently wrong with either woman. They both stand in the kitchen, ducking their heads when he speaks, watching him with anticipation when they think he is not looking at them. He supposes their passivity is a cultural thing, but still, it's unnerving. He becomes overwhelmed by the task of having to think of every exigency the women might encounter so that he can assure Eleanor's safety. What if they answer the phone and she escapes? What if they leave her unattended in the bath and she drowns? How can he admit his brutish secret: that caring for his wife is no different from caring for an infant and that it requires the vigilance of a newly besotted parent, and even he cannot rise to this task? When he turns the women away, he is pained by how easily they accept his rejection.

He second-guesses his decision to hire help. He puts off the acting school until the next series of classes begins, and does not run the ad again. Isn't hiring help the same as abandoning Eleanor? And isn't that the one thing he promised her he would never do again?

He continues to care for his wife. He fetches her the water or crackers she asks for, reads her the historical romances she's always loved, even though her face is a screen that reflects the vacancy beneath it. Many nights he simply sits in a chair by their bed, listening while her mind roams the dense thicket of her past. She cannot remember the way around the kitchen of forty years and accuses him of moving the silverware just to confuse her, but she can remember a certain vein that ran up the back of her mother's leg, or the exact ash blond color of her first doll's hair. These are not facts she ever shared with Vincent when she was well. Their marriage was not intimate in that way; she frowned upon an excess of revelation. When they were young and attended the bottom-tier Hollywood parties they were occasionally invited to, he sensed her disapproval when friends dredged up the dirty laundry of their childhoods as a way of excusing infidelity or drinking or the general dissolution of their dreams. "All that personal business," she'd say on the drives home, brushing invisible dust from her lap.

It is only now, with the onrush of her dementia, that Vincent is actually getting to know his wife better, or at least in more interstitial ways. The disease introduced itself gently over the past five years, then suddenly foisted itself upon her during the last nine months like a pushy party guest at one of those long-ago affairs, standing too close, demanding her attention. Her lifetime is cleaving open, and he is being allowed a glimpse inside the seams and chasms of her past. But when he arranges these new discoveries, expecting them to form a portrait of this woman, this *wife*, hoping they will explain how his life has ended up here, in a house he once fled, caring for a woman who is disappearing as fast as sand through fingers, he is disappointed. As Eleanor unravels her hidden history, he understands that he does not know her or his marriage more emphatically, only more sadly.

Three weeks later Eleanor escapes again, and Vincent realizes he cannot care for her properly on his own. And, if he is honest with himself, he knows he doesn't want to.

Amador Aguilar speaks only a little English, but he looks Vincent in the eye when he shakes his hand and takes a seat at the kitchen table even before Vincent offers it to him. Vincent is suspicious of having a man care for his wife, the term "male nurse" still conjuring boyhood homosexual jokes, but desperation talks him out of his prejudice. He reassures himself that the solidity of Amador's strong hands resting on the marbled Formica tabletop says, *See? I have nothing to hide.*

"Do you have any medical experience?" Vincent asks.

"My wife's mother, she was a . . . I don't know how you say . . . a *curandera*," Amador says. "In my country." Longing runs like a thick stream of honey in his voice.

"No witch doctor," Vincent says. "No *santería*."

"*No entiendo*," Amador says, pointing to his ears in confusion.

Vincent knows he's gotten the country wrong, but does not want to apologize to this man he barely knows. "No crazy potions. No voodoo," he adds.

Amador smiles, but it isn't a smile that begs forgiveness for his shortcomings. Vincent wonders whether the man is sympathetic with Vincent's language problems or coolly derisive of them. The exchange embarrasses Vincent, then makes him uncomfortable, and finally angry, the emotions piling one on top of the other in waves. He wants to send this man away, call him insolent or arrogant, call him a hundred names the man won't understand. He wants to feel as angry toward this man as he does toward his wife's disease and toward himself for feeling his life has become a trap. But Amador is his single prospect, the only one who might release him from the burden of care.

In the week that follows, before classes begin, Vincent observes the new nurse. Amador treats Eleanor with humor and respect, despite her condition. She spits at him, yells at him, squeezes his crotch when she is angry. Amador reacts only by wiping the spit off his cheek, or removing her hand as casually as if he is picking lint off a jacket. Amador is able to master the feat of acting that Vincent can only fake: to be present and not present at the same time. It is the single quality, Vincent has come to realize, that recommends a person to such unrequited duty.

*A month later* Vincent receives a phone call at the acting studio just as he is about to begin his eight o'clock class.

"How did she get away?" he asks, after Amador has explained the situation. He is careful to remove the accusation from his voice. *You lost my wife?* Who is he to accuse? And anyway, he has become reliant on this stranger.

"I take out the garbage," Amador says. "She move so quick. Like *un conejo* . . . a, uh . . . rabbit."

Vincent hears no apology in the man's voice. It galls and mystifies him that Amador does not share his own sense of guilt.

"Is okay," Amador continues calmly. "I go find her now." She would not have had the chance to get far, he says. "She move like waxing floor with her feet." He laughs gently.

"Slide, slide, slide." His laughter reveals his appreciation for her, even for the pathos of her disease. But Vincent is depressed by the image of his wife shuffling along the sidewalks of North Hollywood, never allowing her thonged feet to leave the ground lest she lose contact with earth altogether. He hopes Amador will not suggest he come home to search for her.

"It will not be long, *Señor*," Amador says. "We get her back."

"All right," Vincent says, resisting the urge to thank the man for doing a husband's job. "I'll be home after class."

"Okay, *Señor*," Amador says.

Vincent wonders if the honorific is genuine. Both men know that it will be hours before Vincent makes the slow, liquorous drive home. He returns to his class and engages the students in improvisation exercises. This is the default he resorts to when he runs out of ideas, the way a football coach sends his team out on laps. The students fumble through bursts of ideas followed by half sentences dwindling into strings of "yeah's" and "oh, man's." They slide in and out of character like a high school band struggling to stay on key. Most often, the characters resemble the students themselves. Their improvised dialogue reveals their youth—allusions to television shows or rock bands Vincent has never heard of, or the kind of petulant fighting that is only a half step removed from whining over a stolen childhood toy. Vincent finds the simplistic way the students express happiness and sadness both pathetic and heartbreaking. Their emotions are weighted with no ballast, no sense of the chilly desolation Vincent feels every day of his life. He could teach them to find these moments. He could show them how to mine a playground memory for jealousy and loneliness. He could make them see that what they take for parental love is simply the manifestation of adult self-regard. But tonight, preoccupied by thoughts of his wife wandering the dark sidewalks in her translucent gown and flip-flops, he thinks the students might be lucky to believe that happiness is smiling, that sadness is a frown.

*It is not difficult* to find Mrs. Eleanor this evening; she takes the same route each time she leaves the house on her own. Amador finds her standing on the corner of her block.

"The night is warm, Mrs.," he says, approaching her, careful not to startle her. She looks at him. He can't tell if she recognizes him or not, but she isn't frightened.

"I get lonely in the house," he says. "So I come to find you."

"Don't be lonely," she says, patting his arm with her delicate fingers.

"No more, now that you are here," he says, and begins to walk her back to the house. He prepares what he will say when he calls Mr. Vincent. These conversations make him nervous. Mr. Vincent says little, and he can never tell if he has done the right thing. Well, he knows he has done the right thing this time. But he and Mr. Vincent have different ideas of how to care for Mrs. Eleanor, and Amador does not want to insult the man. He needs to hold on to this job. The old lady will last—she is not sick in the body, only in the mind, which is crumbling like an old clay pot. He saw it happen to his own mother. Not even Inocencia, his mother-in-law, that old *bruja*, could stop his mother's mind from fleeing. In the end she wandered the village, murmuring about spirits and scaring the children.

Amador likes Mrs. Eleanor. She once became confused and called him "Amor" by mistake. She giggled, covering her mouth with her hand. He was pleased that she understood at least one word of his language. This is more than he can say for the husband. Mr. Vincent speaks to Amador in broken English, cutting the language into child-size pieces for easier digestion. But Mrs. Eleanor talks to him as if he were an old friend, worthy of her secrets. Mrs. Eleanor's eyes are like topaz stones. He always knows when her mind is good because the lights of her eyes come from inside her skull, as if she has two candles glowing back there.

"We swam in the river today," she says, as they walk slowly toward the house. "Mother gave us her permission."

"Oh, it must be cold!" he says, humoring her memory.

She continues her story. He doesn't mind listening to her recall her childhood. He charts a path among the words he recognizes as though he is walking across a creek on uneven stones. Her soft voice carries him back to his own childhood. He thinks about his parents who are dead, about the plot of corn they tended in back of their house in Ocampo. He recalls the sweet, woody smell of the dried grass harvested for hay each winter and how, on his way to school, he hid from his older brother and sisters among the pyramid-shaped bales.

Once back at the house, he undresses Mrs. Eleanor and lowers her into the bathtub. He is careful, as always, to look away from her body; nakedness is something a woman should give, not something that should be stolen from her. He remembers bathing his own children, Rogelio, Miguel, and Berta, when they were babies. He tries to summon the smell of their clean hair and the soaps his wife, Erlinda, uses. But he cannot call up the particular scent of his clean children. He prefers their daily smells, anyway, the odors of food on their hands, their acrid morning mouths, the sweet puffs of their gasses in the bed they so often shared with him and his wife.

When Mrs. Eleanor's body is submerged beneath the filmy water, he feels more comfortable looking at her. Her skin is like wrinkled silk, draped loosely across her prominent breastbones. Although he cannot see them, he knows her breasts hang low, the areolas nearly translucent. She lies back in the tub with her knees drawn up to her chest, her kneecaps forming two pale islands above the waterline.

"You wash now," he says, handing her the cloth so she can scrub her legs and the lower parts of her body. He moves away and gathers the towel so she can have her privacy. Erlinda does not let him see her body without darkness to act as a curtain. He knows his wife by touch more than sight, knows the dip and rise of her waist, the reassuring heaviness of her warm breasts, the bumps like hills on the terrain of her wide, luxurious areolas. Mrs. Eleanor is not so inhibited, or maybe her disease renders her heedless, like a child. Once he mistakenly glimpsed her crotch and noticed the pale, thinning hairs there revealing the cleft, her old age returning her to girlhood.

"All done!" she says, brightly. She holds the washcloth out of the water, presenting him with her dripping trophy.

He spreads the dry towel across his own chest, then leans down and gently pulls her from the water. She is surprisingly heavy. But he knows about the paradoxical heaviness of lifeless objects. His own first baby boy felt like a sack of wet sand when he lifted him to place him in the coffin.

He holds Mrs. Eleanor tightly as he wraps her.

"Cold!" she says through clenched teeth. She tilts her head back and smiles up at him, thrilled with the sensation.

"I make warm," he says, rubbing her through the thick towel until her body relaxes.

He encourages her to do as much for herself as she can. If she refuses to feed herself, then she does not eat. He makes her use the toilet alone, only calling through the closed door to remind her to use the paper and to flush. Occasionally he must change her underclothes when she does not do the job properly, but he feels that her embarrassment is nothing compared to the mortification of having a stranger half her age wipe her backside.

Mr. Vincent recommends television. "She loves the game shows," he says. "She'll stare at them for hours." But Amador is troubled by her vacant expression as she watches the bright colors and white smiles of the hosts, pools of spit collecting at the corners of her half-open mouth. He encourages her to listen to the radio instead. Together they follow the soccer games on the Spanish-language stations, and she claps and he hoots every time the announcer screams, "¡GOL!" She likes to listen to a man named Howard Stern, who speaks too quickly for Amador to understand. But he enjoys Mrs. Eleanor's mischievous grin as she listens and can only wonder what the man says to make her smile so. It reminds him of his baby girl, Berta, swallowing a forbidden sweet after Erlinda's back is turned. Mrs. Eleanor likes when he reads to her, too. She is not bothered by the broken trail of sentences he makes as he struggles to sound out words, or that, by the end of a page, neither of them can be sure what has taken place.

Her escapes have become more devious lately. She waits until he is in the toilet. Or she slips out the front door when he is studying at the kitchen table, the rumble and belch of the dishwasher drowning out the soft click of the door lock. He wonders, with some parental pride, if she pretends to sleep so that he will be lulled into a temporary state of relaxation. Usually the alarms alert him before she travels more than a few steps down the front walkway. But occasionally, if he forgets to turn on the alarm, or when he stands outside the kitchen door to smoke a cigarette, she might make it all the way down the block before he realizes she is gone.

After the bath she says she is tired, so he puts her to bed. He is surprised when, an hour later, she appears at the kitchen door.

"I'm hungry." She is barefoot. Her feet are pale as moth wings.

"What you want to eat?"

Her shoulders rise and fall in a shrug. "Pudding," she says.

"You know where," he says, looking back at his English grammar text. She pouts and makes small complaining sounds, but he does not rescue her. She pads to the refrigerator and opens it.

"Look on the bottom," Amador instructs. The pudding

sits in a white dish covered by plastic wrap. He imagines the unbroken chocolate skin.

She closes the door without removing the bowl.

"Not hungry anymore?" he asks.

"I want to go to bed!" she whines. For a moment, her face looks like that of a young child struggling against tears, and then it returns to itself and she is an old woman again, confused and angry.

He walks her back to her room. He helps her into the bed, lifting the covers over her chest. She stares at him. Her eyes are full of water, two glittering blue lakes.

"I don't understand," she says.

"I know," he whispers.

*Vincent ends his* class early and spends the rest of the evening at a bar on Moorpark, hoping not to run into anyone he knows, no one who will shake his head in prerequisite pity as Vincent describes Eleanor's descent. How can he hope to make someone else understand what it is to lose a wife, really *lose* her? Her situation is an even worse trick than death. There are so many times when he is talking to her that he realizes she is simply not there.

He returns home much later that evening. He stands outside the kitchen window for minutes before entering. As a boy he experienced this combination of elation and dread when he stood before the great arched doors of Queen of Peace Elementary School in South Jersey. He would listen to his father's Cutlass sputter toward the tool-and-die shop and experience a sudden panic of abandonment. Then the fear would subside, replaced by a calm that he rarely felt either at home or in school. It was the solace of in-between spaces, of being effectively nowhere in the world, a nonplace where nothing was required of him, where he did not have to be responsible to a mother or father or priest, and where he could invent a self more powerful and capable and better looking than he knew was true.

Amador sits like a statue at the kitchen table. His textbook lies open before him. His short, muscled forearms frame the book, the tendons tensing and relaxing as he squeezes and releases his fists. Vincent wonders briefly what Amador's life was like back where he is from. He's heard of professors becoming street cleaners, of doctors forced to use their deft hands to work sewing machines in sweatshops. But Vincent will never ask. He does not want Amador to become particular to him.

Amador.

Thank God for Amador.

Although, if he were to be honest, he'd admit that he sometimes hates Amador. The man is a silent rebuke. He is irked by Amador's insistence that Eleanor feed herself or get up from the bed and cross the entire room in order to retrieve her bathrobe. He knows these demands are a passive condemnation of Vincent's own, less stringent care. And Vincent is not sure that causing Eleanor frustration is especially kind or palliative. After all, there is no "better" anymore. There is no "well." He wants to tell Amador this, but he cannot risk the man taking offense and quitting.

To smell another man's body odors hanging around in the rooms, to sit down on the toilet seat knowing that another man's ass has been there—these are irritants that never disappear. Two nights earlier Vincent was taken aback to find a can of condensed milk in the refrigerator, a product neither he nor Eleanor ever use. The can felt like a squat intruder, its flowered label peeling to reveal the metal beneath. A teardrop of pale white liquid sat, plump and hardened, at the triangular opening, looking like nothing so much as come. Vincent picked up the can in order to throw it out, silently preparing the speech he would make the next evening to discourage further incursions on Amador's part. This was his house, for Christ's sake. Amador was hired help. But in the end Vincent replaced the can on the shelf where he'd found it.

Amador's mouth moves to form the unwieldy new language. Vincent hears his low, stumbling voice, muffled by the window. Amador reads a passage out loud, then looks up from his book and offers his hand to an unseen visitor.

"I am fine. How are you?"

Vincent coughs intentionally as he works his key into the kitchen door lock. Amador stands and immediately closes his book and pushes in his chair. He whisks his coffee mug from the table and washes it out in the sink, drying it with a paper towel and replacing it in its proper cupboard. With the damp towel he wipes the ring from the table, erasing any trace of himself. Vincent reaches for his wallet and begins to count out the bills. Neither man speaks. They have become accustomed to the awkwardness of this transactive moment. In the beginning Vincent tried to make small talk to cover the uncomfortable silence. But Amador never responded, and after a few weeks the men fell into a habit of silence as money changed hands.

"Where did she go?" Vincent asks, pocketing his wallet.

"Down the street."

"She's sleeping?"

"Yes."

Amador puts his money away and collects his book while Vincent shuffles purposelessly around the small kitchen, relieved that this humiliating moment when another man tells him the story of his wife has quickly disappeared beneath the blanket of worldly noise.

"A telephone call come," Amador says, handing Vincent a scrap of newspaper on which he has written in gnarled letters.

"Caroline?" Vincent says, almost disbelieving the message and the messenger. "For me?"

Amador nods. "She say call tonight."

"It's late," Vincent murmurs. He is embarrassed to reveal his uncertainty in front of Amador, but he has been blindsided by this message.

Amador shrugs. "She say call her tonight," he says again, and then leaves the house.

Vincent pours himself a drink and stands in the dark living room, holding the phone in his hands. Finally he gets up the nerve to call. At first he doesn't understand her. He knows Caroline is telling him something unhappy, something that should make him react with a certain set of expected responses. Her voice is thin and hardened by distance and the thirty-year-old aqua Princess telephone Eleanor managed to keep in working condition. His daughter is talking, but all he can think is that, during all the years of Caroline's absence, she has never called to speak to him.

He imagines her small face. Her features are as precise as her mother's, but where Eleanor's are modest, Caroline's are emphatic and dangerous. Her chin, the gently sloping bottom of a heart on Eleanor's face, is a pointed dagger on Caroline's. Her eyes are dark, the iris nearly as black as the pupil itself. He'd been shocked, thirty-five years ago, when the doctor pulled a black-haired being from between his wife's legs and held it up for Vincent to see. He'd imagined their child would be a fair-complected and docile carbon of his wife, cowlick and demure nature included. He hadn't banked on the sheer otherness of a child. When he held his screaming, olive-skinned baby in his arms for the first time, he felt only a sense of complete bewilderment. He could have been holding a stranger's child. But of course the baby had his skin, his restless, impatient disposition. Caroline came out with her fists clenched in front of her small face, ready for the fight.

Now this tiny, downy-skinned infant is grown and tells him that her husband has left her. As Caroline explains her situation, Vincent tries to recall Frank. A scientist. Something having to do with stars. Something without much of an income—he remembers that, and the photos of the small, uninspired house Eleanor took during one of her visits. Vincent remembers meeting Frank for the first time. He was taller than Vincent. He had the kind of nonspecific, straight-edged face that seemed to have all ethnicity wrung from it. He made Vincent feel immediately self-conscious of his own knobby face, his flat-footed accent, his brusque, unrefined manner. The young man filled silence with silence, which Vincent took to be judgment. What had Caroline told Frank? Everything, he supposed. And he supposed, too, that everything had been exaggerated by her and misinterpreted by the new husband so that Vincent was the selfish cuckold, the cause of all her childhood misery. Well, he thought, marriage allows you a co-conspirator for your delusions. It had been the same for him when Eleanor was well. How often did she assure him a role was just around the corner?

"Are you there?" Caroline asks with irritation. She has finished her story and he has not responded.

"Yes," he says. "I'm sorry to hear that." The response feels too generic. What will his regret do for his daughter? What has it ever done for her? A stranger can be sorry. Even a friend. But a father's commiseration needs to do more. It must fix the thing. But he was incapable of righting his own wrongs during Caroline's childhood. He'd left his wife and daughter too, and his absence dug a hole in Caroline's heart. What does she expect of him now?

"When did this happen?" is all he can think to ask. He feels like he is telling his acting students how to set their scene in some imagined reality.

"It's been three months," she says.

He's startled that she has kept this information from him for so long, but he does not have the right to feel hurt. They share no history of confiding in one another. "How are the boys taking it?"

"Oh," she sighs. "I don't know if they understand what it means. You know? Although everybody's parents nowadays . . . ," her voice trails off.

He senses an accusation. He offers a grunt in response and is relieved when she does not hang up. Suddenly the silence feels strange, as though air is being sucked from the line. A shifting in his stomach tells him she is crying. Finally she gasps for breath. He feels helpless. How he wishes for Eleanor to come and gently take the phone from him, the way she did for years when he and his daughter could not fashion a conversation beyond the opening greetings.

"Shhh," he whispers, then immediately regrets the disapproval inherent in the sound.

Caroline growls angrily at her tears as if she could frighten them away. "I want to come home," she says suddenly. And there are the tears again; her voice is as high as a girl's.

"Of course," he says awkwardly. "Anytime. Just let us know."

"I mean come back," she says. "To live."

He makes the mistake of pausing.

"Forget it," she says.

"No, no," he says. "You just took me by surprise." Caroline is like a roomful of funhouse mirrors. He doesn't want to get trapped and end up staring at his elongated or horrifically fattened self.

"We don't have savings," she says. "Frank left his job. He just left, Dad. He disappeared."

"You have no idea where he is?"

"He calls. Occasionally," she says. "To talk to the boys. He's always somewhere different. I don't know if I can count on him for anything. The boys' doctors cost a lot. I'll have to get a full-time job." She stops abruptly.

Her voice is a bullet. He understands the implicit condemnation the way a shot man understands he is going to die even before he feels the pain of the wound: He has failed Eleanor. He will fail Caroline too.

"Never mind," she says, her voice uncharacteristically fragile. "Forget I asked."

"Caroline——" he says, not sure what to say next. He has never known exactly what to say to her, and she has always misunderstood him. "Come home."

"I miss Mom," she says, her voice graveled by her choked tears. "I miss Mom."

*When he hangs up*, he fingers open the center part in the curtains and peers at the empty street. He is reluctant to separate the curtains farther for fear some neighbor might be awake to witness the aftermath of this awkward failure. His face reflects back at him in the glass. And then, superimposed on it, he sees Caroline's face at seventeen: mouth set, eyes hard as obsidian and just as black, defiantly willing herself to reveal nothing as she leaves home for that preposterous choice of a midwestern college, dragging her army green duffle bag to the waiting taxi, defying him one last time with her unwillingness to accept a ride to the airport. How did he raise such a cruel child? But of course he didn't raise her. He abandoned her. He left when she was twelve, an intense, passionate child, devoted to ballet. She spun around the small living room in her tutu and pink tights in a fury, her face grimly set as though dance were an adversarial sport: Caroline versus gravity. When he returned four years later, she'd relinquished this obsession, along with her grace, in favor of rage. The year between his return and her departure for college felt dangerous. Her outbursts were unpredictable, her sullenness unmanned him. She would no longer tolerate even the slightest hint of his concern or his righteous parental anger. Her dismissal of him weakened him in ways he could never have anticipated. He could not perform an audition without imagining his daughter in the room, silently shaking her head as though she no longer believed in his act.

He lets go of the curtain and sits down on the sofa, holding his drink between his knees. Maybe it was an act, too, he thinks. His whole damn career, if that's what it can be called. He was a messy and garrulous young man, given to heights of temper and lows of despair. He had stormed the gates of Hollywood barely out of his teens, ready to be Cagney or Bogart. But he soon found the manners and customs of the place as forbidding as he would have had he stumbled into a cotillion in New York City. When he met Eleanor, he thought she, with her neatly combed hair and delicate hands and her resolute, unearthly calm, would act as a buffer between him and this city, which demanded such unattainable perfection. She cleaned dishes as she used them. She wore rubber gloves to protect her skin. She reused paper towels. She washed herself after sex. He was a loser of things. He lost telephone numbers and addresses and shoes. He lost friends and jobs. And children. He lost them too.

At first he was grateful for her order. But the gap between his stuttering career and her efforts to plump up their lives like old couch pillows began to make him angry.

"This house, this life . . . ," he'd complained during an argument provoked by her asking him to wash his hands before touching the newly painted bedroom walls, ". . . they're like . . . Everything is so—" he extended a flattened hand along a plane of air to indicate the bland reasonableness of their world.

"We don't want fingerprints is all," she'd said, folding down the bedcover in three neat gestures. She kept her voice low and even, not wanting eleven-year-old Caroline to hear them through the wall that separated the two bedrooms.

"It's like that!" he screamed, pointing at her. "You don't even yell!"

"Why in the world should I yell?"

"Because it feels good!"

"Not to me."

He let out a frustrated howl.

"Vincent," she said. "Why don't you tell me what you want?"

"I want . . . ," he began. But he could not find the end of the sentence anywhere. He'd lost that too.

He convinced himself that leaving Eleanor was necessary to his idea of himself. Her efficiency rendered him useless. He felt as dispensable at home as he did in the world, where casting directors had begun to greet him with tight-smiled impatience. While other men he knew worked regular jobs, accruing power and a sense of usefulness with age, his own profession made him feel that age was an embarrassment. By forty he was in the discard pile.

"I can't be myself here," he said to Eleanor a year later,

when he told her he was leaving. He paced their small kitchen from refrigerator to stove and back again.

"Who are you, then?" she asked.

"I'm not this," he said, waving his hand around the kitchen. "I'm not avocado-colored dishwasher and linoleum floors."

She suppressed a smile, and he became enraged. "Why don't you react?" he said. "I'm leaving you. Why don't you cry?"

"Because I'm not the one who's leaving," she said evenly.

To Caroline he said, "Daddy has to go be by himself for a while." He watched her expression change from surprise to confusion to hurt then back to confusion, as she searched through her arsenal of feelings for the right one.

"Okay," she said finally.

Okay, she understood? Okay, he could go and she would still love him? But he knew these possibilities were fabrications of his selfishness. "Okay" was the resigned acknowledgment that life consisted of things happening to her.

Panic floods his body from chest to bowels. Sitting on the toilet, his face cupped in his hands, his trousers crumpled at his ankles, he feels trapped. Caroline and her boys will arrive in two weeks. His wife is disappearing daily. Caroline has offered to take over the care of her mother. Certainly he could use the money he'd save by not having hired help. But he does not want Caroline to become necessary. He wonders if it is right for a father to have such ambivalent feelings toward his own child.

He finishes in the bathroom and stands in the open door

of the bedroom. His daughter is coming home. He needs Eleanor to get it together and take care of the situation, keep peace, make meals, even out the rough edges of this tangled life.

She lies underneath the covers, her hands flat on either side of her as if she is readying herself to be sliced in half by a magician. Her nimbus of hair fans out on her pillow like rays of an aged sun. She is my wife, he tells himself. I have touched every inch of her and inside her, too. But the words only make him feel more separate and remind him that he is just as responsible for the empty corridor that exists between them as any disease. Illness is a great distraction, he thinks, making you forget all the other injuries that have come before.

He backs out of the room quietly.

"Amador?" Eleanor says.

"It's me," he says, stopping. "Vincent."

"Good morning?" she asks.

"It's nighttime," he says. "Time for sleep."

"Come closer."

Reluctantly he crosses to her side of the bed and sits down. She looks up at him with an unnervingly present smile, but he reminds himself that he might be anybody to her at this moment, and that he should not be disappointed if she refers to him as her brother or father or some stranger from her youth.

"Eleanor. Look at me," he says, gently brushing her cheek. "Are you listening? Caroline is coming home. Did you hear me, Eleanor? Carrie is coming back."

"Who?"

Desolation spreads through his chest like a puddle of spilled milk. "*Care-oh-line*," he says, more forcefully than he intends, as if volume will startle her brain back to normal. "You have to try harder, Eleanor."

After a moment her confusion transforms itself into a look of pleasure.

"That's lovely," she says.

He begins to explain about Caroline's marital situation, but stops himself. This disturbing news might cause Eleanor to retreat or become confused, her own history conflating with her daughter's in a terribly ironic way. And he doesn't want to lose her yet. He has an entire night and day ahead until Amador arrives for tomorrow's shift, and he doesn't want to spend those hours trapped in her memories or, worse, his own.

"They're good boys, Vincent. You don't have to be scared of them," she says, closing her eyes.

"I'm not scared of them," he says, taken aback. But it is true. He has stared uncomfortably at the photographs Eleanor brings back from her trips to Missouri. The two little boys in their heavy black glasses look . . . well . . . freakish. He is scared of them just as, when he was a child, he was scared of a group of wheelchair-bound, slack-jawed children he saw at the circus. During the entire performance he stared at them, horrified and mesmerized by their spastic laughter, their bobbling heads.

"Eleanor," he whispers urgently. How is it that he needs her now more than ever before? "Please."

She opens her eyes and stares at him fearfully, as if he is a rapist who has just climbed through her window. Then she resorts to her atavistic habit of flirtation, her only defense. She lowers her eyelids over those magnetic eyes whose unfathomable color ensnared him so many years earlier. Trying to name the color had been like trying to fix the scent of a complicated perfume in your mind. You had it, and then it would scurry away from your perception like a spider. But she isn't really flirting with him. He knows that. She is simply trying to tame this stranger who has unaccountably called her name.

"Take a walk with me?" he asks.

She doesn't respond.

"I need to take a walk," he says. "I need air." He sits on the edge of the bed and lifts her toward him. He places her robe around her back and works her arms into the sleeves. Her body is limp and unresponsive, and his fear turns to anger. "Help out here, Eleanor. For God's sake, help me!" Wetness soaks into the material of his shirt. Her shoulders shake. Is she crying because he has yelled at her? Or are her tears nothing more than the result of a misfired brain synapse? He holds her to him, stroking her brittle hair. When she calms, he takes her to the bathroom and sits her on the toilet. Gripping her shoulders, he steadies her while she urinates.

The winds kick up as a greeting when they walk out the front door. The trees whisper to one another.

"I want to go to the river," she says.

"There's no more river here," he says, patiently. "I've

told you that. You're thinking of Los Olivos." She has often spoken of the creek that ran through her family's ranch.

"No river?" she asks.

Her voice wavers with the wind, and he senses her confusion making her fragile. He has the feeling she might crumble underneath his grip. "It's too windy for a walk," he says, watching the tumbleweed of an empty plastic grocery bag roll down the street, its white translucence illuminated by the headlights of a passing car. Eleanor sucks in an audible lungful of air.

"Walk," she says gently.

With one hand around her back and the other holding her arm, he leads her down the sidewalk. The wind blows her hair around her face. He stops for a moment and draws the strands out from between her lips. He notices the subtle shift in her eyes as her disease recedes and the smooth plane of her mind surfaces. She looks around in wonder, as if she has just been transported to some magical place.

"Everyone's asleep," she says. "We're the only ones up, and we're the oldest ones left in the neighborhood!" She laughs.

His heart lightens to see and hear her sensible to the same world he lives in, and he grasps for this feeling of companionship, realizing at the same time, by contrast, how deep his solitude has become.

"Mama?" she says.

"I'm Vincent," he says. But he has, once again, been tricked into complacency by her momentary stopover in his universe, and his words come too angrily. "I'm your husband," he reminds her more gently, aware that these words are like cupped hands holding air.

"It's hard," she says, her teeth chattering in the wind.

"It's late. You're cold."

"You can go if you want."

The words pinch like a bee sting. He feels the casual surprise of the bite, knowing that later, even hours later, he will experience the dull throbbing pain. Is she talking to him? And if she is, what does she mean? Go home? Go away? Where would he go?

"I don't want to go," he says.

"I'm tired now," she says.

"Yes. Of course," he says. "It's too late for a walk."

3.

*The school bell rings*, sharp and angry as though it's pissed off and wants these kids out of this building *now*. Marlene is startled out of her precalculus haze as notebooks click and seats scrape across the floor and her teacher yells something about problems number two through five and show your work. Marlene can't remember anything that's happened in the past forty minutes, and when she glances at the chalkboard, the swooping arcs of lines and numbers make no sense to her. She doesn't understand math. The idea that math explains something about the world is idiotic since there is nothing she can point to in her life that matches up perfectly or makes a neat equation, or that you can boil down to one correct answer if you *show your work*.

She decides to skip the school bus. The bus smells of

Naugahyde and vomit, and today she cannot summon the effort it would take to dance around the boys who deliberately sit in front so they can rub up against passing girls. A bunch of hormonal freaks, she thinks, as she turns down the street and begins the long walk toward her neighborhood at the far side (the wrong side) of this school zone. She's seen boys jerking off in the eleventh-grade classroom, pumping one hand up and down below their desks, holding wadded-up lunchroom napkins in the other. If the teachers know what is going on, they choose to ignore it, talking across the tops of the students' heads as though they are teaching a class in a state other than Ohio.

Well, maybe growing up here makes boys desperate for sex. This is a pathetic excuse for a town, she thinks, as she passes the Qwik Stop, considers buying a Coke, then decides against it because today the idea of buying another Coke from the same Qwik Stop, seeing the same girl with the braces behind the cash register who will, no doubt, make some stupid remark about the twelve-headed baby on the cover of the *Enquirer*, flattens her. There's really nothing to do in this town except ride in cars, get drunk, or go out into the fields and get high and give someone a blow job. She won't drink because her mother does, and drinking makes you stupid. And although there is no hard evidence to support this, Marlene does not think she's stupid. After all, doesn't her father/not father have letters after his name? And forget drugs. She knows a girl who raved all night and dropped dead, her heart exploding, her body as dehydrated as a dried up dish-rag. As for the blow jobs, she'd rather eat live rats.

She passes the bail bonds office where her mother works. She leans against the window and cups her hands around her eyes to cut down the glare. There is her mother, behind the bulletproof glass window, looking like a department store mannequin. Her mother is pretty, though, Marlene concedes, as she absentmindedly fingers a zit on her forehead and suppresses the urge to squeeze. Diane's beauty is so conspicuous that even Marlene can accept it without tarnishing it with the pity or disgust she customarily directs toward her mother. Diane's beauty just is, the way a mountain or the sun just is. There is no sense in denying it or trying to find something wrong with it. The long, gray Ohio winters solidified Diane's face at just the right moment, like a perfectly baked cake, so that each feature holds a memory of all the wholesome ingredients.

Diane has never done anything useful with her limpid brown eyes and the beckoning curl of her lips. Over the years friends and perfect strangers have told her she should try modeling. Diane snorts off the compliment, and air honks through her nose in a way that embarrasses Marlene extremely.

"Everyone always wants you to be something more than you are," she tells Marlene. "Someone's got to run the post office, fix the cars, get the bums out of jail. People like us make the world go around." Marlene resents being included in this assessment, but she can never get her mother to entertain her ambitions to be a writer. "Not likely, sweetie," Diane says, smiling tenderly at Marlene's fantastic self-regard.

Marlene doesn't know how her mother can stand dealing

with all those people trying to spring their brothers or husbands out of jail. Her mother always says "innocent until proven guilty" as though her job is an integral part of the United States Department of Justice. But Marlene figures nine times out of ten, they did it. She has no idea if this is true, but it seems true, based on most of the boys at her school who are already delinquents or at least criminals-in-training. In her opinion people are guilty until they lie or cheat well enough to convince someone they are innocent.

Marlene peels away from the bail bonds office and crosses the broad strip of what locals laughably call "downtown." Diane defends her job saying it's a clean office and no one bothers her. "You could do worse," she says. Marlene's classroom is decorated with motivational posters that shout "Reach high!" and "Your mind will take you where you want to go!" and "Just say NO!" She considers ways to apply this last lesson. Just say no to . . . flunking out and ending up working at Pizza King. But that's a lie. She's known plenty of kids who worked hard in school, were class president, or ran around getting people to sign petitions about fur or no fur, and now they are gainfully employed in fast food. Clean office. No one bothers you.

Just say no to sex. That's the big one, in Marlene's opinion. That takes care of everything else. She refused to have sex with her last-year's boyfriend even though he moaned about having "those urges or whatever" like he'd skimmed the health book the night before. Once she almost gave in, but the minute she laid eyes on his thick red penis, she backed out. She didn't want that thing to touch her. She's not embarrassed about being a virgin either. She'll do it when she's ready, and she will, for sure, use a condom. Girls in her class talk longingly about babies, as though this is the only next step they can imagine. And even if you are careful and don't get knocked up, sex just slows people down and makes them unwilling to leave a place. Sex is the Super Glue of the soul.

Diane wouldn't even have a kid if she hadn't made a mistake sixteen years ago. Marlene can't imagine leaving her whole life up to chance, especially in a place like this, where nothing happens that hasn't happened a thousand times before.

When she arrives at her house, she nukes a slice of leftover pizza, gets her bike and eats as she rides one-handed out toward the farms. It's a long ride, but she has energy—too much energy that she doesn't know what to do with. It will be at least two hours before Diane comes home and she and her mother launch into their evening of inevitable misunderstandings and arguments. These have become their principal modes of communication ever since Diane announced that if Marlene is considering college, she better be considering two years at the JC. It's this kind of situation that brings the father/not father problem center stage. How can you know, Marlene thinks, as she takes a corner, what your life is really supposed to be when half of it is missing? Maybe she's supposed to go to a JC. Or maybe she's supposed to go to Harvard goddamn University. All her life she feels like she's been looking behind her, waiting for the rest of her to catch up.

Twenty minutes later she turns off the highway onto a dizzyingly straight farm road. Tractors make their way up and down rows of crops like exhausted dinosaurs. Irrigation wheels spray rainbow arcs of water. Her geography book talks about the "quilted farmlands of the Midwest," but that is utter bullshit. Maybe if you're in an airplane, things look like someone sewed the land in orderly patches for maximum coziness, but down here on earth, all this endless land fills her with a terrifying chill. Where are the borders that hold you in? How are you supposed to know where you begin and where you end? She gets off her bike and lies down in a field of newly turned earth, soft as a blanket. She closes her eyes. Sometimes she feels like an entire person who makes sense. Sometimes she feels like a water glass with a hole in it.

By the time Marlene gets home, Diane has already settled into her sun-faded pink butterfly chair on the porch that fronts their old, peeling house. She's hiked her work skirt high on her thighs so that Marlene can see the bright yellow triangle of her underwear. Traffic from the nearby freeway on-ramp hums like a mechanical insect.

"Got a check," Diane says, dangling a green rectangle of paper from her fingers.

Marlene lays her bike down on the dirt, takes the porch steps two at a time, and grabs the check out of Diane's hands.

"Careful," Diane says. "A ripped check doesn't do us any good."

"A hundred dollars?" Marlene says, incredulous.

Diane shrugs. "He must not be doing too well."

"Or he's cheap."

"Could be."

It irks Marlene that her mother is willing to accept that Marlene's father could be one way or could be another— that she doesn't care who he is exactly.

"I don't know why you bothered to even tell him about me," Marlene says, sitting heavily on the top porch step.

"For a while I didn't. But that was when you were a baby and I didn't know how much money you were going to cost. Although maybe I knew all along that I'd end up telling him. I mean, why would I remember where he worked after all those years?"

She says all this as though she doesn't have anything to do with her own life. This is one of Diane's qualities that drives Marlene insane with frustration. She doesn't want to be one of the mistakes her mother made because she wasn't paying enough attention, one of the missteps her mother will muse about later on with this air of fleeting curiosity.

"You know, there's laws about deadbeat dads," Marlene says.

"You always act like he's your father, but he's not," Diane says.

"What is he then?" They've had these discussions countless times, but still she can't help dragging herself back into them even though she's never going to get a new answer.

"He's the guy I messed up with one time I was messing around," Diane says.

"You should have been more careful," Marlene says.

"Then you wouldn't be here, sweetie."

"No great loss to the world."

"That's just sixteen talking," Diane says. "I remember sixteen. . . ." She tilts her head toward the fleeing sun.

Her mother always manages to insinuate that Marlene's existence is just a rerun of Diane's, as if her future is already being lived for her in the form of this woman, lying back in her frayed chair, legs stretched out, toes turned in, carelessly awkward, pointlessly lovely.

"So maybe you're not so happy after all," Marlene says.

"Who said anything about being happy?" Diane says, her eyes still shut. "Why does everybody think they deserve to be happy? Maybe happy is just like doing a triple axel in the Olympics. Maybe it's just something a few people get to do."

"You're drunk, probably," Marlene says.

"Well, no I'm not, probably. But you're rude."

Marlene doesn't feel angry, but she wishes she did. She wants to feel *something* that will counteract the knowledge that her mother is right. She launches herself off the porch step and storms into the house, letting the screen door bang behind her.

In the kitchen she opens the cupboard below the sink, where the garbage can stands nearly full. "Recycle!" she yells as she picks out the bottles and cans Diane refuses to put in the recycling box. Underneath an empty can of Diet Coke she finds what she is looking for: the crumpled envelope her father's check came in.

She smooths the envelope on the kitchen table. There is never a return address. He probably doesn't want the letters to ricochet back to his house, for lack of postage or some other official foul-up, where they will land with bomb-size explosions. Marlene studies his precise handwriting. Every letter of the address is of even height and width, the *e*'s and *t*'s and *s*'s exactly the same each time. Marlene's own handwriting is an inconsistent jumble of shapes, some of them recognizable only because of their proximity to other, more legible letters.

She takes a scrap of paper and a pen out of her schoolbag and tries to replicate his handwriting. The focus required to reproduce his perfect letters is so complete she feels she has to change her personality. She must become someone who cares about washing her face before bed, who wears matching bras and panties just in case. She has to be someone who tries to obscure everything about herself, whose message to the world is that there is no message. She enjoys imagining herself as his perfect replica, a self-contained, mysterious girl, someone who doesn't need to *talk* all the time the way she does, babbling just to make noise, to remind herself and everyone around her that she exists. But when she cannot imitate the perfect swish and dagger of his capital *R*'s, her fantasy buckles underneath her and she gives up, crumpling the paper and pitching it back into the garbage can. She is still the obvious, yearning girl she's always been, lank-haired, halfway pretty, smelling of cheap perfume she buys at the import shop next to the used CD store. She smells her wrist and wishes she hadn't put on perfume today. The smell irritates her. It is no more indicative of her than her father/not father's maddeningly perfect handwriting. It is just something that occasionally sticks to her life.

4.

*It is after midnight.* Amador sits at the back of the brightly lit bus, relaxing into the long ride to Panorama City. It was an exhausting evening with Mrs. Eleanor running away like that. This job is harder than any he's had in this country so far, harder than the heat and flies in the lettuce fields or the cramped, airless days in the factory. It is not the physical part that is difficult, of course. What is difficult is the caring. He thinks about Mrs. Eleanor when he is home. He worries about her. He came to this country to escape his care and here he is, worrying about someone he barely knows and who sometimes doesn't even recognize him.

The bus is filled with men and women like himself. It amuses Amador that Los Angeles public transportation exists to serve people who aren't even supposed to be in the country. It is another instance of the ironic hospitality he has encountered during his four years here. It was the same on the farms. His old *patrón* in the fields near Dinuba made weekend barbecues for his men and offered rides into town on Sundays for those who wanted to attend church. But this same man told the workers that they would receive their final pay at five o'clock on the last day of the harvest. By some miracle the police arrived at noon that very same day. They arrested every single worker, and the *patrón*, whose harvest was complete, kept the final paychecks for himself.

Amador made a single request when he came to Mr. Vincent and Mrs. Eleanor's house for the interview: "You pay in cash." This was the advice of one of the three men with whom he shares a trailer. He knows how rude and suspect his words must have sounded to the distinguished-looking American who sat in a house full of frozen things—appliances on countertops and empty vases that looked as though they had not been touched in years. But Amador has no papers, and if Mr. Vincent mentions him in his taxes, Amador will be thrown back over the border like a bag of trash. He's been through that twice before. The first time because of the tricky *patrón* in the fields. The second time he'd been cutting molds at the candle factory in Santa Clarita when the doors of the workroom burst open. All the workers looked toward the bright rectangle of light as shadows rushed in, filling the overheated space with their noise. *"¡Pongan las manos en la cabeza!"* More-experienced workers climbed out of the windows without even shutting off their machines. But Amador, new to the factory, sat at his workstation with his hands on his head like a turkey who stares in open-mouthed wonder at the rain, filling his gullet until he drowns.

The third time Amador entered the country, he made a decision. He would remain a tiny parasite on the back of the cow. No more fields. No more factories. An informer can hide in a group like a brown butterfly on the bark of a tree. Amador resolved to lose himself in a city.

That last crossing was the most difficult. He rode from the border to Los Angeles in the covered bed of a pickup truck. Nine men lay on top of one another like flour sacks. The only possibility of air came from two small sliding windows that were covered with cardboard. The *pollero* warned them not to open the windows. "They see these windows slide open," he said, "they know someone inside is trying to breathe."

The sun beat down on the aluminum roofing. The bodies began to stink like meat left too long in the sun. No one spoke. The smell of sweat and flatulence became so unbearable Amador thought he would suffocate. He discovered a crack between the roofing and the sidewall of the truck bed. It was no more than an eighth of an inch wide, but when he pressed his face to it, he felt a minute breeze graze his skin. The impression of space on the other side of the truck gave him the necessary hope to imagine his survival.

The city bus shifts gears and begins its freeway journey. Amador is always amazed by how much traffic there is, even this late at night. There is something wrong with a city that does not sleep, where stores remain open for business in the dead hours of early morning. He thinks people go crazy in a place where time makes no sense. He remembers arriving in El Rosario on his last visit home at two in the morning. How nervous he was made by the silence!

The trips to El Rosario leave him restless. When he arrives, he stands outside the door of his house for minutes before entering. The sense of yearning for and dread of the next moment is so palpable he feels weak. Then the door opens and he is swept into his life, his *real* life. There is Erlinda, her normally wide platter of a face more lined than he remembers, her wary smile full of the knowledge that each homecoming is also a leavetaking. The children are usually asleep. Rogelio and Miguel lie together in one bed, Miguel's hand resting protectively inside the waistband of his pants. Rogelio sleeps with his knees up, as if sleep overtook him just as he was about to flee. Berta sleeps on a pallet in one corner, her thumb in her mouth, her black, curly hair matted to her sweaty cheek.

"I'll make her a bed while I am here," Amador said in a whisper the last time he was home, feeling, as he said it, the insufficiency of the gesture. Erlinda smiled in a way that let him know that "while I am here" had more meaning to her than the promise of a new bed. Erlinda is careful. She wants nothing more to bind them together, not a handmade bed, not a baby. During the three months of his stay, they make love often, but he must be careful to pull out, and when they finish she leaves the bed to clean herself and resume whatever housework or sewing she has not completed during the day.

The children treat Amador with the kind of mute courtesy they might afford a visitor and Amador watches the activity in his house as though witnessing a television show.

Doors open and close. People enter and exit, all with intentions he can only guess at but that rarely concern him. That his family survives in his absence is obvious. The money he sends home helps pay for food and clothing. The roof, which once leaked during the rains, is now patched with new sheets of metal. On sunny days he can tell his house from a distance because it glints, as though studded with occasional jewels. But in truth the money has not made any measurable difference in the life of his family, not a difference a stranger from up north might detect.

When his sense of dispossession overwhelms him, he walks to the town square. He visits old friends at their businesses and watches acquaintances tinker with broken cars, argue about the state soccer championship, or prepare the town square for a *fiesta*. Old Don Virgilio lives forever and is always sweeping the plaza in slow, arcing movements with a broom made of palm fronds.

On these endless, aimless afternoons, Amador thinks over and over about his choice to leave. Old friends greet him and ask him about *el Norte*, nodding their heads even before he answers. They assume that he is like all the others—that he left for work but that he only feels whole when he is back home. But he knows that he is different, and that he feels a relief when he is on the other side that strangles him with guilt. He loves his family, he reminds himself. Of course he does. He yearns for his children and is torn by his sense that he has abandoned them. And Erlinda. He remembers his love for her in fleeting moments, a memory of lightness so burdened by failure and loss that it hardly feels

like love but more like shared regret. And when he is in Los
Angeles he can convince himself for hours at a time that the
past lives with him no longer, that he is not the man who
lost one baby, who abandoned three children, who left a
wife, but that he is a man who is doing what is expected of
him. He is providing for his family the only way he can, by
taking care of someone else's. And if he feels a sense of
relief at being alone, at being allowed to forget the mistakes
of his past, is this not his right?

One afternoon, during the last visit, Amador watched a
carload of tourists drive around and around the plaza. He
imagined they had probably gotten lost on their way to
see the butterflies at the nearby sanctuary, the region's
only tourist attraction. The car stopped and a woman
emerged halfway from an open door. She snapped a picture
of Amador as he stood against a wooden post outside the
mayor's office, then slipped back into the car like a turtle
into its shell. Amador was horrified that his life was now the
subject of these tourists' curiosity, that he would forever represent "lazy Mexican" in the photo albums they would
show their friends. He wanted to run after them and tell
them that they had taken a picture of the wrong man.

He is happiest when Berta consents to sit on his lap and
tell him wonderful, improbable stories about talking pigs
and flying horses. He is happy, too, when he plays baseball
with Miguel, for the boy's total devotion to the sport and his
earnest exuberance seem to extend to Amador as well.

But Rogelio is an accusation. Amador feels his eldest son
watching his every move, as if Rogelio condemns him for

the way he holds a spoon or pours a glass of water. Privacy surrounds Rogelio. Amador cannot penetrate it. When he reaches out to touch the boy on the shoulder, Rogelio is always just far enough away to elude his father's fingertips. Rogelio might smile if Amador attempts a joke, but the expression is a presentation, a rueful gift. It is as though Rogelio has learned the same lessons Amador has mastered during his years up north: If he delivers a set of expected responses, no more can be demanded of him.

Amador senses the bricklike press of fate bearing down on Rogelio's newly muscled shoulders. It upsets him to see his son running after a truck each afternoon to beg a ride to the butterfly sanctuary. There he tricks tourists out of pesos, convincing them that they need his guidance in order to see the yearly convergence of the black-and-orange-winged insects. One evening, after a string of rainy days, Rogelio returned home, proud to tell his father how he'd collected money from unsuspecting *gringo* drivers who believed they needed his help in fording a flooded portion of the road. *The water was no more than two feet deep!* Rogelio exclaimed, laughing at the tourists' ignorance. Amador slapped his son.

That night, he lay awake, feeling his son's cheek on the palm of his hand. Why, he wondered, was it so hard for him to love that child right?

The next day Amador took a bus to the butterfly sanctuary. He walked up the steep narrow path lined with small kiosks. Adults sold sodas and chips to the tourists or tended food stands. Children ran among the tourists' legs, urging them to buy the butterfly pins and postcards that lay on cardboard trays suspended from their necks by yarn. Amador ignored the children and walked toward the trailhead.

Rogelio stood with four other boys his age, leaning against a low wall. He wore a homemade slingshot around his neck. When he saw his father, he stopped talking for a moment but then turned his attention back to his friends.

"What are you doing here?" Rogelio asked, when Amador drew close to the group.

"I've come to see the butterflies."

Rogelio shrugged. Mexican tourists passed on their way up the mountain. The boys did not move; they were waiting for *gringos*.

"Walk with me," Amador said.

"I'm waiting for a customer," Rogelio said.

Amador suppressed his urge to chastise his son for his rudeness. "How much do you make?"

Rogelio shrugged. "Twenty, maybe thirty," he said. "A person."

"Really?" Amador asked, knowing the answer was an exaggeration, wishing he had allowed the boy his lie.

"I can do five trips in an afternoon if I'm fast and if the people are not too old and fat to keep up with me," Rogelio said defiantly.

"That's good," Amador said.

Rogelio nodded. They were silent. Two boys wandered back from guiding tourists and resumed their desultory poses against the wall. Amador reached into his pocket and pulled out a handful of change.

"Thirty pesos," he said, holding the money out to his son. "Take me up."

"It's cold up there," Rogelio said, gesturing with his chin toward the top of the mountain. "The butterflies are not flying today. You're wasting your money."

"Or one of your friends can take me," Amador said, extending the coins to the other boys.

Rogelio grabbed the change from his father's hand, turned, and headed up the uneven mountain path at a furious pace.

"Let's stop for a moment," Amador called out after a half hour of steady climbing. He was winded, and this trip was not turning out as he had planned. He had hoped to talk to his son, to find some peace they could share.

Rogelio leaned against a tree. Amador caught his breath. "How much farther?" he asked. He had not come up here in years, not since before Rogelio was born, when he and Erlinda made a silent journey to plant a cross for Rubén, their first baby, their dead baby, among the high trees and the tumult of monarch butterflies the boy had loved to watch.

Rogelio shrugged. "Farther." He turned and began walking again.

Ten or fifteen people stood in a clearing where the trail came to an end. At first Amador saw nothing in the trees. Rogelio was right. The air was cool; the butterflies were not flying. But when his eyes adjusted, Amador saw hundreds of thousands of sleeping butterflies hanging from the branches, piled on top of one another in giant, living nests.

Rogelio squatted on the ground. He removed the slingshot from around his neck and began to stretch and release the rubber thong.

"You use that to scare them from the trees?" Amador asked.

Rogelio looked at the nearby guides. "That would kill the butterflies," he said witheringly, as though Amador were an enemy of nature. But Amador understood from his son's low voice and furtive gaze that if there were fewer people around to witness his misdemeanor, and if someone was willing to pay for the service, Rogelio would get those butterflies to fly.

"The butterflies that come here to mate don't live long enough to make the journey back," Amador said, remembering something he had once read.

Rogelio shrugged, uninterested. "Seen enough?" he said, rising from his squat. Amador understood there was no conversation to be had. Rogelio was a businessman. Too much time with one client meant a loss of income. He ran ahead of his father down the path, nimbly avoiding tree roots that elbowed out of the ground.

When Amador reached the bottom of the mountain, Rogelio had already rejoined his friends. He acknowledged his father's departure with a nod. As Amador made his way past the vendors and food stands, he heard the voices of the boys behind him crackle with laughter. He thought they must be laughing at him. But then he realized they were probably not talking about him at all.

*The bus exits* the freeway and begins to swing in and out of stops along the boulevard, disgorging sleepy passengers, taking on only a few. Amador steps off and begins the four-block walk to his trailer. In daylight the boulevard is a recognizable place. The signs for the bodegas and cut-rate furniture stores are all in Spanish or Persian, shop windows burst with colorful bolts of cloth, mountainous displays of low-cost shoes and plastic kitchenware. The sidewalks fill with chains of teenage girls walking arm in arm and mothers pushing baby strollers. The sound is not the choppy start-and-stop of English but the rapid waterfall of his own tongue or the percussive din of Farsi. Amador feels nearly comfortable walking these streets. But in the middle of this illusion of home something undeniably American appears, like the palatial supermarket, a confusion of aisles and choices that makes his eyes blur, or the Krispy Kreme doughnut shop, its technical advantage advertised by the visible ovens that produce perfectly identical glazed and jelly-filled confections. The salespeople in the doughnut shop wear beige-and-green uniforms as if they are people he needs to be wary of.

The Laundromat is busy as usual, even at midnight. The dry white fluorescent light makes everyone inside look like faded photographs of themselves. A woman pulls a tangled length of melon-colored sheet from a washer. A child spins around on a rolling laundry basket. Two teenage boys sit on dryers with their backs to the street, the tops of their boxer shorts visible above the low waistband of their oversize blue jeans. Mónaco, the manager, refills a dispenser of soap packets near the door. There is no phone in Amador's trailer, and he has made an arrangement with Mónaco: For a small fee Mónaco has allowed Amador to give the number of the Laundromat to Erlinda. She can call Amador there in case of emergency.

"Any messages?" Amador asks as he enters the Laundromat.

Mónaco shakes his head. Amador detects arrogance in the man's expression, a smirk beneath his heavy mustache. Amador never receives a phone call from his wife. Erlinda is not the kind to ask for help or advice, and she has only grown more independent during his absence. What can he do in an emergency anyway? How can he hope to affect his family so far from home? Amador makes a silent resolution not to come to the Laundromat looking for messages and finding only humiliation.

He rounds the corner to his street and walks past the small houses decorated with children's toys and giant pinwheels motionless in the night air. Despite the late hour, the faint blue glow of televisions seeps through where draperies separate from window frames. A pit bull stirs in his pen, but, unimpressed by Amador, does not bother to stand or even growl with any conviction.

Amador crosses the street and walks down a driveway of cracked pavement. The two-room trailer sits behind a small, wood-frame house. The four men who share the trailer sleep two to a room on thin mattresses set on the floor. Francisco and Juan are cousins from Jalisco and nephews of the owner of the house. When he first moved to Los Angeles, Amador met them at a lumberyard where all three waited each morning to be chosen for a construction crew. The fourth man, Hugo, works on paint crews. He leaves the trailer each morning wearing white carpenter pants, a white shirt, and paint-splattered shoes. He returns each night and washes his outfit in the small bathroom sink, hanging his clothes over a curtainless rod that spans the small window in the room he shares with Amador. After each laundering Hugo scours the sink with powdery green cleanser. Amador appreciates the man's fastidiousness, although Hugo's gesture of domesticity remains forlorn in its singularity. The apartment has no kitchen. The men eat out or bring in food. The empty containers pile up in the cardboard box that serves as their garbage can. The smells of packaged tomato sauce and grease linger in the air of the trailer day and night.

Amador knows little about the men he lives with. They share nothing more than greetings and, if one or the other is feeling flush with a paycheck, an occasional beer. Sometimes the owner of the house allows his relatives or friends fresh from crossing over to stay in the trailer for their first days in Los Angeles. Those nights Amador is often awakened by the music of garrulous conversation and laughter. Amador cannot remember the sound of his own laughter.

The bathroom light is on. The cousins lie asleep in the main room. In Amador's small room Hugo sleeps, air whistling through his nostrils. At nineteen he is already married to a girl in his village. His wedding picture hangs over his pillow. Amador stares at the girl's face, illuminated by the bathroom light. She is young and plump. She has a beauty mark that hangs over her upper lip like a punctuation mark. She is pretty in the way that all young people are pretty—because they are convinced by their ideas of themselves.

Amador goes into the bathroom, closes the toilet lid, and sits down. If he stretches out his hands he can touch the metal sink, the stall shower, the door. Sometimes he feels the world is so big that he is lost inside it. But at other times the world is just this small.

He is ambushed by thoughts of his first child, his no-longer child. Rubén. The memories attack him when he least expects them, and he cannot stop telling himself the story he wishes with all his heart to forget.

He and Erlinda took Rubén for a picnic by the river. It was summertime. The heat was so heavy that men and women walked with their heads bent, taking the weight of the sun on their shoulders. Rubén was one year old that day.

The bus to the river was crowded with families seeking respite from the heat. Amador held Rubén up to the open window. Rubén squirmed with delight at the passing scenery. "*Un caballo*," Amador whispered into the baby's ear. "*Un árbol.*" He loved to name the world for his son. With each label he felt he was casting a magic spell, causing sleeping trees and horses and dogs to awaken and become real.

They found a shady patch of grass on the bank of the river. A vendor was selling plastic cupfuls of *licuado*, and they splurged on the thick, sweet drink. Erlinda fussed with the baby's clothing, taking off and putting on a hat and shirt as the sun dipped in and out of clouds. Amador was charmed by the way motherhood had made his young wife both more womanly and more girlish at the same time. With the birth of his first child, Amador felt he finally knew all of his wife, her past and present. And her future. This child.

She protested when Amador stripped the baby of his

clothes and announced that it was time to take Rubén for his first swim. "The water is like ice!" she complained.

But Amador was already standing, having taken off his shirt. The feel of Rubén's rubbery skin against his own sticky chest was marvelous. He could not tell where his own body ended and his son's began. He licked a teardrop of papaya juice from Rubén's cheek. He squeezed the boy's spongy buttocks, felt the warmth of the baby's soft genitals against his ribs.

The sound of the river made Rubén squeal even before he touched the water. Erlinda was on her feet, begging Amador to bring the baby back to her. But Amador did not turn back. He spoke softly to his son until Rubén's noises subsided and his fear gave way to a stiff, soldierly attentiveness. He stared down at the light glinting like specks of mica on the water, and his breath calmed. Amador took a few steps into the river. The bottom of his trousers became wet, but he did not care. He turned back to the shore where Erlinda stood, shielding her eyes from the sun with both hands.

"*Es un valiente,*" he said proudly.

Rubén made a noise and pointed at the water with a stubby finger.

"*El agua fría,*" Amador whispered into the boy's ear. "*El río.*"

The boy reached toward the water, his fingers splayed, as if begging the river for a hug. Amador held Rubén tightly in his arms and crouched down so that Rubén's bottom skimmed the surface of the water. Rubén gasped, and

Amador swooped him back up into the air. Rubén pointed down again, and Amador lowered him to the water, going farther each time until the baby was wet up to his belly.

"Amador!" Erlinda warned from behind him.

Amador stared down at his miraculous baby. Rubén's eyes were wide. He did not cry or try to wriggle away from the water as the river moved across his skin.

One week later Amador rose early in the morning to catch a ride to his job in a nearby onion field. The baby had been feverish all week and lay in the bed, nestled in Erlinda's arms. Amador leaned over to kiss Rubén's forehead, but even before his lips touched the child's cold skin, he knew the baby was dead.

"There will be other children," the doctor said quietly as he left the house after tending to Erlinda.

"There will be no other children," Amador said quickly. *Because I will not allow myself to touch a child again. Because I killed my son.*

Amador stands and stares into the bathroom mirror but does not see himself. Instead he sees his baby lying in the bed, curled in Erlinda's arms, more still than sleep. How could he have continued dreaming during the night while his own child lay dead beside him? How could he have dared to dream?

After Rubén's death, Amador was scared to touch his young wife. He wanted nothing more than to disappear, to remove himself from the dangerous possibility of procreation. When the second child grew within her, he prayed, foolishly, that the baby would be just like Rubén, that his face would be round, his eyes wide enough to suck in the whole world, that his laugh would sound like bells, and that Rubén would be alive again. But Rogelio was thinner and darker than the first child, with eyes that were wary, as if he didn't believe he could take life at its word. Amador stood over the baby's cradle, unable to reach a hand to touch the boy's cheek. When Rogelio cried, Amador wanted to run and he did not stop wanting to run, even when two other children came into the world unburdened by history. Miguel and Berta were part of a new idea of a family, and Amador could hold them without thinking of the dead child. But still, in that town, in that home, he could not escape himself or his unforgivable mistake. He could not help but turn his self-loathing on Rogelio. That boy would always suffer the fact of having bridged the two stories of his family: He was the child who was meant to heal but who couldn't, for how could he hope to fill his father's endless well of sorrow?

5

*Caroline, Will, and Ethan* are moving to California in two days. Caroline takes the boys to one final eye exam. "Before the insurance runs out," she says as she drives them through the arrow-straight strip of franchises and giant discount food stores that leads to the university hospital. Ever since Will's father disappeared, they have been using up the vestiges of his life—his pass to the university pool, a credit at the bookstore, the loose change in his desk drawer.

Dr. Vandenberg exhales warm peppermint-scented breath into Will's face as he peers deeply into first one eye, then the other, through the lens of his complicated machinery.

"Can you see into my brain?" Will asks. Ever since he learned that the pupil is a hole, he is both frightened and amazed by the vulnerability of his thoughts.

"You have a *veddy beeg brain*," Dr. Vandenberg says, mumbling softly in a bad imitation of Dr. Frankenstein as he scans Will's eyes. When the examination is over, Dr. Vandenberg tells the boys to go to the waiting room. Ethan and Will sit on low plastic kindergarten chairs, while other bespectacled children flip, uninterested, through *Highlights* magazines and smudged board books. Will reads *Hop on Pop*, filling in the remembered text where the pages are ripped or missing. Ethan pulls one end of the cord belt of his sweatpants and watches the string slither into its hole.

"You're never gonna get that back," Will says.

"I don't care," Ethan says.

"Mom cares."

"You really think she cares about the string on my sweatpants?" Ethan blames their mother for everything lately.

When Caroline finally emerges from the examination room, she squints into the brightness of the overhead fluorescents as if she has just emerged from a movie theater into the surprising light of afternoon. Will is used to her gaze scooping up him and his brother at once, but now she looks at them as separate boys, and he feels sick to his stomach.

"I always thought you'd be together in this," she says on the drive home. "That made me feel good, knowing you had each other."

Later that night, as they eat turkey tacos off paper plates, she says, "It seems Ethan's eyes are doing better these days." She fingers her can of Dr. Pepper.

The remark makes no impression on Will at first. Ethan nods, then turns back to the messy predicament of his meal. Will breaks off a piece of his taco shell and dangles it under the table for the two remaining puppies—the runt and the one with the lazy eye, who have lived in the house for months, unnamed.

"But mine are worse, right?" Will says, suddenly getting it. He wipes his hand, now covered in dog slobber, on his shorts.

"Not worse," Caroline says. "There just seems to be a remission in Ethan's case, that's all."

"Remission?" Ethan says, confused.

"But that's a good thing, right?" Will says. "That's like going backwards."

His mother's eyes become glassy. "Yes," she says. "Like going back."

Will stares at his plate. For the first time he realizes he is not part of a family, or a class of fourth-graders, or even a group of children with eye disease. He is by himself.

The phone rings in the middle of dessert. Caroline picks it up. Will can tell by the way her voice grows unnaturally high that it is his father. He rushes to the phone before Ethan can get to it. "Dad," he says, turning to the wall, hoping to hide his happiness from his mother.

His father speaks too fast and too loud, as if he has cranked himself up and is trying to get everything in before the mechanism winds down.

"Where are you?" Will says.

"I'm moving around," Frank says. "I went to Chicago."

"Are you gonna see the Red Sox?" Will asks.

"I'm not there anymore," Frank says.

"Where are you going?"

"Umm . . . not sure."

"Don't you have a job?"

"Not for now, buddy. Taking a break, I guess."

"I saw Jupiter last night," Will says, stealing a glance at Ethan who thankfully isn't paying attention to the lie.

"Is that right?"

"Didn't you see it?"

"I don't watch the sky much these days," Frank says.

"Why not?" Will asks, alarmed that his father has stopped doing the single thing Will associates with him.

"I just can't look too hard at things right now. You can understand that, can't you? You're a smart boy."

"Sure, Dad," Will says.

"You didn't talk to him," Will says to his mother after Ethan has had his turn and hung up the phone.

"He called to talk to you, not me," she says, smiling uncomfortably.

The next day Will and Ethan stand in front of the grocery store with the last two dogs. After three hours and after lowering the price from fifty dollars to twenty-five to free, two men walk the dogs toward their red sports car.

"We don't even know them," Will says, watching as one of the men lifts the runt by his haunches and it pitches headfirst into the narrow backseat. "What if they're mean?"

"The dogs will have to deal with it," Ethan says, as he folds the handmade for-sale sign and stuffs it into a trash can.

That afternoon Ethan, Will, and Caroline have a yard sale. The lawn is a history written in pots and pans, Legos and Hot Wheels, plastic animals and winter boots. "None of this is worth the price of hauling it cross-country," Caroline says, gesturing to the overgrown hills of action figures, basketball cards, and books that once proliferated on the boys' bedroom floor and shelves. She has cleared everything from her own room except for the desk and oak bed, both of which were too heavy for the three to maneuver outside.

While neighbors and strangers finger through his belongings, Will slips back inside the house and into his parents' room. His father's desk is an old-fashioned rolltop, scarred with ink stains and pencil etchings. Will loves this desk for its secrecy. Small drawers open, revealing hidden compartments. Wooden leaves slide out of narrow slots to form impromptu writing surfaces. Will lifts a heavy book from the bottom left drawer. This dictionary-size compilation of medical afflictions is his favorite. The thousand pages are as thin as tissue. He fingers past photographs of physical deformities and schematic drawings of hearts and lungs. He peels apart the transparencies of the male and female body. He is awed by the complicated network of veins and arteries on one, and the braided muscles on another, the way the body unlayers itself before his eyes until it is nothing but organs. Turning more pages, he stops at the section devoted to skin diseases and gazes calmly at the close-range photos of lesions and pustules. The eruptions look like volcanoes exploding on the surface of the body. He flips more pages. There are so many entries in the book that it is impossible to believe a person can be healthy. Defects are as ubiquitous as gopher holes—sooner or later, you are bound to drop down into one and twist your ankle or worse. But when he thinks about the people he knows—

his mother, the kids at school, even Ethan now that he is better—Will realizes that his condition is exceptional.

He locates his disease. It has a Latin name he has to say aloud in order to sound out the strange syllables. The book describes the stages of the disease, which include night blindness, although this is supposed to occur in young adulthood, not at the age of ten. He thinks about that night when he could not see the stars and whispers angrily to himself. *Stupid. Stupid.* He can't even get his disease right.

The book also describes the "usual course" of the disease, leaving room for the odd, the unexpected, the mistake on top of a mistake. According to the book, eventually Will will not be able to see in the dark at all. Night will become the opposite of day, an absolute thing. A no thing. *Night blind.* One day he will find himself in a world of darkness, and he will have to use all his wits to survive. Already he is a detective. The objects of the world—bodies, furniture, trees—fade into the deep background of his perceptions. He focuses instead on their effects—their smells, the heat or chill they cause, the alteration in volume one person's words cause in another's, the way a father disappears because of what his son can't see.

"Blind," he says aloud. He closes his eyes. Then he opens them. Shut, open. Shut, open. He waits for his eventual blindness with the same dread and eager anticipation he felt when he was seven and Ethan persuaded him to climb a ladder to the roof of the house and stand at the edge. Will had wanted to jump, even if it meant hurting himself or dying. Sometimes, when he is lying in bed at night, he wills his blindness to come.

He puts the book back in the desk drawer and goes outside to watch the sale. An old man wearing his father's beige overcoat walks toward an idling car. His mother looks after the man, narrowing her eyes as he moves farther off as though watching a boat slip over the horizon. Then she crosses her arms over her chest and shakes her shaggy hair, reminding herself not to care that strangers are walking away with her life.

Two college-age boys come out of the house, struggling under the weight of the desk.

"You didn't empty it out!" Will cries, waving his hands to get his mother's attention away from Mrs. Duchinsky, a neighbor, who is turning a platter over in her hands, searching for cracks. The boys set the desk down at the curb. Caroline quickly empties the drawers, pulling out papers and pens, a calculator and a compass. Will reaches for the medical book.

"Can I keep this?" he asks.

"If you want it," she says and watches as Will lifts the heavy book and holds it to his chest.

"You're like him that way, you know," she says, tapping the book.

"In what way," Will asks, thrilled.

"You like the facts."

"Is that good?"

She looks as if she is going to tell him one thing but changes her mind. "Sure it is, baby," she says, laying a hand gently on his back.

They stand together and watch as the young men struggle to fit the desk onto their truck bed.

"Bye-bye, desk," Caroline says.

Later, after the last of the browsers has wandered away, Caroline and the boys take a final tour of their empty house. Will stares at the denuded kitchen. Every dirt streak and wall crack stands out in high relief without the mask of foreground coffee pot and bowls of softening fruit. The room looks flimsy. Will cannot imagine how the shelves were once strong enough to hold dishes and pots. The counter tile is stained with rusted rings where sugar and flower canisters sat for so many years. Four small black circles on the linoleum floor tell the story of the kitchen table. Will wonders if the next tenants will be able to reconstruct his family's life from these clues.

"Some people get emotional about houses," Caroline says. "You know—this is the house I raised my babies in, and all that. They feel like they're abandoning something, I guess."

Will and Ethan follow her into their bedroom. The room looks too small to have contained their twin beds and mismatched dressers on which she once painted the planets.

"I used to feel that way," Caroline continues. "But I don't anymore. Does that make me a bad person?"

She does not wait for an answer but moves into the house's only bathroom. The boys follow her. Patches of white scar the cobalt walls where she has removed pictures of magnified beetles and spiders that she loves and which will now hang in Lisa Lamb's bedroom down the street. Ethan crouches down and tries to peel a skateboard sticker off the tile on the side of the tub.

"It will look worse without it," Caroline says.

The boys follow her past her own bedroom. She does not open the door. Finally they stand in the living room. The carpet underneath where the couch and chairs sat is a lighter shade of tan than the surrounding area, as if the furniture has left behind the opposite of a shadow.

"Someone else will live here now," Caroline says, staring out the window at the items lying on the grass no one has bought. "And then, after them, some other people will live here."

"I'll miss the woods," Will says.

"Yes," she says. "There won't be many good hiding places where we're going."

*They are driving* through Kansas. Will closes his eyes. First the darkness becomes sound: the air hissing by outside the Subaru's window, then the song on the radio, played so low it is only a wandering buzz, occasionally punctuated by Caroline's low, off-key hum, her wedding ring tap-tapping impatiently on the steering wheel. (The ring, evidence of her belief in Frank's eventual return?) And then a sleeping sigh from Ethan, who lies across the backseat, his sweaty socks pressed against the window making a design, Will envisions on his screen of darkness, of toes and a blobby foot.

Next the darkness becomes a picture. Amoeboid puffs float and rearrange themselves until they form the unmistakable shape of his father. The figure is tall, with arms that swing loosely next to his sides. His legs kick out at the knees as he walks, as if he is formed from bolted parts. *Frank. Dad. Daddy.* The words no longer slip into their meaning without a shove.

It is hard for Will to remember his father's face, even after six months. When he stares at photographs, he cannot connect the frozen features with the man who went to work one day and didn't come back. Will should have looked at his father more carefully when Frank was around. But you don't look at a father. A father is not simply a face, but a whole idea that lives in your mind more than in your sight. Frank is the coolness of newly washed hands; the sharp inhale while he chews his food; the scattering of dull pennies, orphan keys, and old watchbands inside his dresser drawer. Will can remember the face of the checkout lady at the supermarket better than he can his father's. Polished red cheeks, blue eyes rimmed with dark lashes, a mole he has always wanted to scrape off the bottom of her chin with his fingernail. He could recognize this woman in a moment, in the middle of a crowd. But will he recognize his father if he ever returns?

Will recites to himself the words his mother uses to describe his father, words she seems reluctant to say: *tall, thin, clean, careful.* She uses these words as if she is tiptoeing around other words she doesn't want to say, words that will make Frank present and regrettable all over again. She does not describe the confusing downward twist of his mouth when he laughed, as though he second-guessed his pleasure, or the heavy weight of his distraction. *Dad, Dad, DAD!* Will would say, then finally yell, when he could not get his father's attention. And where was his father in these moments? What private country did he go to all by himself?

Caroline never reminds Will that Frank was ticklish on the bottoms of his feet and that he always hated to be touched there by his sons' spidery fingers when they stood at the foot of his bed, waiting for him to look up from his freckled celestial maps. *Caroline, I can't deal with this*, Frank would call finally, sending the boys scurrying away, giggling, hollow. And she never reminds him (how could she know?) of the reassuring hardness of Frank's lap when Will sat upon it, his face pressed against the cold metal of the university telescope on those lucky Saturdays when Frank would take Will and Ethan to work. How could she know the pleasure of Frank's breath warming Will's cheek or the tense excitement of Frank's body when Will said, "Yes Dad, I see." She knows nothing of the rare intoxication Will felt at being the cause of his father's happiness.

Maybe blindness will be like this, Will thinks. There are pictures you can make yourself see in the darkness—the speckled white trunk of the birch tree that stands in the center of their backyard, (their *old* backyard, he reminds himself), the mint-condition Larry Bird rookie card that he coveted in the card shop, its details all the more indelible for his longing, the precise curve of the hood of his father's Chevy truck ticking warmly under his hand as the engine cooled down. And then there are pictures that escape just as they are nearly apparent. Like this man, this father. The image evaporates at the very moment Will's mind closes around it, the way his hand grasps a firefly, only to capture air.

"Are we there yet?" Ethan says, sleepily.

"Ha, ha, ha," Caroline answers to this age-old and unserious question.

"What will it be like in California?" Ethan says, sitting up. He searches the seat cracks for his glasses, then gives up.

"It will be like . . . ," Caroline begins, but then her voice drifts off.

"Like what?"

"I need to concentrate on the road," Caroline says, leaning forward, her hands tightening around the steering wheel as if driving is a sport that requires strength. This trip seems to demand something from her that she does not possess in abundance. She slips a CD into the player.

"Johnny's life passed him by like a warm summer day," she sings loudly along with the song.

Will is embarrassed by the way she sings and shrugs her shoulders, as if she's forgotten she's their mother. He wonders if she will ever forget completely, the way his father has.

"The question is," Caroline says happily, "who is Johnny?"

The freeway sign reads, "You are leaving Kansas. Come back soon!" and is followed immediately by one that reads, "Welcome to Colorado." Will wonders how one place can suddenly become another. Is it the same as your life being one thing one day and then something else entirely the next?

He rests his head against the cold window, listening to the soft clicks and beeps of Ethan's Game Boy. His mother kicks off her left shoe, lifts her foot onto the seat and massages it with her free hand. Then she turns the volume down on the radio.

"Listen," she says. "Grandma Eleanor . . . she's not the same as when you last saw her."

"You told us. She's sick," Will says.

"Not sick in the body," she says. "In the mind."

"You mean she's crazy?" Ethan asks.

Caroline smiles. "Not crazy. Your grandmother would never go crazy. She has a disease that makes you forget things. Like she might not remember you guys. She might not remember me. Sometimes. Not all the time. Do you understand?"

"Like being blind in the brain," Will says, as a billboard advertising God floats past his window.

"What?" Caroline says.

"Grandma's disease," he says. "It's like going blind in the brain. Little by little."

"That's not right," she says, urgently, as if Will has stepped into oncoming traffic. "It's not like that at all."

Will thinks his grandmother's brain must be like a piece of Swiss cheese with holes where thoughts used to be. His grandmother will see but not know. He will know, but not see. Again the terrible thought seizes him. What if his father comes back and Will cannot see him? His stomach flips over and he is instantly terrified.

"Mom?" he says.

"What's the matter, baby?"

"Nothing,"

"You can tell me."

"I forgot."

"Tell me when you remember."

"I will."

6.

*Rogelio has saved the money* he's earned at the butterfly sanctuary, except for what he gave his mother for food and school supplies. He feels badly about holding back the pesos he buried beneath a rock in back of the house because it makes him angry to see how hard his mother works ever since his father left. But he knows he will need the money. He knows, too, that his savings are pitiful. He hears the boys at the sanctuary talking about *polleros* who charge a thousand U.S. dollars to take a person across! And then you can pay all that money and still get caught and be sent back over the border with nothing to show for yourself but an empty pocket. He knows, too, about *bandidos* who will ambush you and take all your money even before you have a chance to cross over. What scares him the most, though, are stories of men who kidnap children and hold them until their parents can buy them back. But this will not happen to him, he assures himself.

Amador does not see how hard Erlinda works each day and night, how her hands are rough and pricked with sewing needle marks. He does not know how much has changed. Erlinda used to sing all day, her voice an accompaniment that Rogelio cannot separate from the memory of his own childhood. She used to sing as she made small toys out of paper, folding a plain square so ingeniously that it would turn into a cricket or a star. He misses the music of her laughter. Just a week ago, when he and Miguel and Berta returned from the market in Ocampo with their mother, the bottom dropped out of her worn bag. Onions and oranges rolled down the hillside as if they had all given one another a signal to run away. Once Erlinda would have laughed and chased the errant fruits and vegetables, calling out to them as if they were mischievous children, and Rogelio and his brother and sister would have joined in the chase, delighted by the way their mother could turn disaster into adventure. But this time she stood at the crest of the hill watching the food escape and said, "There's nothing I can do about that either."

She will not tell his father to come back home. She is too proud for that. It is up to Rogelio. Didn't his mother herself tell him to do this? Didn't she wake him in the middle of the night and lead him outside, whispering, "Come see the comet"? They sat outside the house, tilting their faces to the sky. He followed the path of his mother's outstretched finger. "*Mira*," she whispered, as if a loud voice might frighten the comet away. Together they watched a bright light hurtle through the sky. "The universe moves," she said, her breath hot in his ear. "We are not fixed in one place. I want you to understand that, my love. Do you understand?" And he did understand: She was telling him to be like that comet. He should hurtle across the horizon to find his father and bring him home.

He leaves El Rosario on the back of a truck carrying dried cornhusks. The bales are packed so tightly he has to squeeze in next to the back gate. With each bump the husks and rough twine bite into his ankles and arms. At first the sweet, grainy smell is comforting and familiar. But after a while, the close odor begins to make him gag. He tries to breathe only through his mouth, but he can taste the smell on his tongue. He pulls his shirt over his face, but the lack of oxygen makes him dizzy. Each time the truck heaves over a buckle in the road, the impact shoots from his ass to his spine. He stiffens his body to withstand the assault but finally gives up and lets himself flop back and forth with the truck's belching movements as though he is one of the cloth dolls Berta swings by her side.

It is impossible not to think of his family. Berta and Miguel are part of him in some important way, just the way his organs are part of him, even though he cannot see or touch them. And Rubén, the one who did not survive, is an invisible bruise somewhere on his body. Sometimes, when Amador looks at Rogelio in a certain way, Rogelio feels the dull pain of something not quite healed.

Berta accepts Amador's arrivals and departures with no more anticipation or regret than she does Alberto the salesman's occasional visits to their house. She knows her mother has no money or inclination to buy things from this small, boisterous man who smells of bubble gum and cigarettes, but still, Berta enjoys the wind of excitement and expectation that accompanies Alberto. When the man finally leaves, no richer or poorer than when he arrived, Berta barely reacts to his departure. This salesman, like her father, is just an event of the day that will soon be replaced by another event, more or less pleasing than the first.

Miguel is an even bigger mystery. He and Rogelio walk the mile to school together each day. Rogelio walks slowly, observing the decay of one house, the repair of another, noting a car that has been newly painted, or a father who has returned home. He cannot help computing how these changes factor in to his life, which seems to be controlled by everyone and everything except himself. Meanwhile Miguel runs, head bowed, like an arrow bent on its destination. Miguel didn't even notice when a bright yellow tractor got stuck in the mud after a big rainfall. The tractor stood out in the landscape like a shout, but it wasn't until Rogelio pointed it out that Miguel stopped to look at it for a moment, then nodded and ran ahead. For Miguel the object of going to school is to get to school. There is no room in his mind for the tributaries of ungraspable and unexplainable feeling that cut endless, twisting pathways through Rogelio's brain. When their father comes home, Miguel plays with him. When Amador leaves, Miguel finds someone else to play with. Rogelio wishes he could be like his brother, but Rogelio cannot play a simple game of baseball without wondering what the other players are thinking, what their expressions mean, how senseless it is to run around bases in the midst of an even more inscrutable life.

The truck stops, farts exhaust, then makes a left-hand turn and continues. Rogelio thinks about his mother and his throat tightens. Erlinda's round, open face appears in his mind. She covers her mouth when she laughs to hide her crooked teeth. She has a beauty mark under her right eye. Her hands are stronger than any man's, but their touch, on a cold night, can feel like the warmest, softest blanket. She is shorter than he is now; her head ends where his begins. Suddenly he wants to call out above the sound of the engine and tell the driver to stop. He will leap out and run back to his mother. He will bury his face in her lap and smell the rich mixture of soap and coffee that is her irresistible perfume. He will tell her that he will stay, he will be both father and son, he will stay with her forever.

He wipes the water from his eyes and curses himself. He is fourteen. Boys his age have taken this journey and not run back weeping to their mothers. They have returned home having been transformed into men, strutting through town in new jeans and clean shirts. He sucks in a lungful of bitter air, hitches his arm through one of the wooden railings of the truck, and lets the journey reverberate through his body.

The driver drops him along the highway at the edge of a town he does not know. He watches as the overweight truck lumbers off the main road onto a rocky path that leads from the highway toward the distant farms. He is as far from home as he's ever been, and the distance between himself and Los Angeles seems endless, unbridgeable. Suddenly, he is gripped by a stomach-churning panic. He is in the middle of a huge ocean without a raft to hold onto and with no way to catch his breath. He looks around for a covert place to release his bowels. Then, as quickly as the terror overwhelms him, it disappears. His insides solidify. For the first time since leaving El Rosario, he feels a peacefulness in his body he has never felt before. He wonders if his father felt this same terrifying and thrilling loneliness of being stranded in the world.

It is nearing sundown. The sky turns an indecisive gray on its way to becoming something else. Rogelio's hunger builds like a distant storm. He knows that if he does not find something to eat soon, it will overtake him and he will miss his mother again. The center of town will be busy this time of day with people shopping and strolling, making the most of the day's last light, so he wanders down an outlying street. A woman leaves a shop carrying a plump brown paper bag. The scent of bitter chocolate follows her, and Rogelio inhales it and thinks of his mother's *mole*. A few men loiter outside a *cantina*. An old, wrinkled woman sits on a low stool just inside the door of a market, catching the negligible breeze of early evening as she sews on a dark blue *rebozo*. Rogelio crosses the street and peers inside. The shelves are stocked with crackers and dry cereals, laundry soaps and cans of milk. A cardboard box on the floor spills over with onions and browning bananas. Crates of soda bottles are stacked against one wall, the bright enticements of their logos dulled with dust. A box of chocolate bars lies like an open palm on the counter.

"What do you want?" the woman asks, without looking up from her sewing.

Rogelio salivates, thinking of the candy. But he must save his money. "You need someone to do work for you?" he asks. "I can sweep. Or clean your counters."

"If you're begging, you can try somewhere else."

"I could watch the store for you," he says.

"No one needs to watch this store," she says. "Not even me."

Defeated, he leaves the shop. The sweet smell of cooking meat draws him down another street. Older boys and men work underneath cars, their trunkless legs protruding into traffic. Mothers call out evening orders to their children from within courtyards hidden behind doors. Rogelio imagines walking into any one of these doorways and resuming his life as it was, just a day ago, before he left El Rosario. His mother will be cooking beans and rice and maybe a little meat. Berta will be playing her make-believe games with a box and some marbles. And there is Miguel, tossing his ball up and down, up and down, his face passive as his mind plays out a fantasy game.

For a moment the idea occurs to him that he does not belong in El Rosario anymore. But he banishes the thought. Of course he knows where he belongs, and when he finally returns home his family will be whole once more.

Later that night, while the town sleeps, he takes a fist-size rock and breaks the window of the old woman's market. He steals two candy bars and a bottle of warm orange soda. He stuffs the bars into his mouth as he runs toward the highway. Certain the police are already after him, he avoids the passing car lights by walking in the bushes alongside the road. After a few hours his legs feel like water, and he heads away from the highway toward a stand of trees. He pulls dried leaves and branches around himself and sleeps.

Each day he travels north, either by truck or by foot. Each night he sleeps on a bench in a deserted *zócalo* or behind a Pemex station, underneath a blanket of discarded boxes. If he is not able to reach a town by nightfall, he sleeps near enough to a road to avoid roaming animals but far enough away so as not to be run over by a drunken driver weaving his way home. Some nights he sleeps a corpse's dreamless sleep and wakes not remembering who or where he is. During the first conscious moments of these mornings he is relaxed, and he relishes the feeling of being without past or present. Other nights he startles from his sleep frequently, his body an overanxious alarm clock. During these wakeful dark hours he feels the torment of his conflicting feelings about his father. Each time Amador leaves El Rosario after one of his visits, Rogelio endures his mother's rage. "You don't talk to your father? You don't even look him in the eye! You have no respect!" How can he tell her that he cannot make words that will express the fire that burns inside him when he is around his father? How can she understand the obliterating heat of his longing?

He remembers the bready, wet smell of his father's neck when he was a child and his father held him. He can smell his father in the house, days after Amador leaves for the north. He cannot escape that smell no matter where he goes.

It is on him, it seeps out of his pores. Why does love feel like hate?

As he travels north, he drinks from silt-stippled creeks or from the runoff of drainpipes after a night of body-soaking rain. He eats whatever food he can find or what he can steal. He does not allow himself to take food off roadside altars. He knows his life could end around any unremarkable bend in the road, just as it has for the people whose names are painted so carefully on the crosses of splintered wood.

The land is part of his skin now. It has turned him a darker shade of brown.

*After four days*, a truck carrying porcelain toilets deposits him at the border. Stupidly he has imagined the border as a thin line Miguel might draw in the dirt to stand for home plate. One giant step could take him from Mexico to the U.S.A. and he would be that much closer to Los Angeles. Rogelio has imagined the step as though it is part of a child's game, something Berta might play with her little friends. *Walk like an elephant!* and the little girls bend over, their arms swinging slowly below their faces like trunks as they take lumbering strides. But when Rogelio finds his way down to the riverbank, he sees that even an elephant could not take a step that big.

He spends the day wandering through the *barrio*, a fortress of homes made of cardboard, corrugated iron, truck tires, and carpet remnants. Still water hangs sullenly in the gullies of the uneven dirt alleyways. Children dart in and out of the dark shacks into the light of the day like fireflies as they play games of chase or run with empty buckets banging against their thighs. The smell of fried meat from the outdoor stalls fills Rogelio's nostrils. His jaw aches with the desire to chew and taste the juice and fat.

He walks past a mirror hanging in a *zapatería*. The mirror is small and low, meant to reflect the chunky sole of a boot or the knifelike point of a high heel. Rogelio bends down and looks at his reflection. A dirty, sunbaked boy stares back, hair matted, eyes as untrusting as a rat's. A dark shadow crosses his upper lip. He rubs his finger carefully over the new hair there. Maybe he looks like a man now. When he tells his father to come home, his father will listen.

"*Bete*," an old man's voice snaps from within the store, and Rogelio runs.

When it is dark he stands by the edge of the river. Vendors sell *tortas*, candy and sodas, plastic bags for covering your feet. He buys one small bottle of water. The river begins to fill with people. Men and women sink down until they are knee deep in water. Mothers lift babies and small children high on their hips. Grandmothers ride on the backs of young men. A small group of men and women stands on the bank near Rogelio, studying the paths of those midway across. Then, in what seems like an unspoken agreement, they begin. Rogelio follows. The rocks near the shore give way to mud. The sticky bottom of the river grabs his shoes. He trips once and falls to his knees, but gets to his feet as fast as he can, struggling with the extra weight of his soaked pants. His water bottle is tucked into his waistband. With each step, the hard plastic cap digs into his belly. He is grateful for the distraction of this bearable pain. The woman in front of him lets out a frightened cry as she stumbles. Rogelio reaches out to catch her. Once she is steady she does not let go of his hand. He thinks of his mother's hand folded around his like wrapping paper around a birthday gift, and his resolve weakens. He shakes the woman's hand loose from his own.

On the opposite bank the men and women run from the river as if it is a monster that will reach out and grab them back. He follows them into the desert. When they freeze at the sound of a helicopter, he does the same. No one speaks. In the moonlight, Rogelio sees the helicopter's wasp tail suspended above its fat body. The broad beam of its searchlight stings the land not twenty yards from where the group hides behind a clump of desert brush. The beam arcs away just before exposing them, and the noise of the plane disappears into the night.

Two hours later, the group drops into a shallow ravine to rest. Rogelio counts three men and two women. They drink from their water bottles and readjust their packs. A tall wiry man with cheeks as sunken as craters gnaws on a rod of sausage. He wears a cowboy hat and old, scuffed boots. He stares at the women in the group, then at Rogelio, trying to make a connection. But the women ignore Rogelio as they attend to their belongings.

"*¿Cómo te llamas?*" the man asks, his voice rough with grit.

"Rogelio."

"*¿Estás solo?*" the man says.

Rogelio nods.

"*¿Adónde vas?*"

"*A Los Angeles*," Rogelio says. The destination sounds as phony as one of Berta's fantasy kingdoms.

The man smiles. Bits of sausage cling to his teeth. His expression is meanly triumphant, as if he is already gloating over the unsuccessful outcome of Rogelio's naive journey. "Eat something," he says.

Rogelio shrugs. He does not want to confirm the man's assumption of his ignorance by admitting he has made the crossing without food and with only a small supply of water.

"*Mira aquí*," comes a woman's voice.

The woman Rogelio helped in the river offers him a *tortilla*. She wears a San Antonio Spurs T-shirt, an unzipped nylon jacket, and a full skirt.

"*Gracias*," he says.

An argument breaks out about the route. The man with the sausage wants to continue in one direction. Another, younger man, wearing a sweatshirt and a baseball cap, disagrees.

"Look at the stars," the younger traveler complains. "We're going *east*. We're going the wrong way." As the argument continues, Rogelio scans the sky. He searches for the constellations he knows: Orion, Pegasus. He is comforted to find the Big Dipper, scooping up a ladleful of heaven. He lies down on the ground. In this place where he knows no one and nothing, at least he knows the stars. The sky is the only thing that has accompanied him from home.

*They travel by night* in a lazy line. No one speaks; it takes too much energy to make a sound. They follow the sausage

man. Néstor is his name. Felipe is the one with the baseball
cap. There is María Elena, the woman he helped in the
river, and her sister, Esperanza. The other man is very old
and seems to belong to no one in the group. Rogelio does not
know his name.

During the day the heat of the desert sun slams down on
them like a hammer. Rogelio's brain aches. He has no hat.
He takes off his T-shirt and ties it around his head. He can
practically feel his skin baking like a chicken's on a spit. His
water is gone. He reswallows his own spit. His lips crack
whenever he moves them. He licks them to take away the
sting, but when the air hits the newly moistened skin, the
pain worsens. Thoughts of water invade his mind: a glass of
water, a bath, the swimming hole near his home filled to the
brim with rainwater. He imagines jumping into the hole
with the other children. He hears their laughter, the sound
of the first body breaking the still surface of the water with
a crack. He thinks of his mother holding the brown jug over
Berta's soapy hair. His mouth waters at the thought of his
own stream of piss.

The second night the group gathers beside a rock shaped
like an enormous arrowhead.

"You're leading us to our deaths," Felipe argues.

"Go your own way, then," Néstor says.

Felipe grumbles that he will. María Elena and Esperanza
speak tensely to themselves in Nahuatl. Rogelio can't understand the language, only recognizes the clacking sounds
from his grandmother's speech—like dried beans rattling
inside a gourd. Esperanza begins to weep softly.

"The boy," María Elena says. "Look at his eyes." She

walks toward Rogelio and grasps his face in her hands. Her fingers feel dry and rough and cold. He wonders what she sees in his eyes that causes her own to widen in alarm. As he stares into her face, her features rearrange themselves. Her mouth takes the place of her nose. She has eyes for ears. He laughs.

"He needs to drink," she says.

"He's going crazy," someone says.

"He needs water!" María Elena cries. Her exclamation seems to exhaust her, and she drops her hands.

Words surround him like fluttering bird wings. Who knows the boy, anyway? What business of theirs is he? The voices grow louder and more percussive until he imagines they take the shape of a blackbird that is swooping toward him and attacking his face. The bird is going to kill him. The thought calms him. He is going to die, and he will not be thirsty anymore. He looks up to expose his face to the bird. He sees no stars, only darkness. Gentle darkness, like a blanket. Okay, he thinks. I will let it cover me, and then I will die. And I will not be thirsty anymore.

He feels something hard against his mouth. It is the bird, pecking him. Something wet slides down his chin. His blood?

"Don't waste! He's wasting the water!" It is Felipe's voice. Felipe burned himself in his family's kiln. The skin of his forearms is shiny and hairless, stretched taut like the film on top of boiled milk. Why is Felipe here? Rogelio thinks. Has the bird pecked him to death too? Tepid liquid runs down Rogelio's throat, warming the inside of his hot chest. He imagines his body is a river. It is water, rushing, rushing.

Rogelio opens his eyes and sees Néstor's face hovering above his own. He smells the man's stink. Néstor shakes the bottle.

"Drink," he orders.

The water smells of foul breath and spit, and Rogelio has to stop himself from retching. But he can hardly swallow before his tongue and throat beg to suck down more. After he has taken four long pulls, Néstor yanks the bottle away. He stares into Rogelio's eyes, searching for something. His own dark eyes dart back and forth like guppies. "This one won't make it," he says.

He is interrupted by the crunch and slide of tires over rock. No one moves. And then, as though a gun has signaled the beginning of a race, they run, fanning out in all directions. Rogelio stands uncertainly. He is dizzy. He tells himself to run, but he cannot make his body move. The sound of a motor grows at his back. He turns and is blasted by twin beams of white light. He thinks the sun has fallen down to earth.

7

*August, and the high school* feels like a place full of wilted people. The students who failed out during the school year move through the corridors like indolent fish. Others, like Marlene, who work cleanup for summer pay, move just as listlessly in the un-airconditioned buildings. What Marlene likes best, likes singularly, about the work is that she arrives at three and leaves at eight and so is nearly always alone. The two other kids who work her schedule work in other buildings, and the three rarely run into one another except in the supply room, which reeks of pot and cigarettes.

Tonight Marlene finishes early but if she clocks out, she won't get full pay, so she sneaks into the library and fingers past the rows of books, finally pulling out a copy of *Siddhartha*. She writes a note to the librarian that she took the book even though she knows no one is on staff until the school year begins. But she is no thief.

It's still light out as she bikes home, and the heat is dense; breathing makes her sweat. She likes the long, boring ride each night. She thinks of nothing. She concentrates on pushing the pedals around until she feels like the bike itself. It is a relief to feel like a thing whose sole purpose is to go someplace else.

A half block from her home, she passes a man sitting in a parked car. His presence unnerves her because she doesn't recognize the car and because she has the feeling, as she rides past, that he is watching her. Her mother will be out late this evening, eating with friends from work. If Marlene stops at her house, the man will know where she lives. She passes the car and circles her block.

When she returns to her street, he is there. She turns and rides away, her heart pounding. Five minutes later, he's still there. She considers going to a neighbor's house. But her mother is not friendly with the neighbors, and she doubts anyone will help her. She could call the police. But they'd probably laugh at her. It's a free country. A man can sit in a car and look at whoever he wants.

Suddenly the car door opens, and the man steps out. It takes him some time to unfold his long legs from the bucket seat. He turns toward Marlene, and in that second when her heart is pounding, her mind clears, and for reasons she can't explain, she knows who he is, and she knows that he doesn't mean to hurt her. She gets off her bike and walks it slowly toward him.

"Marlene?" he asks, tentatively.

"Who wants to know?" she says, trying to hide the tremble in her voice.

"I'm your . . . well, I don't know exactly what to call myself."

"You're my father," she says.

"Well," he says.

She's only two bike lengths from him now. He doesn't look her in the eye when he talks. He holds on to the car door as if it is the only thing keeping him standing.

"Don't worry," she says. "It's just a word. Like 'book' or 'table.' It doesn't mean anything personal."

He says nothing.

"I thought you were, like, a sex fiend or something," she says.

"No," he says, upset. "No."

He's very tall, she thinks. And thin, like her. And he's pale. His eyebrows are so light she can't see them on his face. His blue eyes sparkle as if out of a snowy field.

"My mother's not home," she says.

"I didn't come to see your mother," he says.

"You came to see me?"

He nods.

"Why?" she says.

"I'm not sure."

She is confused and happy and for some reason incredibly sad. Here he is, the man she has wondered about all her life. And he is . . . not sure.

"I've been doing some traveling," he says.

"And your itinerary takes you through here?" she says, gesturing ironically at her neighborhood, her town.

He smiles briefly. "I guess I came a little out of my way."

"You have kids," she says. "Other kids."

He looks as though she has struck him. "Yes, I do," he says. He glances at his car as if he'd forgotten they were inside it. "Boys," he says. "Good boys." He winces.

She feels immediately jealous. "Well, I failed math this year, so I guess I didn't get that part of you," she says. "But they're probably real smart, those boys."

When he doesn't answer or crack a smile, she feels like an idiot. She's making him want to leave. She wishes she hadn't told him about the math, especially since she got a C-plus, but she just had to say something and that was the first thing she could think of. She wishes he would ask her a normal, boring question about what grade she is in or what her favorite subject is, something she knows the answer to. Her nose begins to tingle, and tears collect behind her eyes. She bends down to adjust something on her bike that doesn't need adjusting. By the time she straightens up, her heart is hard.

He looks around the street distractedly, as though he's not really seeing any of it. He's like an apology for himself, she thinks.

"We don't know each other very well," he says.

Her throat tightens. "You don't know me at all."

"Maybe it would be better if I hadn't come," he says.

*This is my father. My father.* The word seems at once too much and not enough to describe the man before her. She feels as if she is reading out loud in Spanish class when she doesn't know what the words mean but tries to say them correctly so the teacher will move on to the next student.

"Do you have a lot of kids? I mean all over the place. Sprinkled," she says.

"Sprinkled?" he says. "No."

"So I'm the only one. The only *other* one."

"Yes."

"I don't know if that makes me special or not."

He doesn't answer, and her heart caves in.

"Why are you here?" she asks again.

"I guess I got lost, somehow," he says.

"You sure did," she says. "Nobody comes here unless they've got a good reason, and there aren't too many of those."

"I don't mean that literally," he says.

Now she feels really stupid. She's sure his other children would have understood what he meant. She imagines that phantom family standing on the street, laughing at her.

"I'm having a hard time right now," he says. "I'm trying to figure out what . . . I have lost," he says. "That probably doesn't make any sense to you."

She says nothing for fear of saying the wrong thing.

"You seem like a nice girl," he says. "You look . . . lovely."

"Not really," she says, feeling her face redden.

"Thank you for talking to me." He begins to get back into his car.

"That's it?" she says. "You're leaving?"

"I'll let you go," he says.

"You're the one who's going."

"What?"

"You said 'I'll let you go.' But I'm not going anywhere."

She feels momentarily triumphant, having rendered

him speechless. Then she feels sorry for him. "I'll let *you* go," she says, releasing him.

He tucks himself into the car and closes the door. He sits for a moment with his hands on the steering wheel, but doesn't start the car. She hopes he is reconsidering, and that he will get out again and that he will stay and live with her and teach her math and be her father and——. But the car starts and he pulls away from the curb and heads down the street. She watches as his car disappears around a corner. She shivers and realizes that the air has finally given way to coolness and night has fallen around her without her even realizing it. She mounts her bike and heads out toward the farms.

8.

*North Hollywood is an* optical illusion. It reminds Will of the drawing that looks like two profiles facing each other but is actually a picture of a wineglass. Or the other way around. The neighborhood appears familiar—there are houses with shingled roofs and painted shutters. There are trees and front lawns and sun-bleached plastic jungle gyms that are probably too small for whoever used to play with them but that nobody has bothered to remove. But something is different about this place. It's not just the palm trees, which look like Miss King, his old P.E. teacher, who was so tall and thin he used to think she'd snap in two every time she caught a ball. The clue to the difference is the color of the trees and bushes, which is a weather-beaten version of the deep, trusting greens of the forest behind his old house.

The car smells of oil and junk food and the Cherry Coke Ethan spilled outside of Las Vegas that has seeped into the creases of the seat cushions and that will probably forever remain as a reminder of this long, sodden trip. For the last five hours Caroline drove with all the windows down, trying to avoid the smell of too-much-time-in-an-old-car. Still, as much as he is happy this drive is over, Will is vaguely disappointed when Caroline stops the car in front of a small house on a quiet street. The house is beige and rectangular. The shutters are brown. A strip of lawn spreads out between the house and the sidewalk like a tablecloth that's too small for the table. Dry-looking dirt rings the edges, and the flowerbed bordering the sidewalk looks thirsty. A single blood-red rose reaches up out of a bramble of dead stems.

"He let the garden go," Caroline says.

She does not remove her hands from the steering wheel, and Will wonders if she is going to start the car again and keep on driving. He decides that it is much better to be on your way somewhere than to get there. Once you arrive, hope vanishes.

"You always remember things differently," Caroline says. Her jaw muscles work as though a small beetle is rustling around in there, trying to get out.

Will understands what she means. A few months earlier his teacher asked him to deliver a message to the kindergarten classroom. When he opened the door to the room, he was surprised to see a tiny, drab space where he remembered a vast miniworld whose dress-up corner and shelves full of blocks were as distant from one another as continents. Children sat in a circle on a blue carpet, counting by tens. A cardboard tree hung from the ceiling, and the children's names were written on apples made of lamp-faded red felt that swung lazily in the wind from the heating vents. Will delivered the message and walked back to his own classroom with a sick-to-his-stomach feeling that his whole impression of his life was wrong. He wondered whether his fourth-grade classroom, decorated with Indian totems and portraits of regal-looking chiefs, a room that made him feel proud and important and old, would seem pathetic in a few years. Did growing up make everything that came before a big lie?

He closes his eyes on North Hollywood and tries to freeze the image of Missouri in his mind. There is his old house, the outside cream-colored walls interrupted by purple shutters he helped his mother paint one year. Spongy grass circles the house like a green moat. In the spring he can suck drops of sweetness from the honeysuckle flowers that grow there. He sees his woods, private and endless as any imaginary world. This is the home he remembers, and he is as certain of it as he is of the color of his skin or the shape of his nose. He opens his eyes and looks at his grandparents' house. Maybe he has been wrong all along and his own home was stale-smelling and too small, his woods nothing more than a strip of foliage separating back-to-back houses. Perhaps, in time, even this boxy, lifeless structure standing before him, this new "home," will become a culprit of his stupid longing.

His grandfather appears at the door. Will doesn't really recognize him—he's seen him only a handful of times in his life, but he knows it must be him. The man wears dark slacks and a green sports shirt, open at the neck. His arms and face are tanned. His slicked-back hair shines in the sun like the hood of a silver car.

"Get out and say hello," Caroline says.

Shaking hands with an adult is a test Will always fails. In his grandfather's hand, his feels small, his arm too weak to deliver even one solid pump.

"Ethan," Vincent says, staring at Will.

"I'm Will."

"It'll take me some time to get used to twins."

"We don't look anything alike," Ethan says.

Vincent's eyes sweep over Ethan. "Yes," he says. "You're the shorter one. Ethan short. Will tall." He looks past them toward the curb, where Caroline struggles to lift a heavy suitcase over the lip of the open trunk. "Help your mother," he says.

*Will's grandmother sits* in a stuffed chair in the living room beside an empty fireplace. A brass clock hangs on the wall above her head, its pendulum nodding back and forth in a slow rhythm. Her cheeks are stained with patches of pink makeup; she looks like the girls in Will's class when they dress up for school plays. She looks nothing like the grandmother he remembers who visited yearly with her red rolling suitcase and her rectangular makeup bag, the grandmother who would walk into their house, announce she needed to change from her "city mouse" to her "country mouse" shoes, and exchange the shoes that perfectly matched her traveling outfit for a pair of fresh white Keds. He can't imagine that this is the same woman who would immediately fill his house with smells of stews and baking chicken and who taught him how to finger-knit. She looks like a big doll or a wax statue version of his grandmother, the features right and wrong at the same time.

When she used to visit them in Missouri, Will would always share Ethan's bed so his grandmother could sleep in his. He liked the fact that, after she left, her scent of spearmint gum and flowery perfume lingered on his pillowcase for days until the next laundry. Those smells were her, more than anything she did or said and, if he ever smelled that same gum on a kid at school or on the breath of a clerk at a store, he would look around, his heart leaping with hope that his grandmother was near. Now she doesn't smell like anything at all. She wears slippers that have no shape to them, so that her feet look like two unbaked cookies.

Caroline kneels down in front of her mother and takes her hands. Eleanor's eyes wrinkle into a thousand folds when she smiles. Will recognizes the smile. It is an imposter. He uses it himself whenever his eyesight makes a situation uncertain. The smile takes up space, it gives him time to figure things out. He knows his grandmother does not recognize her own daughter.

"Eleanor, it's Carrie," Vincent says loudly. He stands in the doorway, his arms folded, his hands hidden beneath his armpits so only his thumbs stick out. His forearms are thick and muscled. "Remember? And the boys?"

Eleanor notices Will and Ethan, and looks confused.

"Hi Grandma," Will says, tentatively.

The last time he saw her in Missouri she showed him how to make a tree out of a Styrofoam ball and Popsicle sticks and stud it with hard candy for leaves and fruit. She told Will he was "blind as a bat" when he couldn't find a butterscotch lying on the table right in front of him, and he laughed, relieved by her frankness. She was the only person he'd met outside of his brother who wasn't scared of him. His father was angry with him. Will had heard it in his voice that night, beneath the stars. His mother worries in a way that makes her overenthusiastic when he does something like throw a baseball in the right direction. His grandmother was always a relief. She could somehow manage to acknowledge the problem and not care one bit about it in the same breath. She made him feel normal. He loved her wrinkly soft skin and the warm, embarrassing mush of her breasts when she hugged him each night. But now he cannot connect his love with the old woman sitting in front of him.

"You look good, Mom," Caroline says. Her voice shakes. She stands on her knees and puts her arms around her mother. Eleanor raises a hand and strokes Caroline's hair.

"It's all right," she says.

Caroline pulls back from the embrace and turns to Will and Ethan. "Come," she beckons. "Give Grandma a hug."

"Hi, Grandma," Ethan says, staring at the carpet without moving.

Will moves toward her, reaches down and hugs her awkwardly around her shoulders. "Got any spearmint gum?"

"Gum?" Eleanor says. "I don't . . . we don't . . ."

"In your bag," Will says. "Like you always have."

Eleanor grows agitated. She begins to wring her hands as if she is washing them with invisible soap.

"I don't think she remembers, honey," Caroline says.

"Sorry," Will says, embarrassed.

"It's not your fault," Caroline says. She turns back to her mother. "We've come to live with you for awhile, Mom. Isn't that great?"

When Eleanor does not respond, Caroline looks back at her father.

"Didn't you tell her?"

"Of course I told her. It will take her time to get used to you," Vincent says.

"I'm her *daughter*," Caroline says, her eyes glittering. She turns back to her mother. "Okay, Mom? Is it okay that we're here?"

*Later Will and Ethan* unpack their bags and stuff their clothes into the narrow dresser drawers in the room that used to be their mother's but is now filled with piles of papers and boxes and framed photographs of their grandfather with his arms around the shoulders of strangers. He looks happy and young in the photos. Will and Ethan have occasionally spotted him in reruns of old TV shows although their mother never comes to look and verify the identification. It is hard to match up the man in the living room with the man in these photos, harder still to think of him as their grandfather and not an actor playing the role of a grandfather in a TV show on *Nick at Night*.

Ethan gives up on unpacking quickly and lies on the low trundle, groaning. "I hate it here," he says. "It's like a place for old people. Or dead people."

On the trip Ethan stole a pack of Gummi Bears from one of the gas station convenience stores. Will saw the theft but said nothing. Tomorrow is Monday, the first day in their new school, and he will need his brother on his side.

"I wish we were still back home," Will says, trying to ally with his brother in some safe way.

"Back home sucks too," Ethan says.

"Where do you want to be?"

Ethan is quiet for a moment. Will imagines standing in his old shower, running his hand over countries on the map-of-the-world shower curtain, choosing India or Kenya or Turkey.

"Nowhere," Ethan says.

*When Amador enters* the house on Monday evening, prepared for a night alone with Mrs. Eleanor, he discovers a kitchen full of strangers. Two young boys, perhaps no older than Miguel, sit at the table, eating cereal, their heads bent low over their bowls as they shovel sloppy mouthfuls toward their faces and splatter the table with raindrops of milk. A woman stands by the stove, watching the boys eat. Her hair is a waterfall of black curls. Her lips are full, the color of pink geraniums.

"You're here to take care of my mother?" she asks, taking a protective step toward the boys.

Before Amador answers, Vincent comes into the kitchen.

"This is my daughter," he says hurriedly, not looking Amador in the eye, patting pockets, looking for wallet, keys, looking for a way out. "She's living here now. My wife is resting. She ate." His report concluded, he leaves the house. He does not say good-bye to the boys or the woman.

The woman introduces herself and extends a slender arm toward Amador. He takes it, surprised by her touch. He feels as if he has touched an exposed wire and that his body is immediately disrupted. He drops her hand abruptly and notices a small look of hurt flee across her face, chased by an effortful smile.

"*No hablo español,*" she says, her inflection ironing out the rises and dips of the words so they are flat and unmusical. "It's stupid in this day and age, I know."

He doesn't understand the phrase and hopes she will not ask him anything that he can't answer. He wants someone to explain to him what is going on. It is typical of Mr. Vincent to tell him nothing.

Caroline doesn't look at all like Mrs. Eleanor. Her nose is long, her skin dark like her father's. And that hair. It is as if there is so much life in her body that it bleeds out of her scalp, causing her hair to twist and turn in a hundred different directions. She stands with her arms crossed over her chest. When she smiles her eyes turn down like her father's.

She introduces her sons. They look up from their bowls and greet him, mouths glistening with milk. Miguel is an intent eater too, Amador thinks. His attention cannot be diverted from a meal even by fireworks at Christmas. The act of eating consumes him, causes him a driven pleasure. Amador stops himself from remembering more. His thoughts are always abducted by other thoughts; he can never exist in only one place but is pulled backward and forward like the object of a tug-of-war. He has no right to coddle this memory of his own child. Who knows how Miguel eats now? Who knows if he still looks like these boys, with their soft faces of childhood?

"I hope my boys will not be in your way," Caroline says. "Although I can't guarantee it."

"Is no problem," he says, half understanding her rapid speech.

"They can be loud," she says. "Loud is their biggest characteristic, I think. And smelly."

"Mom!" Ethan says.

"They don't like when I talk about them in the third person."

"I don't like when you talk about us, period," Ethan says.

Amador sees a familiar manufactured rage in the boy's face, a need to be angry even if he doesn't feel exactly angry, even if he feels something else he cannot name. Rogelio's face floats through his mind, and Amador chastises himself for caring about what these strange boys feel. To care for even an instant is a betrayal.

"We're in the room, you know," Ethan singsongs to his mother.

"Don't be smart," Caroline says, rolling her eyes for Amador's benefit, revealing the pride that all parents take in their children even in their worst aspects. He'd like to tell her about his children, to share their exasperating appeal. But he cautions himself: He works for her now, too. You can make big mistakes in this country thinking anybody is interested in the full fact of your existence. The only person who knows him at all in the entire U.S.A. is an old woman with half a mind.

Caroline tells the boys to clear their dishes and get ready for bed. They leave the room quickly, but Caroline stays. Amador begins to fill the teapot with hot water in order to make Mrs. Eleanor's customary hot cocoa.

"Oh, let me," Caroline says, moving across the room and reaching for the teapot.

Instinctively he draws the pot closer to his body. "I do it," he says.

"Of course," she says, shrinking back.

How quickly he becomes the servant who knows his place and knows that if he gives it up, he will have no place at all. He is ashamed of himself. Her presence makes him aware of every one of his movements. He feels uncertain, as if he has not made this very same cup of cocoa one hundred times in the last four months. He wonders if she will correct him or judge his actions poorly and tell Mr. Vincent that he is not good enough for the job. Now he will not be able to do anything without imagining how he is being seen by her, this stranger, this woman who is making an effort to be . . . what? Nice? Or is she offering him that defensive kindness he sees on the faces of so many white people who do not know if he can be trusted? He does not want to be stared at, observed, like some curious zoo animal. He's spent three years getting to a place where he can work without feeling like an ant under a microscope. And now this woman is going to take that away.

"You need me, Mrs.?" he asks.

"No," she says. "I'll let you get to work."

She leaves the room, but returns a few minutes later holding her mother by the arm. "Here she is!" she says brightly. "Ready for cocoa."

Mrs. Eleanor looks confused as her daughter sits her at the table. Amador does not tell Caroline that she has disrupted the nightly ritual of cocoa in bed that Mrs. Eleanor has come to expect. What is worse, Caroline has not bothered to brush Mrs. Eleanor's hair or dress her in her bathrobe. The old woman's hair flies out from her head; her flimsy nightgown reveals the contours of her body beneath it. He is certain Mrs. Eleanor would be upset to be seen in such a way. From observing the photographs hanging on the walls throughout the house, he knows that Mrs. Eleanor is a neat and careful woman, and he is determined to help her maintain her personality even as her mind fades.

But it is the daughter's turn now. Her arrival signals some shift in the order of the house. He places the cocoa on the kitchen table.

"Here, Mom," Caroline says. "Let's have some hot chocolate."

"I don't want it."

"Yes, you do," Caroline says. "You like cocoa. Right, Amador?"

Caroline looks up for his help, but he does not know what she wants from him. A caretaker would handle things the way that is best for Mrs. Eleanor. A servant would remain silent. Mrs. Eleanor pushes the cup away, and some of the brown liquid spills over the top and onto the table.

"Oh, Mom!" Caroline exclaims, then catches herself. "I mean, it's okay. Everyone spills, right?"

Amador takes a dishrag from the sink and cleans up the mess. Caroline tries to remain in control, but her mother's behavior frightens her. Amador can see it in her eyes, in the tentativeness of her gestures. She fills her anxiety with aimless chatter. *Did you have a good day, Mommy? We're so glad to be here with you.* Amador never speaks to Mrs. Eleanor like a child. If she spills her cocoa, he simply asks her to get a towel and clean it up. It is a matter of respect, not for him but for her.

"Just take a little sip," Caroline urges. She holds the cup to her mother's lips. Mrs. Eleanor bats the cup away with surprising strength, and it falls from Caroline's hands, spilling its entire contents. While the women react to the spill, Amador lays a kitchen towel over the lake of cocoa on the table, sopping up the excess.

"I just thought—oh, Jesus," Caroline says, looking on helplessly as the brown water sluices off the edge of the table and onto the floor.

Amador's resentment evaporates when he sees her eyes fill.

"Does she always act this way now?" Caroline says.

"Yes," he lies. "With me sometime it is more worse."

She smiles at him gratefully. Her teeth are slightly crooked. Two of them on the side overlap in a way that momentarily paralyzes him. The teeth make him understand her imperfection and her fragility. Her smile begs something of him, some kind of medicine she needs. He can feel it in the air between them even if she does not express it. Now he understands why she holds herself in her own arms. She is cold on the inside.

For the rest of the night Caroline's unnerving presence forces him to stay in the kitchen. The boys sleep in the extra room, the mother on the couch in the living room. He tries to study his English textbook but is distracted by the unfamiliar sounds in the house—doors open and shut, the toilet flushes, the bathroom sink handle squeaks. He feels trapped. He resists checking on Mrs. Eleanor in order to avoid an embarrassing encounter with the daughter. The television in the living room comes on, and then almost immediately the sound disappears and he is left trying to conclude a character from this indecisiveness. The springs of the sofa creak under her weight. She coughs. She sighs.

*She should never* have come, is what Caroline thinks as she sits on the couch watching the image on the television screen snap into blackness. She drops the remote control on the cushion next to her. She should never have brought her children across the country to this bewildering place. When she turned off the lights in their bedroom, Will looked terrified, as though she had just abandoned him in the middle of a crowded airport and disappeared into a thicket of strangers. Her father doesn't want them here, that much is obvious. And her mother. Oh—she cannot think about her mother. If she does, it is too much, too big. It is a cavern of guilt and sadness she cannot allow herself to fall into. So much has changed since she saw her mother last, when she flew out to California a year earlier to hear the doctor's diagnosis for herself. But even then her mother was present. She had come up with ingenious tricks to aid her memory. She kept Post-it notes all over the house to remind herself to turn off the oven or call the dentist. She wrote "Now, make breakfast," on the bathroom mirror with a Write-n-Wipe pen. And each night she bravely went through the house collecting her notes and congratulating herself on a day full of remembering.

Caroline stands and unfolds the sofa and stares at the thin mattress for a moment before she begins to make up the bed. She embarrassed herself in front of her mother's nurse. What must he think of her—a woman who does not even know how to take care of her own mother? She feels inappropriate in the house, too big for it, her voice too loud. She thinks about the house's decorations—the china figurines, the set of Franklin Mint plates above the dining room table, painted with children holding puppies or playing marbles, and wonders if this place ever felt like her only known world. But of course it was her universe once. She had hiding places and favorite chairs. She filled the rooms with the howling anger and hyperbolic tears of her teenage years and never once felt that she was in a place that ultimately couldn't contain her. But now she feels as if she's attending a party full of old friends and she can't remember anybody's name.

*Will lies in* his bed, attempting to map this new geography of darkness. Shapes emerge, then disappear, as he tries to identify the desk, the dresser, the thickly curtained window.

The first day in his new school was horrible. He felt sick all day. He had to memorize a whole new landscape of corridors and classrooms. He was exhausted by how much effort it took not to make a mistake and crash into an open locker door or miss a step and go flying down a staircase. In his old school the fact of his thick glasses and his physical awkwardness was taken in stride. In this new school he feels like a malfunctioning car alarm. He endures the stares of classmates for whom newness is like a disease. When he told one boy he was from Missouri, the boy looked at him blankly, as though he were waiting for the rest of the joke. Will has already learned to keep his hand from leaping into the air each time a teacher asks a question. Being smart won't do him any good.

He is nervous about the next day and cannot sleep. He gets out of bed and, arms extended, feels his way to the door. Down the hall, the kitchen is lit up, and Amador stands over Will's grandmother, braiding her long gray hair and fixing it with a rubber band at the end. Will draws closer.

"I no choose. You choose," he says, patting down the flyaway hairs.

Eleanor pouts. "Don't make me."

"It's your stomach, Mrs. How I know what it wants?"

Will's foot hits the door frame, and Amador looks up. He raises his hand to stop Will from entering, bends at the waist and speaks quietly to Eleanor.

"What you want to eat?" he says coaxingly. "Roast pig? Bananas on fire?"

"Cream of Wheat," she says at last.

Amador pops up as if from a jack-in-the-box. "Cream of Wheat!" he says triumphantly, turning to Will. "*Su abuela quiere* Cream of Wheat."

This seems to be an invitation for Will to enter the room. His grandmother looks at him, then catches Amador's hand.

"It is your grandson," Amador says gently. "Ask him to sit with you."

Eleanor looks at Will. "You like Cream of Wheat, boy?"

"I guess so."

She lets go of Amador's hand, reaches across the table, and pats the place opposite her. Will takes the seat. He stares at the confusing fact of her. She is like a fast-disappearing impression in the sand. He will have to memorize her quickly before she fades. Her skin is nearly translucent. Veins branch through her cheeks and up the rise of her nose. Her eyes are the perfect blue of the university swimming pool back home.

"You can talk to her," Amador says as he stirs a pot of cereal on the stove.

"Does she understand?" Will asks.

"She understand what I say," Amador says.

"Hi, Grandma," Will says.

"Ask her a question," Amador instructs.

"Did you have a nice day?" Will asks awkwardly.

"Oh, yes," Eleanor says. "I'm glad it rained."

It was a hot and sunny day. Will looks to Amador for help.

"Tell her the truth," Amador says, his back to Will.

"It didn't rain today, Grandma."

"No?" she says. Her eyes dart back and forth uncertainly.

"No rain," Amador says as he carries two bowls of steaming cereal to the table.

Will can't tell if she feels stupid or saddened by her error. His mother tells him it is better not to know you are losing your mind. She says knowing will drive a person crazy.

"Olive trees need rain," Eleanor says. "We have hundreds and hundreds. See out the window?"

Will looks at Amador. "What should I do?"

Amador shrugs. "Sometime she disappear. Then it is better to go with her into her dream."

Will walks to the kitchen window. The view is brief: a narrow alley between the house and the one next door. A spotlight illuminates a chain-link fence and a trio of garbage cans, green, blue, and black.

"Do you see the trees?" Eleanor says.

Will takes off his glasses and rubs his eyes. Now the garbage cans are pulpy masses of color, the outdoor light a halo. He shuts his eyes and summons the image of trees. He sees the birch tree standing in the center of the yard back home. He travels up its pocked trunk. He sees its light leaves flip in the wind like tossed coins.

"Yes, I see," he says.

"Aren't they pretty?"

"I guess."

"And the smell," his grandmother says, inhaling deeply.

"I think you are smelling Cream of Wheat, *mi amiga*," Amador says.

Will opens his eyes and replaces his glasses. He sits down at the table while Amador ties a napkin around Eleanor's neck, patting down the peak at her throat. Will twirls his spoon in the thick mush.

"I've been in California two days," he says, addressing the bowl.

"Me, four years," Amador says.

"Do you like it here?"

Amador doesn't answer, and Will wonders if he has said something rude. His mother has told him not to bother Amador, to let him do his job. "We're never going back to my home again. That's what my mom says. She says there's nothing to go back to." He scrapes his bowl with his spoon. "We had a dog but she ran away. Do you have a dog?"

"No," Amador says, shaking his head. "Where I come from, there are many dogs but no owners."

"Who feeds them?"

Amador shrugs, "They just—" he stops, searching for a word. "*No más existen.*"

"I don't know Spanish," Will says.

Amador's eyes travel to the right as though he is searching for language in the air. "The dogs, they just live," he says, finally.

Will wonders if language, to this man, is like blindness— if it is a void out of which you conjure memories.

Back in his bedroom Will lies in the dark and listens to the soft sound of his brother whimpering in his sleep. Nelsie chased rabbits in her sleep. The dog made short, strangulated yowls while she pawed the air and shook imaginary prey back and forth in her soft mouth. The dog's dreams always made Will feel that something frightening was going to happen: that night would become day, sleeping would become waking. Everything he thought he knew and could count on would be the opposite of what it was supposed to be, and he would be left alone, unable to negotiate this new, inside-out world.

He reaches out a hand and touches his brother's body. "Ethan, where are we?" he whispers.

9.

*"Helio!" Berta calls sharply.* The girl stands in the doorway of the house. Her dress, clean only this morning, is smeared with dirt.

"Rogelio is not here," Erlinda says, trying to contain her worry. She sits on a stool, sewing holes that appear in Miguel's trousers as frequently as blisters swell on his feet. There is not a day he does not return from school covered in mud and dirt. "Baseball," he says, by way of explanation, as though the game takes possession of him like a spirit. Rogelio's interests align much more with her own. He likes to read, and when she presents him with a book borrowed from the *padre,* who himself is a great reader, he seizes it the way a dog snatches a proffered bone, taking it into a corner and devouring the book before anyone can take it from him. And he loves the stars as she does. On the night of the comet they sat on the lawn underneath a single blanket, shivering, silently enjoying the deliciousness of waiting. And when they saw the bright streak! It was as if God were drawing with light! Rogelio froze, not daring to move and chase away the moment, and she knew he was feeling what she had once felt: that the world was huge and that there was magic that existed outside of El Rosario. She wanted him to feel the almost painful ecstasy of possibility; she wanted to plant in him the seed of yearning.

"I want Helio," Berta repeats, stamping her bare feet on the floor.

"Stop that now!" Erlinda snaps. Her anger is only curdled fear, but she cannot help lashing out at her daughter. Anything to cover the quiet terror that roots inside her.

When Rogelio was gone the first day and night, she felt his absence as a minor, familiar irritation—Miguel forgetting to feed the chickens, Berta refusing to eat her dinner. Rogelio had disappeared before, she reasoned. Sometimes he would spend the night up at the butterfly sanctuary if he could not find a ride home, although she knew lack of transportation was only a partial excuse.

He has become unreachable this last year, remote even when he is beside her. She reminds herself that he is fourteen now, and that all boys need to be separate from their mothers. Perhaps, without a father at home, Rogelio needs to make that separation emphatic in order to overcome the confusion of being the only man (and not yet a man at that) left. She reminds herself that he is still dutiful. He takes care of small repairs around the house. He turns the soil in their garden. He collects and delivers the sewing she takes in. But when he doesn't return home a second night, she cannot deny the knot of anger that has congealed inside him, which he carries everywhere like a dangerous treasure.

He has grown so tall in the last year, surpassing both her and Amador in height. The last vestiges of his boyish fat are now stretched tautly over his chest and back. His face has narrowed, his gaze on the lookout for certain disappointment. He shrugs off her embraces as though they are as irksome as flies.

The last time Amador came and went, he took what remained of Rogelio's childhood with him. Rogelio stayed inside the house while she and the other children stood at the door, waving to Amador as he disappeared down the road. When Erlinda turned back into the room, she gasped. Standing before her was a stranger wearing her son's clothes.

"What's wrong?" she asked.

Rogelio brushed past her on his way out the door. "He should not come here again."

"Rogelio!" she scolded.

"He is a poison."

She grabbed his arm and slapped him across the face with her free hand. He looked down at her, grinning. For the first time she realized she had a child who could hurt her.

The following day she and Rogelio repaired a crack in the wall where winter wind snaked through the fissure. Rogelio stirred the thick mortar while she smoothed it on the wall.

"A man can die of not working," she said, gently. She has

given her children only the most obvious excuse for Amador's leaving, an excuse they have in common with their friends. They cannot, *should* not, know the debilitating weight of the marriage since Rubén's death.

Rogelio stirred the stucco so that it would not harden. When they finished the job, they stepped back to inspect their work. Mortar scarred the wood like veins on an old woman's legs.

"Looks good," he said, cracking a smile at their rude handiwork. They both laughed.

"I love you," she said.

"Then why are you crying?"

It was true. Sudden tears collected in the corners of her eyes. Why did she cry? Because the feeling was so huge, so lucky, so terrifying. Because she was bewildered knowing how much sorrow and joy lay in store for Rogelio, knowing how much he would have to *feel* on his life's journey.

On the third day of his absence, Erlinda is clearing the weeds from her small garden when she looks up to see the two stalks of Berta's legs.

"When is Rogelio coming back?" the girl fusses.

"He'll come soon," Erlinda says, although she can barely speak through her worry. "Come, help me."

Berta kneels down and begins to yank at weeds. Her dark hair sticks out at odd angles from her head. That hair is its own living thing, Erlinda thinks, recalling the child's screams the previous evening, when Erlinda combed out the tangled nest. Berta was an impatient child at birth, grabbing for a breast, for hair, for anything to secure her purchase in the world. She was not truly content until she could walk at ten months, her legs bowing under the weight of her torso. Erlinda's mother eyed the baby warily, as if Berta were possessed by some dark spirit. But Erlinda knows the coiled tightness in the chest produced by wanting what is beyond your reach.

"This one is smart," Amador had said of Berta, the last time he was home.

His comment wilted Erlinda. It suggested such distance between the father and the girl. He could have been picking out the distinguishing characteristics in a litter of dogs. Erlinda is sad that he is not around enough to notice the subtle indications of *all* his children's intelligence. It is obvious in the way Rogelio needs to analyze every possible option and likely outcome before he chooses a path through a given situation. It is apparent in the way Miguel associates the shape of a cloud with the face of an old, gnarled woman on the bus. But Amador does not know these things. And it is impossible for Erlinda to try to relate to him the incessant revelations of their children's lives. How to tell him about the mixture of anxiety and delight she experienced during last Sunday's mass, when Rogelio held a candle at such an impossible angle that the congregants were certain he'd fallen asleep on his feet? How to tell him of her pride that Miguel has befriended Orlando, the neighbor boy who cannot hear? How dissatisfying it would be to watch Amador struggle to imagine and appreciate the tense hilarity that filled the small church, or the lovely grace of Miguel as he helps little Orlando steal a base.

Sleeping with Amador after such long separation is awkward. The combination of familiarity and foreignness unsettles her, makes her feel like a teenager—uncertain of herself, too needy of his reassurance. When she was young and they made love for the first time in the field beyond his parents' house, his body was a new country. Her first new country. He laughed as she ran her fingers down his midline, tracing his groin muscles, guiltily enjoying his unbearable anticipation. But now his body travels without her. When he touches her neck or breasts, it is with hands that have touched homes or people she cannot imagine.

In the last few years she has begun to think of herself not as Amador's wife but as a woman, thirty-four years old, raising three children on her own. The sense of a solitary mission strengthens her. She refuses to mark time by how long it has been since Amador's last visit or how long until the next one. She forces herself to notice her life so that the present matters. She isolates the novelty in the most unimaginative activities—hanging out the wash, cleaning Miguel's dirty fingernails, sweeping her floor. The smell of the wind might carry the scent of mesquite or the sweetly compelling smell of tobacco. The rigor mortis of a dead dog on the side of the road is not something to ignore but something to study, the way one might study the sculpture of Christ hanging above the church altar, admiring the tension of the stilled muscles, the peacefulness of expression. Unless she confirms the life she leads then she has no life at all.

Her son is missing. She is suddenly gripped with a glaring understanding of how serious the situation is. She stands up from her gardening, cursing the denial that has kept her from acting. Berta looks up at her, big eyes wide with questions she needs her mother to answer.

While Miguel is in school, she walks the town with Berta, forsaking her shame and asking everyone she comes upon if they have seen her son. She and Berta walk out to the *ranchos* and ask the farmers the same question. The men, bending low to repair irrigation pipes, shake their heads.

They travel to the butterfly sanctuary. It is a place Erlinda visits once a year, to tend to the cross she planted in the dirt there fifteen years ago to put a memory of her first baby in a place he loved. Her journey there to find Rogelio feels perilous, as though she will discover not one wooden cross nestled in a grove of trees but two. But none of the boys has seen Rogelio for days.

"Is he dead?" Miguel asks that night while they eat their supper.

Erlinda is startled. This obvious explanation has not occurred to her. But in the wake of the simple question, she realizes how naive she is. Of course he could be dead, killed by a car, a bandit, or by a drunken fall into an *arroyo*.

"He's not dead," she says, trying to steady her voice.

"Well, he's gone, anyway," Miguel says.

She watches him duck his head between his shoulders and scoop up another bite of rice with his *tortilla*. Dead. Gone. Absence and nonexistence manifest themselves identically in her children's lives.

The following day she walks Miguel to school and leaves Berta with her sister, Yolanda, and Yolanda's four small children. She stands on the side of the highway for forty-five minutes before the bus to Ocampo arrives.

The morgue stands next to a toy shop. Blowup toys hang

from a metal pole: gray-and-pink elephants with enormous ears for a child to grab, a giraffe with a long, sturdy neck. Erlinda makes a deal with herself: If Rogelio is not dead, she will buy a toy for Miguel and Berta. Berta loves giraffes.

The walls of the morgue were once painted turquoise blue, but the color has faded to a dusty cream. The original blue clings only to the eaves of the roof and the window casements. Erlinda enters the courtyard. It is bare of flowers or any decoration save an unmanned metal desk. Heavy wooden doors lead to interior rooms, but they stand closed, and she hears no life behind them.

She looks at her watch. Of course. It is dinnertime. Everyone will be home, eating and resting. She wonders why the door to the morgue is not locked. Just as she is about to leave, a man wearing a white medical coat crosses the courtyard. She waits for him to notice her, but when he does not, she calls out. She is embarrassed by the shrillness of her voice as it pierces the quiet. The man squints at her, as though the sight of a living body is as unexpected in this place as a dinosaur might be.

"I've lost my son," she says, trying to render the awkward phrase casually, as if she's misplaced an insignificant thing, a hairpin or a cooking spoon. The man takes a few steps closer until he stands across the desk from her. His face reminds her of the mask of an angel that she saw as a child, being held aloft during a parade. The man's nose is long, the nostrils defined as if by a craftsman's tool. His hands look too delicate for the work they do. She is struck by his gentleness, and her heart weakens. In a split second, her contemptuous denial that Rogelio can be in this place dissolves and she is overcome by a burning in her throat.

"Our desk clerk is at her dinner," the man says, uncomfortably as though he is not familiar with the protocol at this front end of the office, the living end.

"Of course," she says. "I didn't realize the time. I will come back."

"No, no," he says, waving his hand. "I can help you."

She takes a breath, then tells him her problem. He asks for particulars about her son—his age, his height, how long he has been missing. As she speaks, her mind's eye travels the length of Rogelio from the light green speckles in his brown eyes to his feet.

"He has very long toes," she says. "He is embarrassed by his toes." She tells the man how Rogelio refused to try on a new pair of shoes because he was sure a group of giggling girls in the store would make fun of his feet.

The man smiles awkwardly.

"You don't need to know about his toes," she says, ashamed of herself. It was easier to talk with the useless policeman in El Rosario. His incuriousness strengthened her denial. Perhaps this man's indulgent patience means he knows something.

"Please," the man says, gesturing for her to follow. He leads her across the courtyard, through one of the doors, and into a room that smells of chemicals. The temperature is unnaturally cold. She knows the cold is meant to preserve the bodies and help dispel their complicated deathly odors. She holds her sweater tightly around her chest. How grateful she is that Rubén was never in a place as frigid and unlovable as this. She shivers, shocked that her mind has already opened itself to the possibility of Rogelio being here.

"We have one boy that age right now," the man says.

She grows deaf, hears only the roar inside her skull. Two empty cots shine under low hanging bulbs. There are no bodies in sight.

"Where?" she says. Her voice sounds thick and muffled, as if she is talking through cotton.

He disappears into another room, and in a few moments returns, pushing a gurney. A body lies on it, covered by a sheet. Erlinda's legs buckle underneath her and she has to steady herself on one of the empty cots. She thinks she might vomit and covers her nose and mouth with her hand.

"The smell can be difficult at first," the man says. "I guess I've gotten used to it." He wheels the gurney around and brings it to a stop.

She cannot move.

"Would you like me to describe the body to you?" he says.

"Yes," she whispers through her hand. "Please."

He lifts his side of the sheet so that she cannot see the body. "Male. Maybe thirteen, maybe a few years older. The beginnings of genital and facial hair. Medium height. Brown hair. Brown eyes . . ."

It is useless. He could be describing a hundred boys, a thousand boys. She moves closer to the table. She nods, and he pulls the sheet back.

She begins to weep. At first the tears come slowly, but soon she cannot stop them.

"I'm so sorry," the man says softly.

"No." she shakes her head.

He re-covers the body with the sheet. "Let me help you," he says, moving toward her.

"No," she repeats, stepping back and holding out her hand to stop him.

"I'll get you a chair." He moves toward the door.

"It's not him," she manages to say.

He stops and turns. "It's not your son?"

She shakes her head. "I'm sorry," she says. "I don't know why . . ." she gestures to her tears.

"You're relieved," he says, sympathetically. "It's understandable."

But her heart continues to shatter inside her chest, and her tears will not stop. She shakes her head vigorously. "He's someone else's boy," she says. "Someone's baby."

*She is exhausted* on the bus ride home. She sits in her seat, crowded in by the blowup giraffe she bought and the woman next to her who carries several bags filled with bananas, melons, and giant's fingers of sugar cane. Small field fires burn in the distance, sending up thick shields of smoke. At the edge of a roadside village a group of children run and laugh, seized by the joy of some plan. Erlinda counts the number of buildings that have been abandoned in midconstruction. The countryside is filled with these skeletons, monuments to enthusiasm and resignation.

For the first time in years, she misses her husband in a way that feels more personal than practical. As separate as they were in their mourning of Rubén, they have never been as separate as they are now. *My God!* She shudders. He does not yet know that Rogelio is gone! He is just like any man on the street who knows nothing of her life.

She remembers when she discovered she loved him, and she felt she was bigger, somehow taller than everybody else in the world. Her mother had presented Amador at first by means of an old, creased photograph. The sun-bleached picture, scalloped at the edges, showed two boys and two girls sitting formally, hands in laps, backs stiff, faces grim. The younger of the two boys wore a shirt buttoned up to his neck. His soft cheeks looked unnaturally plump, as though they were hiding forbidden candy.

"He's young for me, no?" Erlinda said slyly, trying to offset the awkwardness of this prearranged moment.

Erlinda's mother blew her lips dismissively at her daughter's sarcasm. She argued that Erlinda's quick-wittedness would do her no good as far as men were concerned. "Of course he's older now," she said. "He's twenty years old, more a man than you are a woman."

Only sixteen, Erlinda blushed. She still thought of herself as a girl. The idea of marrying a grown man terrified her. She did not want to get married yet, anyway. She wanted to go to Morelia or even Mexico City and study at a university.

Amador arrived at her home one Sunday for the first meeting. He was small, only an inch or two taller than she. His arms and chest strained at the seams of his "good" shirt like little boys sitting anxiously in church pews, waiting to be let out to play. His face had thinned out in the ten years since the photograph. His cheekbones were high, and two valleys sank gracefully beneath them. His lips were wide, the upper one resting gently on its full lower partner. He looked as if he knew more than he was willing to say.

She did not want to go to the plaza and face the knowing smiles of her girlfriends and their mothers, so they walked up and down a deserted road near her house, their shoulders a careful two feet apart at all times.

"Do you like your town?" she asked. He lived in Ocampo. Although it was hardly a city, it was bigger than El Rosario, and its energy on market day tantalized her.

"It's good," he said, staring out at the horizon as if he were trying to plan his escape.

"Is it cooler there?" she asked, fanning herself with her hand.

"The same."

They continued to walk in silence.

"How are your sisters?"

"They are well."

"They are in Ocampo?"

"They are in Morelia."

Her heart quickened. "What do they do there?" she asked. The idea of his sisters having traveled excited her. Perhaps he had such ambitions as well.

"They work in a hotel."

"Have you been?"

"No."

At the end of the afternoon, she stormed into her house. "He's mute!" she cried. "He's an idiot!" She fell onto a low stool and hid her head in her hands. Nearby, Yolanda laughed as she folded *tamales*. Erlinda reached out an arm to pinch her sister, but Yolanda danced away.

"I refuse to marry an idiot," Erlinda wailed.

"Then don't marry him," her father said.

Her mother screamed.

Her father lay on the bed. He'd lost a hand to an accident with a saw that year. Periodically the arm with the missing hand throbbed so painfully he had to lie down and rest it on a pillow so that the blood would flow evenly. "Well, she can't marry an idiot," he said, smiling. "We don't want idiot grandchildren."

"You ask a man too many questions," her mother said. "A man doesn't want to feel like he's being investigated by the police."

"How do you suggest I get to know him?" Erlinda asked, her voice rising in frustration. "How did you get to know Papa?"

Erlinda's mother looked at her husband. His pain had worsened; his good hand lay over his eyes. The expression on her mother's face was not exactly love, Erlinda thought. It was an expression, if it was possible, of forgiveness. "We didn't know each other at all," her mother said.

Erlinda's father's breath was steady. He was sleeping. Invisible clouds of sweet air rose from his parted lips. He drank most days to take the edge off the pain. He spent his time in bed or in the plaza, watching the shadow of hours slide across the stones. She bent down and kissed his sweating forehead.

Amador appeared at her house the following Sunday.

"My mother should have told you not to come," she said as she edged out of the door and shut it halfway.

"She did. I thought that was a bad idea," he said.

"And why did you think that?"

"Because we don't know each other."

"It's hard to get to know someone who answers questions with a yes or a no."

"Your questions were not interesting."

"Excuse me?" Erlinda felt her face flush with embarrassment.

" 'What is your town like? How are your sisters?' "

She wanted to slap him for his impertinence. She wanted him to say more.

"Walk with me," he said.

"No."

"All right." He turned and began to walk away. She watched him go, certain he would look back. She was wrong.

He did not come the following week, although Erlinda stayed home all day in anticipation of his arrival, complaining of a headache to excuse herself from church. All morning she tried to find things to occupy her in the house. She cleaned, then cleaned again. She read a book, but her eyes skated over the words while her mind remained elsewhere. She watched her father leave in the morning with a solid stride and come back later that afternoon, well after her mother and sister had returned from mass, wobbling as if he were being pushed on either side by unseen tormenters.

"You can stop waiting now," her mother said when it was five o'clock.

The following Saturday, Erlinda boarded a bus to Ocampo. Once there, she stood outside the old church in the square, feeling foolish. She didn't even know where Amador lived. Was she just going to stand there and expect him to pass by? A few children greeted the bus, hoping for coins from a traveler. She asked a girl if she knew where Amador Aguilar lived. The girl shook her head, but a boy held out a cupped hand. Erlinda dropped a coin into it; then, along with the yelping, skipping group, followed the boy down one street and up another until they arrived at the edge of town. They stopped in front of a slumping house. Chickens pecked lazily at the dirt. Pots of red geraniums stood on the porch railing, their limp beauty a gallant reproach to their surroundings.

Amador appeared in the doorway. He looked at her, and then back at his house, and she realized he was embarrassed. He hissed, and the children squealed and fluttered down the road like papers in the wind. "Why are you here?" he said.

His abrasiveness was unnerving. He was not happy to see her. Her heart was beating so hard she was sure he could hear it.

"I thought of a good question," she said softly.

He continued to stare at her. His face was unfathomable.

"Well?" he said finally. "What is it?"

"What do you want our life to be?" she asked.

He looked into her eyes in a way no one ever had, as though he was trying to see exactly who she was. "More than this," he said finally.

They made plans. They would live in El Rosario to be close to her parents and sister. They would plant the small

field behind her parents' house. When they had saved a little bit of money, they would move to Morelia. His sisters
would help find Erlinda and Amador jobs, maybe at one of
the finer hotels. Eventually Erlinda would begin her studies.
She would like to be a teacher.

But then Rubén was born, and then Rubén died. And
things changed between them. They no longer spoke about
Morelia or about any future. They began to live their days
just as her parents did, resigned to the accumulation of
time. Amador found work on nearby farms and road main-
tenance crews. One by one the other children were born.
Amador was alternately irritable with and overprotective of
them, as if their existence only reminded him how easily
their lives could be snuffed like a flame between the press of
two fingers.

El Rosario grew more and more silent each year, like an
old person who no longer feels compelled to speak because
he knows, finally, the inefficacy of words. One by one families lost fathers and brothers to the cities or the north. They
returned triumphantly at *fiesta*. Their wives and children
would hang on their arms, grins wide with uncertainty, as if
they were showing off treasures that were not theirs to
keep. And then the men would leave again, nearly all at
once, and the town would grow quietly bereft.

"A group is going next week," Amador told Erlinda one
night. They lay in bed. Berta, just two months old, slept in
a basket on the floor. The boys shared a mattress on the
other side of a loosely hung curtain. Erlinda's head rested in
the warm gully below Amador's shoulder. She did not
respond. She felt milk let down in her breasts just as Berta

shifted in her basket. She reached over and lifted the baby and began to nurse on her side, contenting Berta before her cries woke the boys. Amador's fingers rested on her waist. This is the body he will remember, she thought. This is the body he will forget.

As the bus bumps along the road toward El Rosario, Erlinda falls asleep, the inflatable giraffe her pillow. In her dream she sees a great, colorful butterfly flitting among the sun-dappled leaves of a tree. It is primarily orange, but two big green circles decorate the wings as if they are eyes. As it flies its "eyes" fix on her so that even in her dream she is held by its unseeing gaze. When she wakes she feels full of light.

"He is not dead," she says aloud. The woman next to her looks annoyed by her outburst.

Yes. She knows Rogelio is not dead. He is traveling like the butterfly. She knows this in her heart, in her blood. Rogelio is on his way to his father. She must call Amador in California. They must hold their hands together across the continent and form a human bridge so that their son will not get lost. It is impossible. Yes, of course it is. But what can she do? She has three living children and only one who is dead. It is her duty to take good care of them all.

10.

*Marlene and her mother* fight daily. About too much makeup or not enough makeup (an even worse insult, as far as Marlene is concerned) and too short T-shirts and too much vodka and why-don't-you-smile-when-you-see-your-Mama-who-loves-you? Marlene arrives home from school every day and feels as though she is walking into the wrong house. There is her mother, relaxed, satisfied, unable to desire or imagine anything beyond what she has. And the feeling Marlene carries with her is that this is not supposed to be her life at all, that she's missing a key ingredient and the recipe is going to turn out to be shit.

She does not tell her mother about her father's visit. She knows her mother would find some way to diminish the event, to make Marlene feel foolish for finding meaning and even hope in it. And the ideas that have been brewing inside Marlene since her father's appearance must be kept secret, too.

"I'm going to call him," Marlene says, one evening, after a typical argument about her college prospects.

"With what number?" Diane says.

"Ha!" Marlene exclaims and storms into her bedroom. She returns holding the crumpled envelope she rescued from the garbage can months earlier. "I can read a postmark. I can call 411. Only thing I don't know is why it took me so long." But she does know: It is the Diane in her, slowing her down, making her aim low.

Diane stiffens as Marlene reaches for the telephone next to the living room couch. "Don't do it, Marlene," she says.

"Why not?"

Diane stands. "Marlene," she warns.

"What are you so scared of?" Marlene says, punching in the numbers.

"I'm not scared, I'm—"

But Marlene stops her with an outstretched hand. She listens to the ring. Her heart is beating fast. The phone feels hot in her hand. After a moment she hangs up. She stares at the phone.

"You're lucky no one's home," Diane says, sitting down again. "Sometimes making things more complicated just makes things more complicated."

"They moved," Marlene says quietly. "The recording gives a forwarding number. They moved to a whole other area code." She looks at the phone in disbelief.

"I'm sorry, baby," Diane says softly.

"No, you're not," Marlene says. "You're happy. 'Cause now you're right about everything."

"Being right always makes me sad," Diane says.

*Three days later* Marlene stands at the edge of the highway, waiting for a ride. She's never hitchhiked before. She fights her growing anxiety about leaving her mother with her reservoir of age-old complaints. She's glad when the first driver to pull over is a woman.

The woman says she is a photographer and that she is doing an article for a magazine Marlene has never heard of.

"Taking pictures of what?" Marlene says.

"The land," the woman says. "It's beautiful, don't you think?"

"Not really," Marlene says.

The woman's private smile irks Marlene. It means that the woman thinks Marlene doesn't know what she's talking about. The woman wears jeans and a red-checked blouse, so new they're still creased. She probably bought them just yesterday so she could look like her ignorant idea of a farmer.

"Can't think of one thing I've seen in my life worth taking a picture of," Marlene says.

The woman laughs. "How old are you?"

"Eighteen and a half." Her voice slides recklessly over the two-year lie. Adding the half is a mistake. Only little kids care about halves and quarters. The woman nods but does not reveal whether she believes Marlene or not.

"Where are you heading?"

"Los Angeles."

"That's a long way," the woman says. "What for?"

"Not to be rude or anything, but none of your business."

The woman shrugs. "Just making conversation," she says, losing interest in Marlene.

"I'm going to find my father who has a whole other family there so I can tell him he has to take care of me, too," Marlene says. How about *that* for conversation? She is pleased when the woman glances at her in confusion. People skate on the surface of lies, Marlene thinks. It's the truth that lands them flat on their asses every time.

A day later Marlene stands in the ticket line at the Greyhound station in Indianapolis. She's made it this far hitching, but she's tired, and the last driver scared the shit out of her. He told her how lonely he was and how useless and ignorant his wife and kids were. She was surprised that he'd let her out when she asked without laying a hand on her.

She has enough money for the ticket, but she'll have to avoid motels altogether. Aside from the cost of a room, a motel manager might ask for ID, and then the next thing she knows, she'll be sitting in the back of a police cruiser while they call her mother. She reminds herself to call home and leave a message while Diane is at work. She left a note on the kitchen table but she can't be sure Diane will see it before it gets buried under a pile of coupon fliers.

The drive through Indiana is nasty. The bus is air-conditioned, but after twenty minutes the recirculated air carries the odor seeping from beneath the bathroom door. At first Marlene sits at the back of the bus in order to avoid making eye contact with the driver. But she moves seats twice in order to flee the noxious combination of urine and disinfectant and ends up directly behind him. She doesn't have to worry. A small, wiry man, the driver leans forward and hugs the enormous horizontal steering wheel as though he is mounting a giant whore. He couldn't care less about Marlene.

She falls asleep and wakes in the dark center of night. Pressing her face against the window, she sees black shadows of hills sketched in the distance. All the land and darkness make her feel simultaneously safe and frightened, the way she felt as a little girl, in that startling moment after her mother said "goodnight" and turned off the lights in her bedroom and Marlene understood she was alone. The darkness outside the bus is tangibly thick. If she could open one of the glued-shut windows and stick her hand out, she'd come back with a fistful of night.

Suddenly her heart begins to race. Her breath becomes trapped in her chest. She doesn't know where she is. She has no idea what she'll find when she gets to Los Angeles. All she has is this stupid forwarding number with an 818 area code. The operator told her 818 could be Sherman Oaks or Burbank or fifteen other places she's never heard of. She feels both stupid for making this flying leap of a trip and absolutely certain that when she gets to Los Angeles, her father will be happy to see her.

She needs to talk to someone, but there is no one. Her life is a private, isolate thing, like those one-celled creatures that swim around underneath her microscope in biology class. Marlene puts her hand in her bag and feels for the hammer she brought from home for protection. She digs the narrow ridges into her thumb. *Stupid, stupid girl.* She stands up and walks to the bathroom at the back of the bus, holds her breath and pees.

11.

"*Mom needs more stimulation,*" Caroline says as she bursts in through the kitchen door, having just taken the boys to school. "We should take her on an outing."

Vincent, drinking what he'd hoped would be a recuperative coffee at the kitchen table, his head throbbing dully, recognizes the trap immediately. If he disagrees he will seem heartless, fulfilling Caroline's expectation of his character.

"Fine," he says.

"I was thinking of the zoo," she says. "She loves animals."

Her enthusiasm shames him. Why is he so suspicious of her? Isn't she just his little girl, dancing with anticipation at the pony ride in Griffith Park? But the lie of parenthood is this: You don't see your innocent child in the adult she's become. You only see a stranger who is all the more alien because you keep thinking you're supposed to know her.

"Mom should sit in front," Caroline announces an hour and a half later, after Eleanor has been roused, fed, and dressed and all three are heading for Caroline's car. Caroline steers her mother toward the front passenger seat. "Better view," she says, then takes the driver's seat.

Vincent sits in the back seat behind Caroline as she drives to the zoo. The boys' detritus sprinkles the floor— candy wrappers, broken pencils, corrected homework crushed into fist-size balls. He feels childish and overgrown at the same time. He suppresses an urge to push his knees into the seat to see how much pressure he can apply before Caroline scolds him. Eleanor stares out her window. Her silence, and the fact that she does not seem interested in the novelty of the trip, satisfy Vincent in a way that ultimately depresses him.

They rent a wheelchair at the zoo, and Caroline takes control. She stops in front of the flamingo enclosure. A bushel of orange and pink birds stand on spindly, banded legs. Occasionally one dips down to fish a fly out of the brackish, coin-infested water.

"You'd think throwing coins would be against the rules," Vincent says, staring across the chain fence at the quavering nickels and quarters littering the pond.

But Caroline has already placed a penny in her mother's palm.

"Make a wish, Mommy," she whispers. "Anything you want."

Eleanor looks at the penny for a moment, then leans forward in her chair and lets the coin slide from her fingers. It lands in the scrub plantings surrounding the habitat.

"That's okay, Mom," Caroline says as she reaches for the coin and tosses it into the pond. "Don't tell us what you wished," she cautions sweetly. "Or it won't come true."

"I forgot to make a wish!" Eleanor exclaims.

"Try again," Caroline urges, offering her mother another coin.

Two birds begin to fight, and the sudden eruption of feathers draws excited comments from the bystanders. Vincent considers how ridiculous it is that people only perk up when animals start to act like real wildlife rather than the indolent, overheated prisoners they really are. It's the same with acting. People want an actor to portray a character in a way that conforms to their idea of "real life," and they complain when a character does something they would never do. He supposes that parents are meant to adhere to a child's idea of them, too, and that they are destined always to flub their lines.

He tries to identify the motivation for the birds' fight. Is it food? Or a female? But the flamingos quickly lose interest in their tussle and return to bending their long, rubbery necks like umbrella handles so they can groom their backs.

Caroline stops the wheelchair at the seals, the morose, dirty polar bear, then the slow-motion elephants tossing hay onto their broad backs. She kneels down so that her face is level with her mother's. "The Asian ones have ears in the shape of Asia. You taught me that. Remember?"

Eleanor stares wanly at the beasts. She seems as worn down by purposelessness as they.

"I don't think she's interested," Vincent says.

"How do you know?" Caroline snaps, standing. "You don't know what she's taking in. Her mind has to stay active."

He resents her immediately. "Her mind is active. Just not in the way you want it to be."

"I don't accept that," Caroline says.

"You don't have to accept it, but it's the truth."

"She can get better."

"She can't get better."

"Or at least things can slow down. Don't you want that?" Vincent reminds himself to breathe.

"We have to help her," Caroline says. "It's our responsibility, right?"

Responsibility. There it is: the bullet he's been waiting for. Caroline looks away, apparently unaware of her direct hit, and pushes the wheelchair back onto the zoo path.

Vincent follows a few steps behind. The acute discomfort of having his daughter back in his house is physical. As he drives to teach his class each evening, he feels crowded in his chest, as though there are too many organs there, vying for space. He suffers from indigestion. Food transforms itself into fire as it descends his esophagus and winds its way through his gut. He knows it is his guilt, bounding back as if it were only yesterday that Caroline was twelve and he left her. He only hopes that adulthood and her own sufferings have made her less sharply judicious of others. She is a mother, after all. She must have learned by now that it is possible to have ambivalent feelings toward those you are meant to love the most.

He hopes she will find a job soon. He sees her reading the classified section, but she has not mentioned her progress and he dares not ask. She pays for groceries. She offers to give him money as a form of rent, but the loan on the house was long-ago paid off and it would be humiliating to take money from her.

When she is around her children, she is purposeful, motherly in a way that frankly surprises him. It is curious to watch her comfort and reprimand, grow provoked and pleased by them at turns. He can't imagine how she grew from an angry, dismissive teen into this woman with a capacity to take care of other living things.

But when she is away from the boys, she seems unmoored. He's come upon her standing in the middle of the living room in a patch of sunlight, doing nothing but waiting. For what, he wonders? Her sense of dislocation is palpable. Entering a room, she looks as though she has forgotten something she needs, like a sweater or a set of keys. In this way she reminds him frighteningly of his wife. He is living in a house filled with lost people.

He is certain she blames him for Eleanor's illness. He wishes she would just come out and say it: He abandoned his wife, and Eleanor's response to this injury simply appeared years later, like some long-dormant cancer finally manifesting itself. Yes, Eleanor's disease stole upon her when she was too young, her life unspooling practically before his eyes. But none of this is his fault. Christ, he's stuck by his wife when other men might have fled in an attempt to salvage their final years without a spouse's decline hastening their own. They would have taken younger lovers, shrugging off an old, tattered coat in favor of a new one. They would become sixty-five-year-old fathers of newborns. It happens in Hollywood all the time.

*The three eat lunch* at an animal-themed kiosk. Eleanor becomes cranky and pushes away the French fries. Caroline urges a spoonful of yogurt on her mother. Eleanor bats the spoon away, and yogurt splatters Caroline's jeans.

"Shit," she mumbles.

"You shouldn't spoon-feed her," Vincent says.

"*You* do it!" Caroline says. A wet paper napkin disintegrates into dirty white shreds as she tries to wash yogurt off her pants.

She looks up, exasperated by her effort. But her eyes are full. He looks away. This whole trip is a mistake. It only serves to humiliate them all.

"When you were a little girl, the polar bear died," Eleanor says.

Vincent and Caroline look at her, then at each other, both of them ambushed by hope.

"Yes, I remember," Caroline says, turning back to her mother. "But then they got a new one."

"I suppose the elephants and such are happy enough," Eleanor says. "But I don't think a polar bear belongs in Los Angeles."

"I agree," Caroline says.

The pleasure and anticipation in Caroline's expression remind Vincent of his daughter at age five or six, when she loved him most and would run to the door to greet him when he returned home from the work of finding work. She'd charge into him with a body-crashing hug, obliterating the day's tally of rejection. The joy she took in her own passion was equal to her delight at seeing him. They had loved each other then. They had loved being loved by each other. Day after day she had gifted him with the possibility of reinvention.

He feels an urgent need to protect her now. He wants to remind her that Eleanor's lucidity will soon be replaced by the vacancy that preceded it. He must teach her that love trips over its own feet like an awkward dancer, and then you have to bear the dull pain of surprise and hurt and the knowledge that you are a fool to have hoped.

"You were never interested in animals," Eleanor says, looking directly at Caroline.

"No," Caroline says. "I was never one of those horse girls."

"Like Libbet Foster," Eleanor says.

"Libbet Foster!" Caroline erupts. "I can't believe you remember her. She was so snotty with those jodhpurs!"

"Well, with a mother like *that*," Eleanor says, raising her eyebrows in contempt.

Caroline laughs. "Mrs. Foster. Oh my God. That phony English accent. She was from *Downey*, for God's sake!"

Eleanor's eyes drift across the restaurant patio.

"How did the polar bear die?" Caroline asks.

Eleanor is silent.

"Was it the heat?"

"Caroline," Vincent says softly.

"Or maybe loneliness," Caroline muses. "It's cruel to have only one polar bear at a time."

"It's over," Vincent says.

"What?"

"She's somewhere else," he says.

"Mommy," Caroline says, urgently. "Mom."

"I don't like this food," Eleanor says petulantly.

"We'll get you something else," Vincent says, resting a hand on her arm.

"Mommy, what about the bear?" Caroline insists.

Panic spreads across Eleanor's delicate features. "Where are we?"

"We're at the zoo," Vincent reminds her evenly.

"I want to go home."

"They have ice cream," Caroline says. "Would you like ice cream, Mommy?"

"I want to go home!" Eleanor cries.

Nearby, children and their parents stare at the commotion. Vincent stands, releases the brake on the wheelchair, and begins to maneuver Eleanor away from the table.

"Dad!" Caroline calls, catching up. "You're making a mistake. She was doing fine."

He stops the wheelchair and turns to face his daughter. "Don't you understand?" he says, trying to control his rage. "This is just an exercise to make you feel better about yourself. It does nothing for your mother. Nothing."

"She remembered Mrs. Foster," Caroline says. "She was getting somewhere."

"There is nowhere to go," he says.

He insists on driving home. Eleanor sits in the passenger seat and quickly falls asleep against the window. Vincent feels Caroline's knees shift against the back of his seat when she moves. Neither speaks. When they reach the house, Vincent hurries around to the passenger side of the car, wedges his arms beneath his wife, and lifts her from the car seat.

"Do you need help?" Caroline asks.

"I can take care of it," he answers as he climbs the porch steps.

*Hours later*, after Caroline returns from picking up the boys at school, she finds Vincent in the backyard hosing out the garbage cans. Eleanor sits nearby in a chair, shaded by a dusty old outdoor umbrella. He tries to hide the tension his daughter's proximity engenders in him. Silently he calculates the hours until Amador's arrival and his escape.

"She looks sad," Caroline says after embracing her mother.

"She's not sad," he says.

"How do we know?" she says. She sits down on the concrete and rests her head in her mother's lap.

He turns up the pressure on the hose, hoping that the sound will deter Caroline from speaking.

"If you have things to take care of, I can stay with Mom," she says.

"It's fine."

"Really, Dad," she says. "There's no point in two of us being here. You must have things to do."

He starts to protest again but realizes they are engaged

in a game of chicken. The fact is, they are both unnecessary. The world demands nothing of them and expects less. Each new day they compete for the privilege of taking care of Eleanor in order to avoid the hollow fact of their superfluity.

"All right, then," he says, turning off the hose, trying to infuse his voice with jaunty resolution. He will *act* the part of the one with an actual life. "I'll take you up on that offer."

"Stay out as long as you like," she says.

He pulls out of the driveway and drives down the street. He stops at the corner, unsure whether to turn left or right. He can never remember where things are anymore. Is the grocery store to the right? Is the newsstand to the left? Does it matter? Maybe he is losing his mind, too. For a moment it's a comforting thought. With the arrival of Caroline, his whole life has begun to feel like it no longer fits him. He's acutely aware of its splitting seams.

He finally makes a left turn, drives to the grocery store, and sits in the enormous parking lot. People move in and out of the store carrying bags and children, rolling recalcitrant carts toward cars. Two boys slide to the entrance on skateboards, elegantly stepping off their boards and bending to retrieve them in the same movement. He remembers the time when life required so little effort, when grace was as natural as breathing. Cars glide in and out of parking spaces with metronomic regularity, as though they are part of a giant factory machine manufacturing—what? Movement? Purpose? Definition?

Years ago he convinced himself that leaving Eleanor was necessary to his survival. Her irritating calm, her resistance

*No Direction Home* < *173*

to surprise, the grating temperateness she insisted on stood in direct opposition to his idea of himself. What was acting if not the ability to rise and fall like a wave? It was the single occupation on earth he'd found that would validate his enormous internal storms of self-loathing and self-love. He was miserable with feeling. He had to scream and yell and fuck and fight. But when he was on the stage, or in front of a camera, he could force all that emotion into a succession of small moments and his life felt manageable.

He left Eleanor for another woman—a typical excuse (a generic performance, God knows). But this relationship was short-lived. He spent the next four years mostly alone in a rented apartment near MacArthur Park, a place in which, he was perversely proud to think, Eleanor would never set foot. The area, once charming, had given way to drugs. Syringes floated in the pond like inert guppies, rising from the wakes of paddleboats commandeered by Mexican families. Cars swung up to curbs and pulled out again just as soon as two hands met and made an exchange.

He occupied his days with the occasional job, auditioning, or playing basketball at the YMCA. Nights he visited the local bars. He nursed his drinks and listened as mariachi music blew in and out of the neighborhood restaurants like lazy gusts of wind. He felt pleasantly foreign in that neighborhood, and like a traveler, he relished the release from the obligations of relationships. No one talked to him. No other actors asked him how "things" were going and then gloated at the response. During the days he strolled past old people sitting guard in front of their buildings in aluminum beach chairs and clusters of young men huddled against parked cars, taking breaks in their conversations to stare at passing girls. Vincent felt happily invisible. But of course he was irrelevant.

During the fourth year of his exile, he and Eleanor met at a bank in Toluca Lake to sign a refinancing document. It was the first time they'd been alone since he'd left home. Whenever he picked up Caroline for their occasional outings, Eleanor would keep herself busy in her bedroom.

Eleanor arrived at the bank wearing a simple shirtwaist dress and sandals. She looked uncomplicated and lovely, like a white daisy, so different from the dark and supple women in his new neighborhood, whose laughter poured from their throats like rushing streams. He found Eleanor's primness alluring, just as he had when they'd first met and he thought she could smooth his rough Jersey edges and mold him into someone other people would want. The bank officer referred to the house as though Vincent and Eleanor were living in it together. Neither one corrected her.

Vincent held the door for Eleanor as they exited the bank. He walked her across the parking lot. She was silent as she fished through her bag for her car keys. When she finally pulled them out, a wadded tissue fell to the ground. He bent to pick it up. She took it from him quickly, as though she was embarrassed for him to see the stuffing of her life.

"You work hard, don't you?" he said.

"What do you mean? I don't work at all," she said, as she opened the car door and faced him.

"At life. You work hard at life. I admire that."

A bolt of feeling shot across her face. She looked down at

*174 > Marisa Silver*

her shoes. "No you don't," she whispered. "You think it's silly. A waste of time."

"Can I take you for a cup of coffee?" he asked.

"I don't want coffee," she said.

"I understand." He reminded himself how thoroughly he had laid waste to his life.

"No," she said, lifting her startling eyes to him. "You don't understand."

He followed her in his car. She drove along Olive Avenue until she reached the Sahara Motel, a drab affair that offered an unlit neon sign in the shape of a camel and free cable TV. He followed her into the motel lobby where she paid for a room with cash. She did not speak to him when they made love. They did not speak when they parted.

They met at the motel once a week for the next two months. Sometimes they watched the news on television after they finished making love. Or he would lie on the bed listening to the splatter and ping of the water as she washed in the plastic-lined bathroom shower. If he tried to ask her about her day, or about Caroline, she would parry with brief, informational statements.

"What are you thinking about?" he asked one afternoon. The jingle of an ice cream truck filtered in through the open window. It was July and hot. The air conditioner was broken. She lay on top of the sheets, startlingly uninhibited. Her body was thicker than when he had first met her, but in a solid, comforting way that made him less conscious of his stomach's new roundness, of his legs that had grown bandy with middle age. He wondered if she'd taken lovers in his absence. The thought made him jealous.

"I'm thinking about the heat."

"That's what you were thinking about? The heat?"

"And groceries."

"I don't believe you," he said.

"You asked me what I'm thinking—the most banal question in the world, by the way—and I'm thinking about salmon or sausages. But Caroline is on a no-meat kick. So I guess it will be salmon. Which she will tell me she hates."

"Why don't you just say it?" he asked.

"Say what?"

"That I'm a prick. That I've ruined our daughter's life." His voice was too loud for the small room.

Her hand fell to her chest where it played with a tiny mole above her right breast. "Do you want me to be angry with you, Vincent?" she said.

He roared in frustration. "I don't have any idea what you're thinking!"

"You lost that privilege," she said.

In that moment he knew that Eleanor was not a color of hair, a way of wearing a dress, or any set of mannerisms he had once thought defined her character. He had assumed she had no compulsions, that her representation to the world was an exact mirror of her internal life. And now, lying on that motel bed, he knew he would never be allowed to know her differently. He had blown that chance.

"I want to come back," he said.

She sat up and moved off the bed and walked into the bathroom. In a moment, he heard the sound of the shower.

All energy deserted him. The bedsheet fell around his thighs. His penis was wilted and bent. He realized he had not bothered to take off his socks. The sound of the shower stopped. She stood at the door of the bathroom, dripping and naked.

"All right," she said.

He couldn't tell if she was pleased or if she greeted his suggestion as the inevitable consequence of what they had been doing these past months.

"What about Caroline?" he asked. "Is that what she wants?"

"I don't know what Caroline wants," she said sharply.

He had imagined that his wife and daughter had weathered his departure as a team, sharing their hatred and their hurt. It hadn't occurred to Vincent that Eleanor had to cope with the same difficult, resentful child he saw only once a month for a taco or a movie, never both.

"If you come, you cannot leave," she said. "Do you understand?"

He went to her and put his hands on her shoulders, but she stiffened.

"I won't leave."

"Because it's enough," she said. "It's just enough."

"I promise."

*Vincent starts the engine* and pulls out of his parking space at the supermarket. He has only been gone from the house for a half hour. He cannot go home yet. So he will drive up and down the boulevards of this valley teeming with cars and people and a thousand strands of purpose. There are so many nights when he fantasizes about not returning home after a class, so many mornings when he wakes with the shameful wish that his wife were not beside him. But he has promised her. And if he can redeem himself in any way during this lifetime, he will.

*"How many six-packs* of soda are in two hundred and seventy five?" Caroline says, exasperated. "Just divide it. Six into two seventy-five. Long division. Why is this hard?"

"Because we aren't supposed to do it that way," Will says. "We're doing partial sums."

The boys sit at the kitchen table, pencils poised over math sheets. Caroline looks at Will's paper, confused by the lists of numbers he's written down. "Well, I never heard of doing division this way," she says. "This seems needlessly complicated."

"Math is needlessly complicated," Ethan says. He draws a picture of a spaceship with breasts in the corner of his page.

"She didn't explain it right," Will says, of the math teacher the boys have both admitted hating.

"Do you understand it?" Caroline asks Ethan.

"I wasn't listening," he offers.

"What do you mean, you weren't listening?"

"This year doesn't matter anyway," Ethan says. "They're gonna pass us 'cause they think we're blind."

"You're not blind." Caroline says, horrified. "I filled out the form, that I-52 or -53 or whatever it was that says exactly what is going on."

"I guess they didn't read it," Ethan says. "And because

of Dad," he continues. "They think we're, you know, messed up."

"But you're not messed up," Caroline says, and as she says it she hears the fear in her voice. She's just like all those parents who assuage their guilt with talk about children's resilience, as though kids were just hard rubber balls being bounced around the mayhem of their parents' lives. Look at Ethan, she thinks. Her sweet, fearless boy has become so cynical, using his disability to get ahead.

Every morning, when she pulls to the curb outside the school and waits silently for the boys to gather their bags and lunchboxes and slide out of her safe, Cherry-Coke-smelling car, her chest tightens. Ethan throws his backpack over his shoulder and barely grunts a good-bye before he is sucked into the flow of children headed toward the beige-and-green trailers scattered like dominoes across the asphalt. Will always stalls, giving Caroline a final half-ironic smile, sharing the certain hardship that is in store for him, before he slams the car door shut and walks stoically through the security gate. Yesterday evening he told her that a group of boys called him "four eyes" when he put on his protective goggles during P.E. She has yet to hear him mention a specific friend, and she fears he has none. But he never complains.

"Is this true?" Caroline says, turning to Will, who, she is ashamed to admit, she trusts more than Ethan these days. "Are you guys given slack because of your . . . situation?"

Will shrugs. "I guess."

"He wouldn't know," Ethan says. "He gets everything right anyway."

"I do not!" Will protests.

"Yes you do," Ethan says.

"Boys!" Caroline warns sharply. "Cut it out!"

Ethan grabs his math paper roughly and stands.

"Ethan!" Caroline says. "Come back here right now!" But Ethan says nothing and leaves the room. "Ethan!"

He goes into his room and shuts the door behind him. She stands in the hallway, as startled as if she has been slapped. She is suddenly aware of Amador nearby, helping Eleanor, fresh from her bath, into the bedroom. She is overcome with embarrassment. What must he think of her, screaming at her children as they ignore her?

She moves to the doorway of her mother's room. Amador helps Eleanor into her vanity chair and begins to brush her hair. She imagines he has intentionally, decently, ignored her altercation with Ethan. The house feels suddenly overcrowded with people and anger and individual desires all at cross-purposes with one another. She realizes they have all adopted a posture of emotional deafness in order to cope with the awkwardness of being pushed up against one another's frailties.

"*Hola,*" she says. She wants him to acknowledge her. She wants him to stop avoiding her and look at her, *really* look at her. She wonders if he even considers her as a woman, or if she is just the inconvenient daughter of his boss. She is so tired of being lonely among people.

"*Hola,*" he hears her say, from the doorway. "I forgot to say that when you came in."

"*Buenas noches,*" he says, correcting her. He continues

brushing Mrs. Eleanor's hair. He wishes the daughter would not watch him.

"Right," Caroline says. "I have to get a book, or something."

He didn't mean to correct her Spanish. Why does he care if she speaks his language or not? Why does he care how he moves when she is near?

"Ethan is angry," she says. "It's hard to know what to do."

Amador is confused by her casual inclusion of him in the effort to raise her children. How can she presume such intimacy? And where is her husband? She worries her wedding ring around and around her finger as if she wants it to cut her skin.

Her mere presence makes him feel as though she is touching him. He wishes he could look at her, right at her, for a long time.

"Can I help you?" she asks.

He can accept her help and demonstrate that he is not really needed and lose his job. Or he can refuse and insult her. The house feels unsafe since her arrival. Even when she is not nearby, her smells, the sounds of her breath, move through the house like spirits searching for him.

"Where am I?" Mrs. Eleanor says, suddenly. He sees in the mirror that she has lost herself and that she is terrified. He leans down until his eyes are even with hers. "I am here," he says.

Mrs. Eleanor's eyes flicker from the vanity-mirror image of her own face to his. He watches as she tracks his features, piecing them into the puzzle of himself. She turns to him, raises her hand, and traces his cheekbone. Amador feels self-conscious under Caroline's gaze, but it is important that Mrs. Eleanor knows who he is, that she doesn't consider herself an unwanted object being passed from one person to the next.

"Did you meet my daughter?" Eleanor asks, resting her hand on his shoulder.

"Yes. She been here many weeks now," he says, glancing up at Caroline. Her face looks suddenly years younger. She is sixteen and uncertain. She bites her lip.

"And my grandsons?"

"Handsome boys," he says.

Eleanor smiles. She leans closer to Amador and whispers. "The father is gone," she says. "He doesn't want them anymore."

Caroline does not react, and he is not sure she's heard.

"*Tan triste*," he whispers.

"We have to take care of her now," Eleanor says.

"You don't have to take care of me, Mom," Caroline says, moving into the room. She crouches down on the other side of her mother. Amador feels her breath on his face. He has tried to stay far from her, even in the close confines of the house, even though he wants so much to know what it feels like to touch her. But she is not a prostitute or even a woman who has made herself available to him at a bar. She is his employer's daughter. And he will lose his job. And then he will fail his wife not only in one way but in two ways. In America his desire is always split from his purpose. He is like two men, strangers to each other.

"I'm here to take care of *you*." Caroline whispers to her mother. She takes the old lady's hands and pets them.

"Amador takes care of me," Eleanor says.

"You want me to be here with you, Mom, don't you?" Her voice teeters, begging for the right answer.

"I'm hungry," Eleanor says.

Caroline's dark eyes sparkle as she endures her mother's dismissal.

"Stand up," Amador says to Mrs. Eleanor.

"Shouldn't we help her?" Caroline asks, standing, still holding her mother's hands.

"She do it herself."

Eleanor pouts for a few moments, then slowly takes her hands from Caroline's and pushes herself out of her seat. "Which way?" she asks, when she is finally steady on her feet.

"You know the way," he says.

"Oh," Eleanor sighs, distraught about the work ahead of her. Then her face solidifies into a decision, and she heads toward the bedroom door.

Amador looks back at Caroline, who stays by the vanity.

"You come?" he asks, surprised and frightened by his forwardness.

"Is it okay?" she says.

"Yes, Mrs."

"Caroline," she says.

"Carolina," he answers.

"Oh!" she exclaims, her eyes filled with delight as if he has just surprised her with a single perfect flower.

Her smile shoots through him like a little death.

## 12.

*Rogelio is hungry all the time.* The gnawing emptiness in his gut makes him want to vomit, but when he does he produces only spit and foul air. His belly muscles ache from heaving. He escaped from the shelter the police brought him to, sneaking through a window when the guard went outside to take a piss. The meal there was his last real food. It has been scraps and garbage since then. His hunger makes him angry.

As he wanders the *barrio*, he curses his father for going to America. He curses his mother for letting his father leave, and he curses himself for failing. He cannot bear to be with himself. The stinking smell of his own body follows him wherever he goes like a hungry dog. If his body *was* a dog, he would kick it. Delivering pain would make him feel less pain. He is certain of it.

There are other boys like him wandering the *barrio*, boys attached to no one and nothing. He notices them as they search for leftover food in garbage cans. They watch Rogelio, waiting to see what his movements augur for their survival.

Night falls and he skirts the perimeter of a garbage dump, past a group of boys sitting on a pile of discarded tires. A glowing cigarette butt dances among them.

"Hey!" a boy calls out.

Rogelio stops but does not look at the boys. A mistake might cost him the stale bread he found only minutes before, half of which sits snugly in the waistband of his trousers.

"You don't talk?" the boy says as he climbs down the pyramid of tires and walks casually toward Rogelio. "Where's your mama?" The boy's tone curls the end of his sentence into a sneer. He is twig thin, but he walks with the intentional stride of a much bigger, stronger boy. He wears a printed shirt tucked into his pants. A heavy gold watch hangs loosely on his wrist. Unlike the other boys Rogelio has seen who slither around corners and down alleyways trying to mask their existence, this boy moves with a syncopated hitch that announces: *Here I am. What are you going to do about it?*

"How old are you?" the boy asks.

"Sixteen."

"Bullshit."

"Fifteen," Rogelio says.

"Maybe twelve," the boy says.

"Fourteen!" Rogelio says defiantly.

"Ahh," the boy says, pleased at having tricked the truth out of Rogelio. "A baby."

As if obeying a signal, the other boys climb down from the tower of tires and begin to walk away. Just before they round a corner, the boy with the gold watch looks back and beckons.

Rogelio trails the boys toward a cream-colored cinderblock building. The building looks official, like a school or a government office, and Rogelio hangs back warily. One by one the boys disappear like rabbits into a hole near the building. When Rogelio comes closer, he realizes the hole is an entrance to the sewers. Excited laughter and shouts echo in the darkness. He knows in his gut that if he loses sight of these boys, he will not survive another day. He drops down five feet and lands on his backside. When he stands, he hits his head against an uneven rock ceiling. The smell is a rich, nauseating blend of water and earth and rotting garbage, and it takes him a moment to breathe without gagging. He sees nothing but hears the footsteps and voices of the boys disappearing deep inside the tunnel. A pinprick of light bounces off the walls. He crouches and runs. Within minutes, his thighs burn. Each step produces a spray of foul water that wets his face.

When he finally catches up to the boys, they are squatting against the sides of the tunnel. The dull corona of a flashlight illuminates the walls where people have written their names along with crude drawings of naked women and guns.

There are maybe eight or ten boys here. They huddle together as the one with the gold watch points the nozzle of a spray can into the mouth of a wrinkled brown bag. The hiss of the aerosol fills the tunnel like a warning and everyone becomes church-quiet—expectant, restless.

"Tonio, here!" calls a boy in a high voice. "Tonio, me first!" Tonio, his gold watch flashing as he moves in and out of the light, takes a long inhale from the bag and passes it on. The boys take turns. Someone hands the bag to Rogelio. He looks up and sees eyes staring impatiently in his direction.

"Take it or pass it on, man," says a boy. "*¡Guay!*"

"*¡Cállate!*" hisses Tonio.

The boys fall silent. Tonio lifts his chin encouragingly to Rogelio. Rogelio holds the bag to his face and inhales. The fumes burn his nostrils and his throat. His head begins to feel heavy and light at the same time.

Tonio moves closer, and Rogelio smells cologne. The scent reminds him of a time long ago, when his father lifted him onto a carousel horse. Rogelio buried his face in the sweaty warmth of his father's neck and smelled a sweet, spicy odor. When his father put him on the horse and walked away, Rogelio cried, not because he was scared, as his frowning father thought, but because he wanted to stay in his father's arms and inhale that marvelous smell.

Rogelio's head spins. He thinks he sees his father standing before him, and he reaches out. But then Amador becomes Tonio, who is laughing. His teeth sit wide apart from one another, as though he wasn't given the right amount and has to make do.

"What's your name?" Tonio asks.

"Rogelio." His voice is coming from outside his body.

"Where're you from?"

"Michoacán."

Some of the boys murmur and nod their heads. They move closer to Rogelio, inspecting the object of Tonio's interest.

"You have any money?" Tonio asks.

Rogelio feels the bread stuffed into his waistband. He feels, too, the expectant eyes of the boys. "If I had money, would I be here with you?" he answers carefully.

There is silence. The other boys look at Tonio, waiting to see how he will respond to this impertinence. Tonio's dark eyes glitter. He juts out his lower lip in a thoughtful frown. Rogelio feels sick to his stomach.

"That's the fucking truth," Tonio says finally, grinning widely.

The other boys turn back to the business of the spray can. When the can is empty, someone tosses it to the ground where it rolls in a lazy circle.

Laughter. A boy hangs his head between his legs. Someone sings half the words of a song Rogelio recognizes. Tonio stands still, his eyes closed, mesmerized by his inner distortion. When the chatter around him becomes too loud, he raises a warning hand without opening his eyes, and the other boys immediately fall silent.

Rogelio's body feels like rubber. He leans against a wall until his legs give way. He wants to scream or sing or say one word over and over again until it is as hard as a bullet and he can bite down on it and make his teeth hurt. He looks down at his legs. They are too long, his feet too far away. He is more than one person. He is the tunnel. He is space. He is emptiness.

Suddenly he hears heavy footsteps echoing in the tunnel, drawing closer.

"Tonio!" someone whispers.

Tonio snaps off the flashlight. The boys freeze in the darkness. Rogelio stands slowly, willing his legs to return to their normal size.

"*¡La chota!*"

"*¡Corran!*"

Rogelio takes off after the boys. The tunnel narrows, and he bangs his head and arms against the low ceiling and rough walls. He feels cold air collide with something virgin on his elbow, and he knows he is bleeding, but he keeps moving away from the heavy sounds of the policemen's footfalls, finally following the boys up through a manhole. Once on the street, the boys fan out in all directions like a covey of birds after a gunshot. Rogelio runs, charged by the night air, adrenaline, and the drugs. He could run forever.

*During the day* he wanders the streets of the *barrio*, sometimes alone, sometimes with other boys. He hunts for food in garbage cans or in the backs of *mercados*, where he might find rotten fruit or stale bread. If he passes an outdoor spigot, he strips off his shirt and bathes himself. Rolls of dirt and peeling skin collect in his hands. He runs his shirt under the water, wrings out the black dirt, then dresses again.

Tonio tells him that the tunnel stretches all the way to the U.S.A. The boys occasionally rob the small bands of men and women led by *polleros* across the underground border.

The bounty includes crosses and jewelry, sometimes a watch or a few pesos. Rogelio stays close to the boys during these thefts, trying to appear involved, but he cannot bring himself to fish inside the bags or pockets of the men and women.

A boy named Diego joins Rogelio in the theft of some black bananas from the back of a store. The boys part after eating the soft, metallic-tasting fruit. When Diego does not appear in the tunnels that night, Rogelio wonders out loud whether he was caught by the police. Or has he succumbed to the white woman who routinely approaches the boys with offers of a place to sleep if only they will attend her Christian school?

"Who knows?" Tonio says, with little interest in the subject. "They come, they go."

Rogelio cannot imagine leaving the tunnels. His days are busy, consumed with the business of remaining alert to the possibility of danger. He looks forward to rejoining the boys each night and listening to one or another of them spin real or exaggerated tales of bravery. He wonders if this is how life happens. You think you are doing one thing, then you realize that you are doing something else. And the days pass. And this becomes your life. Maybe his mother is wrong, and the universe is not a design of constellations and planets whose movements are mirrored on earth. His own father stumbled out of his life as recklessly as Rogelio stumbled into these tunnels. You make one mistake and then another, and your life becomes the sum of these blunders.

But when he is alone, wandering the streets, he thinks about his father. Amador cried when Rogelio read a poem he had written at school about the moon. Rogelio didn't know what he had done to make his father sad, and when he asked, Amador said, "You can have two opposite feelings in your heart." Rogelio didn't understand at the time, thought only that he had written a bad poem, and was ashamed. He felt as he always did that his father disapproved of him. But now he begins to understand why he cannot hug his father when he sees him, why he can barely utter a sentence in the man's presence. And he understands why, after his father leaves for *el Norte* each time, Rogelio feels that something is forever lost because he was not brave enough or strong enough to say what he meant to say. If only he knew what he meant to say. And then he hates Amador for leaving, and he curses him and he decides that he will stay in these tunnels and never leave because here he matters. But how he longs for the weight of his father's hand on his shoulder.

*Tonio snaps his fingers* to music only he hears. His amped-up gait signals a purpose that makes Rogelio eager to be near him. He is always clean. He wears sunglasses with silver frames. If he is outside the tunnels at night, he pushes the glasses on top of his head and the sides reflect the street-lights as if he is wearing a crown. He looks as though he has no worries, as though the tunnel is the home he's chosen out of all the mansions and castles at his disposal.

"Why are you here?" he asks Rogelio one night, when most of the boys are asleep.

The darkness is thick. Tonio's invisibility emboldens Rogelio. "My father is in Los Angeles," he says.

"Ahhh," Tonio replies, as if he knows the entire story. "Los Angeles is shit, by the way."

"You've been there?" Rogelio's heart beats faster. Perhaps he is closer to his father than he thinks.

"I have a cousin there. I went to see him once." Tonio says. "He's a gardener. Works at all these rich people's houses, you know. He doesn't know shit about gardening." Tonio chuckles quietly.

"Why did you come back?" Rogelio asks.

"I was *invited* back," Tonio says. "*La Migra.* They drove us down to the border in this nice air-conditioned van, man. They gave us Cokes. Hey, you get better treatment on your way out than on your way in, that's for sure."

"I'm going to go to Los Angeles," Rogelio says, with less conviction than he intended.

"You gonna leave me?"

Rogelio doesn't know how to answer. He feels safe with Tonio. He is not sure what will happen to him if he leaves. He shakes his head.

"There's nothing for you there, man," Tonio says.

The next day, when the boys make their way out of the tunnel, Tonio grabs Rogelio by the arm. "Wait," he whispers. He lingers by the mouth of the tunnel as the other boys disappear into the day, then he drops back down into the dark. Rogelio hesitates. He doesn't want to spend the day in the tunnels, even in Tonio's company. He needs air and light. He is hungry.

"Hurry up, you lazy ass," Tonio calls.

Rogelio follows. The boys crouch and move quickly down the dark shaft. After ten minutes they reach a metal fence.

"They put this up, we take it down," Tonio says, kicking the fence once, then twice. Rogelio joins in. The numbing feeling of flinging his body against metal is exhilarating. The boys grunt and swear and double over with laughter.

"Welcome to America, man," Tonio says, when they finally break through. He leads Rogelio to a manhole, and the boys climb out of the tunnel into the daylight.

"Looks like Mexico to me," Rogelio says, as his eyes adjust to the light. A collection of shabby dwellings stretches out in front of him. All the signs are written in Spanish.

"It's all the same for people like us," Tonio says. "You think your father's living like a movie star in Los Angeles? No way."

The thought of his father makes Rogelio's chest tighten. He is in America, closer to his father by only a few hundred meters but closer than he's been in years.

"How far is California?" he asks.

"Depends on your luck," Tonio says. "Why, you gonna leave me for your *papá*?"

"No," Rogelio says quickly. "What do I give a fuck about him anyhow?"

"Like he's thinking about you right now," Tonio says. "Fuck that."

"Fuck that," Rogelio agrees, deflated.

"Hey man, you stink."

Rogelio looks down at himself. The knees of his pants are soaked with sludge. He tries to wipe them off, but the effort proves useless. He feels ashamed, but when he looks up, Tonio is smiling his gap-toothed, benevolent smile.

"Hungry?" Tonio asks.

They weave quickly in and out of streets and alleyways. When they travel beyond the *barrio*, they slow to a walk. They stop in front of a store window to look at television sets and vacuum cleaners and discuss the merits of the appliances as if they have bank vaults nestled inside their pockets.

Tonio grabs Rogelio by the arm. "You can't eat a TV, man," he says.

He leads Rogelio toward a pink building whose windows are framed with frayed green awnings. "Hotel Excelsior" is painted on the front of the building in peeling red letters.

"I'm thinking about a big juicy hunk of *meat*, man," Tonio whispers.

Rogelio's tongue feels thick as he thinks about the food.

Tonio stops and consults his watch. "They're gonna clean up breakfast about now," he says. "We're gonna have a feast." He picks up his pace and leads Rogelio around the side of the hotel. Tonio stops short, holding Rogelio back with his arm as a kitchen worker wearing a hairnet and a stained white jacket emerges from a doorway with a dark green sack of garbage. He heaves it into a Dumpster, then walks back into the building. When the man is out of sight, the boys make a run for the Dumpster. Tonio vaults easily over the edge and drops down. In a few moments the garbage bag lands on the pavement at Rogelio's feet, followed by Tonio.

"Breakfast, *mi hermano*."

Rogelio relishes the endearment.

Tonio tears open the bag. He claws through the contents

until he finds what he is looking for: triangles of watermelon, an untouched piece of toast. "Still warm," he says, biting into the toast. "Fucking *gringos* sure know how to waste food." He offers the toast to Rogelio.

The boys feast on half-eaten sweet cakes and breakfast cookies, an uneaten orange, a piece of ham, and two individual boxes of Frosted Flakes. They eat like rich men, comparing delicacies. They congratulate each other on their prodigious burps.

"*¡Salte a la chingáda!*"

It is the kitchen worker. He starts toward them, waving a dirty rag. The boys shout back insults as they flee around the corner of the hotel. Once they are underground and safely across the broken border fence, they stop, bending over to catch their breath. After a few minutes Tonio unfolds himself and imitates the enraged worker's high-pitched threat, waving an imaginary, impotent wet rag.

"*Maricón*," Tonio says, shaking his hand limply.

"*Maricón*," Rogelio agrees.

That afternoon the boys split up, and Rogelio wanders the town himself. He feels strong. He is the king of the *barrio*. What does he need Los Angeles for? What can his father do for him? He practices walking until his movements are as elegantly effortless as Tonio's. He sees his reflection in the window of a gas station. He thinks he looks like a ship or like an airplane in the sky, something whose actual speed and power seem diminished by distance, its strength a slow-moving secret.

13.

*Marlene arrives at the Hollywood* bus station at three in the afternoon. Her body aches from the unnatural position she slept in, her head bent over her chest, her arms clutching her bag so she would wake if anyone tried anything.

Cupping her hand around her mouth, she blows out and smells her rank breath. She finds the bathroom, washes her face, brushes her teeth, and rubs her underarms beneath her shirt with a wet paper towel. Her face is puffy and discolored. Her hair is limp. She is developing a zit in the crevice above her chin. She considers washing her hair, but the sink faucets are too low, and the hot water tap doesn't work on purpose.

She takes out the folded sheet of notebook paper from her pocket. It is creased and sweaty from the trip, but she can still make out the telephone number. Suddenly she isn't sure about calling. Whoever picks up the phone might not be happy to hear from her, and she isn't ready for that, not after traveling so far. She isn't sure she is ready for the opposite, either. She hasn't fully imagined what it will mean to start up a whole new life with a different family. What if they take her in out of duty but don't like her? What if they think she is stupid and badly educated and embarrassingly plain? What if they send her home?

She's come halfway across the country to discover she is scared shitless. She considers calling her mother, but she called from Barstow only three hours earlier and left a message, and if she calls again her mother will know she's a coward. And if she actually hears her mother's voice, she might start crying and beg to come home because even if she fights with her mother all the time, at least she knows what that's like. She can't go back home now. She must prove that her life is different from her mother's, and that those feelings of possibility that nearly burst from her chest, that certain knowledge that she is more than what she's told she is, are not fantasies.

She is overwhelmed by a sick intuition that she may be wrong about all this. Why is it just when you think you know what you're supposed to do, some little freak inside your head sticks out its tongue and says, *Nyah, nyah, nyah, nyah, nyah?*

She decides there is no rush to make the call. She'll wait until that sick feeling goes away. She wipes her wet hands on a paper towel and pitches it into the garbage can. She is finally in the same city as her father. He is going to have to deal with her sooner or later. She has all the time in the world.

She walks out of the bus station. She didn't bank on a windy day in Los Angeles, and she pulls her thin jacket around her. Litter dances in the gutters. Marlene's hair blows into her eyes. Bus station bums linger around the building, and cars stutter in traffic on the narrow side street. She's the only person walking, and she feels as exposed as if she were naked. She is so self-conscious she can barely walk properly. After a few blocks she sees a girl with blue hair and a boy with no hair at all sitting on the steps of a giant CD store. The girl scrapes her gaze across Marlene as she takes a drag of her cigarette, then hands the butt to the boy. People move in and out of the store, kids with mohawks and chains mixed in with people in pressed pants and polo shirts who look like they sell computers. Marlene leans against the wall of the store a safe distance from the couple. She feels in her purse for a half-eaten bag of M&M's and eats the candies one by one, trying to define the difference in taste between blue and red and brown, deciding that there is none and that once again the world is a big gyp. Suddenly she realizes she feels calm, as if she spends every afternoon of her life hanging out in front of this particular store with these not particularly friendly people. The girl and the boy finish their cigarette, stretch as if they've just enjoyed a luxurious nap on a tropical island, and head down the street. Marlene feels a momentary panic; now she's alone all over again. As if loneliness is something you need to be reminded about, she thinks. She sighs, pushes herself away from the wall, and searches for a pay phone.

She hangs up the minute she hears the boy's voice. She is prepared for her father's wife, or even for her father. But she isn't prepared to deal with the fact of a kid. His kid. His real kid. Her hands sweat.

She calls again.

"That was me before," she says when the same soft voice answers.

"Why did you hang up?" he says.

"I got confused."

They are both silent.

"Who do you want to talk to?" he asks, finally.

"Frank." The minute she says the name, she knows she has no right to it. She feels like a fool to have come all this way to claim something that is not hers.

The boy says nothing.

"Hello," she says, sarcasm coming to the rescue. "Anybody home?"

"Umm . . . Well, he's not here," the boy says.

"When will he be there?"

"I don't know."

"Is there anybody there who *does* know?" She's beginning to feel impatient. Days on a bus, and now she has to deal with *this*?

"I mean, he doesn't live here," the boy says.

"What do you mean?" she says. She stares at the scrap of paper with the number written on it. "Is this his home? I mean, do I have a wrong number? Frank Burton?"

"He doesn't live here," the boy repeats. "He doesn't live with us anymore."

"Where is he?"

"I don't know."

"I don't understand." Her heart races.

The phone makes the sound of hitting something hard, then the boy's voice returns. "Sorry," he says. "My glasses fell."

"You wear glasses?" she says. Suddenly the boy takes shape in her mind. He is younger than she is, with his high child's voice. He wears glasses. He thinks everything is his fault just like she does. He is her brother.

"Who are you?" he says.

She doesn't know if it is worth telling him her story. Her father has ditched her without even telling her or her mother. Probably so he can stop sending money altogether, she thinks. She sees the man by the car in her mind. He said he was traveling. She hadn't understood. So what is there to tell this boy? If she tells him who she is, what will it matter? She'll probably mess up his life even worse than it already is. His father ditched him, too. Telling him will only confirm the fact that she shares this abandonment. She's not ready for that.

If she says nothing, one day the boy will forget about the weird phone call with the strange girl. And then she will not exist for anyone, not her father or this sweet-voiced apologetic boy.

"Are you crying?" he says.

"No."

"You sound like you're crying."

"It's just—I'm tired and I don't have anywhere to go."

"Where do you live?"

"I'm such a loser," she says. She can't stop her tears now. "Oh, shit," she says. "This is all wrong."

"What's your name?" he asks.

"Marlene," she says. Then she makes a decision that isn't a decision but just happens in her heart, like a beat. "Burton," she adds. A lie and a truth at the same time.

"Hey! That's my last name, too!" the boy says enthusiastically. "Burton. Will Burton. Isn't that funny?"

She breathes, trying to steady herself. "Yeah," she says. "It's funny."

*Ethan bursts through the kitchen door* just as Will hangs up the phone. His face is flushed and he carries his skateboard under his arm. He flings open the door of the refrigerator and guzzles orange juice from the carton.

"Who was on the phone?" he asks, after he wipes his mouth.

"Nobody," Will says.

"Will's got a girlfriend," Ethan sings.

"Shut up. It was a wrong number."

Ethan slams the refrigerator door shut, having lost interest in Will and the phone call. "Tell Mom I'm going out again," he says as the kitchen door bangs behind him.

Will heads slowly down the hall toward his bedroom. He feels confused and jumpy, like something bad is about to happen or maybe it already has happened.

"Will," his mother says, from the living room door. "Come listen to some radio with Grandma."

"I was going to go to my room," he says. He wants to be alone to figure things out.

"Will," his mother warns as she brushes past him. "I'm not asking you."

"But Ethan—"

"Jesus, Will. Help out here, all right?"

"Sorry," he says, the way he's learned to say it from Ethan so that it means a host of things that are all the opposite of sorry.

The radio in the living room is tuned to a classical station. Will's grandmother's chin rests on her chest as if she is sleeping. Will begins to leave the room when he hears her move.

"Hello," she says.

"Hi, Grandma," he says. "Can I listen with you?"

"Lovely."

He sits next to her on the sofa, waiting for her to say something else, but she doesn't. Her eyes drift toward the window, where the afternoon light flutters through the leaves. He studies his hands. The girl's voice sounds in his mind. She was angry when he said his father wasn't there. And then she cried like a little kid, sucking up her snot and gulping, and then she was nicer.

The phone call was the first time he's admitted to having no idea where his father is. Saying so has left him with a heaviness that feels as if a thousand-pound weight is sitting on his chest. He should have told her that his father is coming back. His mother never says that he won't. She doesn't say anything about it at all. So probably he will. Whenever he finishes traveling around and doing whatever he's doing that he never really explains in any of the phone calls. He hasn't called lately. His mother says he'll call when he's ready. Ready for what? Sometimes missing him feels like the stab of sudden hunger, like the way sometimes, when he forgets to eat, his body gets jangly and everything seems to be rushing past him and his words sound like they're not coming out of his mouth. If he can settle down, he can remember certain things, like the light dusting of hair on his father's forearms, or how clean he kept his fingernails. But he can never remember his father as a whole person. He can't see him anymore. He squeezes his eyes shut.

"What are you doing there?" his grandmother says.

He opens his eyes. "Nothing. Just playing."

"You'll ruin your eyes that way," she says.

"You remember about my eyes, Grandma?" he asks.

"You're blind as a bat!" she says.

They laugh together. He takes her hand. Her wedding ring feels cold against his skin. His mother doesn't wear her ring anymore.

*Caroline opens the* door to her mother's room. It is a sick-room now, a room of low light, silence, and suspension. She is soothed by its quiet predictability, by the way the pink velvet chaise sits in its place like an overfed uncle at a wedding, by the landscape paintings that face one another with their bland images of pastoral California, the California her mother loves and dreams of in her confusion. She explores the nighttable drawers, fingering her mother's cut-glass perfume bottles, her lipsticks. Eleanor has worn the same shade of flame orange for as long as Caroline can remember, buying multiple tubes at the department store in case the color was ever discontinued. When she was well, she would reapply her lipstick at unnecessary moments—in the middle of a movie, or in the car, when she stopped for a red light. Caroline doesn't know whether her mother was excessively vain, or whether putting on a second face was so habitual that Eleanor wasn't even aware that she did it.

Her father's bedside drawer holds a pair of cuticle scissors, reading glasses, and an accordion of wrapped condoms. The condoms startle her. Do her parents still have sex? She cannot imagine her mother being alive to her feelings in this way, cannot imagine her father's desire. The possibility of their love is almost more unsettling than the opinion she's had all these years that her father killed that love. She had cast them in neat roles: Vincent, the deceiver. Eleanor, the self-negating sufferer. But maybe, despite Caroline's teenage certainty that she understood the hypocrisy of her family, she was wrong. Perhaps her parents chose not to tell her the truth of their lives, that their desire endured in ways that all things endure: imperfect, repeatedly injured, paradoxically strong. After all, what has Caroline told her children of her own marital mess? Not lies, exactly, but only the skin of the truth.

For the first time she wonders if her disgust with her parents was their knowing gift to her. Better she should feel clear-cut patronizing rage than have to untangle the confusions of real compromised love and acceptable disappointment. The notion gives her a moment of peace. Maybe Will and Ethan will be all right, and the half-truths she tells them will save them in the end.

"What are you doing?" Will stands in the doorway.

Caroline turns, startled. "Did Grandma like the radio program?"

"I guess," he says, coming to sit with her on the bed. "I don't know if she was really listening. She fell asleep."

"Thank you for being with her."

"I don't mind," he says. "Grandma's funny."

"I know," Caroline says. "It's what I explained about her brain."

"No. I mean she made a joke."

"She did?"

"Why is six afraid of seven?" he says, smiling.

"Because seven eight nine," they chant together.

"I taught you that one," she says.

"I pretended I didn't know it."

She takes him in her arms. She smells his musty hair, looks at his dirty fingernails, considers reminding him to shower, doesn't.

"Mom, you're hurting me," he says.

She releases him, laughing. It is impossible to get Ethan to hug her anymore. Now Will. So that's it, she thinks. You get ten years to touch them, ten years during which they must be the helpless recipients of your need to love. And then it's over.

"Does Dad know we're here?" he asks.

"Of course," she says, surprised.

"He knows the address and everything?"

She nods, her heart hurting for him. "He has it."

"So he could come here?"

"Will . . ." she begins, then stops. Doesn't he have a right to believe that he is wanted?

"Is Burton a common name?"

She laughs. "Where did that come from?"

"I was just wondering about it."

"It's common enough, I guess."

He thinks for a moment. "Okay," he says. He stands and heads for the door.

"I'll walk you to your room," she says, joining him.

"I can do it myself," he says, alarmed. His hand rises to his glasses.

"I know you can, silly. I just wanted to be with you."

"You're with me now."

"Okay, Will," she says as he goes.

Tomorrow she will start a day job as a waitress at the Smokehouse, a red-booth steakhouse that was the "special occasion" destination when she was a girl. The restaurant smells of more than fifty years of heavy perfumes and hard liquor. She will wear a short black uniform and a white apron, running shoes and hose. Hose! She laughs to herself, remembering the frosty-haired manager using this anachronistic word. At night she will study for the accreditation exam to be a substitute teacher. Her friends back in Missouri were nearly envious that she would get to "start all over again" without the debilitating fact of an unsatisfying husband shaping her life. But this is not a beginning. It is a continuation. Everything—hope and disappointment, relief and despair—has traveled cross-country with her, packed into that soda-smelling car.

14.

*Before taking the bus* to Mrs. Eleanor's, Amador stops by the Save-On to buy presents for his children—a miniature pink plastic grooming set so Berta can brush and comb her doll's hair, a Dodgers cap and T-shirt for Miguel. He does not know what to buy for Rogelio. The boy was once interested in lizards and snakes, but a plastic snake is no present for a fourteen-year-old. He leaves the store with an oversize T-shirt with a picture of a skateboarder on it. At the checkout line, he adds a big bag of jellybeans to his shopping basket, knowing that his two younger children will delight in pawing through the multicolored candies as though they are jewels. Later, standing on line at the post office, he imagines Berta's thick cord of laughter as she bites down on a pink jellybean only to have the unexpected taste of bubblegum explode in her mouth. He imagines Miguel wearing his cap as he crouches, hands to knees, at first base, waiting for the *thwock* of the ball on the bat that will send him hurtling toward second. And he pictures Rogelio's silent dismissal of the ridiculous shirt, proof that his father is a fool.

He has no gift for Erlinda except for the money he is sending home. Other men send small appliances or cosmetics to their wives, gifts the women can show off to their friends to prove they are longed for. But Erlinda would not want such gifts. When he and Erlinda decided he should go north the first time, she nodded, as if the choice was inevitable, not simply because of money but because she knew, as he did, that ever since Rubén's death, their life had been an unraveling.

After finishing at the post office, Amador heads to the bus stop. When he passes the Laundromat, Mónaco pounds on the window. Amador sighs. Does the man need to chase him down to tell him there are no messages? Reluctantly he steps inside.

"*Su esposa llamó. Su hijo viene,*" Mónaco says, handing Amador a message on a torn sheet of paper. He says it with no urgency, but his eyes flick past Amador's, waiting for a reaction.

The message is too unbelievable to make sense, and Amador focuses on the handwriting of the note, which is careful and small. The curls of the *e* and the *j* remind Amador of how his own schoolteacher taught the students to write and how carefully Amador labored and ultimately failed to achieve the style before he quit school altogether to help his family with the farming.

His son is coming to Los Angeles? How? Erlinda would never let one of her children leave her. She does not trust America. Amador is sure she no longer trusts him. Something is wrong. His heart begins to pound.

"When did she call?" he asks.

"One week, maybe more," Mónaco says.

"One *week*?" Amador says, incredulous. "I pass by here every day."

Mónaco shrugs. "But you don't come in."

Amador buys a telephone card from a convenience store on the boulevard, then calls the number of the telephone office in El Rosario. He tries to convey the urgency of his message, hoping that Don Martín will dispatch one of his sons immediately to find Erlinda. He hangs up and paces agitatedly back and forth in front of the phone booth, impatient with the slowness of his town, impatient with himself and how far away he is from what matters in his life. When the phone rings, thirty minutes later, he nearly rips the cord from the box.

"It's you?" he says before she speaks.

"Of course. I've been waiting for your call."

He has forgotten the smooth music of her voice. It pierces him, and then an image of Caroline's throat flashes in his mind.

"*Dime*," he says. How often did he say this to his wife in the early years of their marriage, before their sadness? The word said, *Tell me who you are. Open up your life to me.* And once she had.

She says, "Our son is gone."

He does not hear the rest of the conversation, neither his

voice nor hers. His life, his real life, not this anonymous half-life he has been living in Los Angeles, is ricocheting back to him with such force that it will knock him over. *My God!* He feels like a man who stands looking at his house burning down and does not move to grab his children out of their beds.

An hour later Amador steps off the bus at Verdugo and walks slowly to Mrs. Eleanor's house. *Stay where you are.* That is what Erlinda told him. *Wait for him.* Of course she is right: There is nothing to do *but* wait. Rogelio could be anywhere. To find him would be as impossible as locating a particular piece of sand in the desert. And what if Amador leaves the city to search for his son and Rogelio, by some miracle, arrives? The thought of his boy lost in this forbidding place is almost more frightening than anything he can imagine. Except for death. But no, he cannot not think of that. Erlinda sounded calm over the phone. She did not cry. She told him her dream about the butterfly, and he did not reject her uncharacteristic embrace of the life of the spirits. He wants to believe her dream, too.

*Wait.* It is an action that is no action. Waiting is all that is left for a man who has abandoned his family. Waiting is for a man who has abandoned himself, as he has done, here in California. How could he have thought that he could live and eat and dream as a man untouched by his past?

As he rounds the corner onto Mrs. Eleanor's street, he hopes Caroline will not be at the house when he arrives. And then when she is there he is relieved.

Mr. Vincent has already left for work. Caroline serves her boys pizza out of a box. Mrs. Eleanor sits at the table with them, not eating. Amador notices that Caroline has dressed her mother in her robe and has combed her hair off her face, even applied lipstick, which is unnecessary but kind. Caroline's long, slender arm reaches into the center of the table and pulls a sticky piece of pizza from the box. She laughs as she takes a bite, cheese spreading inelegantly over her mouth. Her lips glisten with grease.

Amador looks away, willing himself not to feel what she makes him feel. He listens to the chatter of the boys. Ethan sits half on, half off his chair, like a runner on the blocks, ready to sprint at the sound of the starter's pistol. The boy moves through the house with pent-up energy. He ignores his mother's demands, wills himself not to hear her as though he wishes to exist in his own private, silent box. The other boy, Will, ignores nothing. He sees everything, despite those thick glasses that make his eyes look like the eyes of fish.

*No.* He cannot allow himself to note the particular characteristics of these boys. They breathe the air he breathes. He could touch them if he wanted. They are accessible, real, certainly alive. But where on this earth is his own child?

Caroline smiles warmly at him. She offers him pizza. She pours him a glass of water. He wants to accept her comforts, to believe that she knows his mistakes but forgives him. But she knows nothing about him.

"I want to walk," Eleanor says, suddenly.

"It's late, Mom," Caroline says, putting a hand on her mother's shoulder and leaning down to kiss her cheek. "We'll go outside tomorrow, how's that?"

"I want to walk," Eleanor repeats, her voice rising.

"Is okay, Mrs.," Amador says. "I take you for a walk."

"I want the boy," Eleanor says, looking at Will.

"No," Caroline says. "That's not a good idea."

"I'll go with her," Will says.

"It's nearly dark," Caroline said. "You're ten years old."

"Come," Amador says, moving to Mrs. Eleanor and beginning to help her up out of her chair. "I take you."

"No!" Mrs. Eleanor says.

"Mother," Caroline says. She looks to Amador for help.

"It's not too dark," Will says. "I can do it, Mom."

"Amador?" Caroline says. She looks frightened, in need of reassurance. If she only knew the truth of his life, he thinks, she would never rely on him for advice.

"It's good, what she want," he says, looking at the floor. If he looks her in the eye, she might read his failure.

"Half a block," Caroline agrees weakly. "That's it, Will. Then come right back. You understand?"

"Half a block," he says.

"I'm not kidding," Caroline says. "And if she gets . . . ," pain strikes her face and then recedes. "Oh!" she sighs, as if she cannot bear to think the rest of her thought.


*Will feels his* mother's eyes on his back as he leads his grandmother out the front door and onto the porch. He is self-conscious about every step he takes—he does not want her to sense his uncertainty in the low light—and he's relieved when he hears the door click shut behind him. As he and his grandmother move away from the house, he realizes that the evening is darker than he expected and the geography of the uneven sidewalk becomes difficult to negotiate. He is helped intermittently by the street lamps, but is helped even more by his grandmother's surprising assurance. She walks slowly, but seems to know where she is going.

"What's your name, boy?" his grandmother says.

"Will."

"Will," she repeats.

"You're my grandma."

She stops and looks at him, her eyes scanning the length of him. She traces the numbers on his soccer jersey. It feels strange to have someone other than his mother touching his body.

"Eighty-eight," she says.

"It's not a real team or anything," he says. "I don't really play sports."

"Why not?"

"I'm not good at them, I guess. Because of my eyes."

"What's wrong with your eyes?"

"You know. 'Blind as a bat.' "

"I don't know what you're talking about," she says.

"That's what you always say."

"Don't tell me what I say," she snaps.

"Why are you angry, Grandma?" he asks, even though he knows. His mother has explained that his grandmother sometimes gets so confused that she has a tantrum. Like a kid.

Will studies the trees, the cars parked neatly in driveways, the mailboxes standing like storks. In the distance he sees a jagged mountain range of half-lit office towers. And then, in the farther distance, he can just make out the

shadow of real mountains. The more he and his grandmother drift away from the house, the more Will realizes
how nearly impossible remembering the world is going to
be. There are so many kinds of trees or shades of green. And
during the day the sky is never crayon blue. It is a blue that
looks like someone has sucked the color from it the way you
suck the flavor from a popsicle until all you have left is a
memory of color trapped in ice. Nature is too various, he
thinks. It is an insult to a blind person. What are the words
to conjure the sulfur yellow of the sky when his mother
drove him to school this morning? Everything looked as
though he were seeing from inside the sun. His mother said
it was because of fires burning far away in the Valley.

Faces are the most impossible to categorize and remember.
His mother's face can look soft and welcoming, like a hug, or
it can be blank, which is indescribable and therefore the most
scary face of all. How can he remember a blank face?

If he never sees the girl, Marlene, how will he remember her? He *must* remember her because he knows she has
something to do with him. He doesn't know why, but he is
sure of it. He thinks of her voice, the way its confident
harshness got caught like a snagged sweater on a tree branch
when she cried.

He understands what he has to do. He must focus on the
mistakes and remember them. The crack in the wall outside
the doors of the school, the burned husk of the tree on the
third lawn down from his grandparents' house. He will fill
his mind with the mistakes, and the whole picture will
always be there for him. And when his father comes back,
he will be able to see everything his father wants him to see.

His grandmother stops abruptly. "Why are you here?" she asks.

"My father went away," he says. "So we came here to live with you. Because of money and stuff."

"I want to go to the river," she says, walking again.

"Where is the river?"

"There," she says, gesturing in every direction.

He thinks she might be going into one of her strange memories, but he is not nervous. She says things that don't make sense. She sees things that aren't there. But if he pays close enough attention, she might be able to show him how to see the world from the inside out, so that when he can no longer see what is there, he will be able to see what is not.

*Caroline stands nervously* in the kitchen. She stares at the clock. It has been ten minutes, and Will has not brought her mother back home.

"I better go out there," she says to Amador, who is cleaning the kitchen counters.

"Everything is okay, Mrs.," he says.

"I'm worried about my mother," she says. "And Will is alone with her."

"She is fine, Mrs. It is good she walks."

"Caroline," she insists. "Carolina," she adds cautiously. "I like the way you say that."

He says nothing.

"You're patient with her," she says.

"She is good lady."

"How do you know?" she asks, moving toward him. He

takes a step back and she stops. Her desire to know these secrets is so great she is scaring him away. "I mean, how do you know what she's like. She's so different than she was. She used to be so . . . I don't know. She used to wash the bottoms of my shoes when I came in after the rain. And lay them on paper towels by the door. And, oh!" she says, as if just remembering. "She used every bit of a paper towel. She'd cut off the dry part with a scissors and use that later." She stops, puts her hand to her mouth as though she's said things she didn't mean to. She wants to tell him so much more. She wants her words to fill the emptiness that is her mother, as if they are little gusts of air, puffing out a balloon to its full, robust size.

"I don't know her before," he says. "I know her now."

"But who is she now?"

"She is like a person who live in two places," he says. "Inside," he says, touching his chest, "and here." He holds his palm out to indicate the kitchen, the world.

She smiles. He appreciates her mother in a way she has never imagined a man enjoying a woman. Not her father. Not her husband. The idea startles her. She realizes she has never understood how a man loves.

"Are you married?" she asks.

"Yes, Mrs."

She stops before she corrects him. "Your wife is lucky," she says.

"No," he says, shaking his head.

She thinks she sees him shudder. But before she can ask why, she hears Will's voice outside the house. "They're back," she says, relieved, putting out a hand and touching

Amador's arm. "Every time my children come back home, I feel safe again."

*Mrs. Eleanor is* exhausted from her walk. Amador sits on the bathroom stool, his elbows on his knees. A film of soap stretches across the top of the water, the pattern rearranging itself whenever Mrs. Eleanor moves. Her eyes are closed, and her head tilts back against the clear inflatable bath pillow he blows up and deflates each evening. Her hands move beneath the water with the indolent motion of jellyfish.

How he envies her! How he would love to be prey to a disintegrating mind, if only to rid himself of the thoughts that gnaw at his brain. He will be struck down for thinking of Caroline when he should only think of his son and family. What a relief it must be to lose just enough of your life so that you forget what to regret.

The conversation with Caroline made him feel crazy inside his skin. He wants to tell her everything—that his wife is far from lucky, that she married a man who has lost two sons. That he can never know the relief she feels when her son comes home from a short walk up the street.

And what does he want from this woman, the first person in the entire country who has asked him about his life? He feels as though he will explode. He wants to be contained, to be surrounded by something—a prison, or her arms. But he deserves no kindness, and certainly no love.

Mrs. Eleanor opens her eyes and smiles. The water makes a light music as she waggles her fingers back and forth on its surface.

"Cold," she murmurs between clenched teeth.

He turns on the hot water faucet. She closes her eyes again and sighs as the heat warms her. Her feet float to the surface of the water like twin buoys.

"Amador," Mrs. Eleanor says, opening her eyes.

"Mrs. You ready to dry?"

"Don't leave me."

She opens her eyes and looks at him, searching his face for the answer she needs. He does not want to lie to her. People lie to children all the time. "I'll see you in the morning," they say, as if they have control over the universe and are certain morning will necessarily follow night or that they will be alive to greet it. "I'll see you when I get back," they say. And then one day they don't come back.

"I no good, Mrs. Eleanor," he says quietly.

She sits up in the tub. The sudden shift and splash of water startles him. Her blue eyes are wide. "Are you leaving me?"

"No," he says, frightened by her outburst. "I no going to leave you." Maybe the lie is necessary, he thinks. How can anybody, child or adult, march forward in the face of such truth?

After Amador puts Mrs. Eleanor to sleep he returns to the kitchen. Caroline is seated at the table, drinking from an oversize mug. He wonders, half hopes she has been waiting for him. His insides churn in a confusion of needs. His son is lost in the world, and he stands here. And yet he wants to be here, can't imagine not being near this woman. His self-hatred heats his blood.

*Wait.* This is what Erlinda has told him. His *lucky* wife! Lucky to have a husband who has no power in the world to save his own children, lucky to have a man who wants more than anything to be in the kitchen of a stranger, gazing at the narrow triangle of her throat where her blouse falls open, and imagining her breasts.

"Sit with me?" she asks.

He shakes his head. If she asks about his sons, he will tell her everything. And then she will know him for the helpless man he is.

"What are you reading there?" she asks, gesturing with her head toward his textbook, which lies unopened on the table.

"A book," he says, silently cursing himself for not looking her in the eye. Years of being in this country have conditioned him to hide, even in the sight of others.

"Well, I know it's a book," she says, laughing lightly.

"A book of words," he says.

She leans over and lifts the cover of the book. She might as well be touching his skin. He wants to inhale her.

"Ah," she says when she reads the title of the book. "You're learning English?"

He nods.

"My degree was in English," she says. "Literature. I wouldn't know how to teach anybody to speak the language. It makes no sense."

"Sure," he says. She's talking quickly, and he does not understand. But he doesn't care. Steam rises from her mug to meet her face. He wishes he were the steam.

"I taught back home. Well, substituting really, which is more like being a traffic cop. But I think I can get a teaching job once I get a certificate. They need teachers here. Too many kids in the schools."

He nods. Too many brown-skinned children, he thinks. He wonders if she understands anything about his life.

"We're okay here," she says, digging into her sweater pocket and taking out some folded bills. "It's silly for you to stay, especially when my mother is sleeping."

How can he tell her that he wants to stay and he wants to leave at the same time, that being here with her boys, her life, is a kind of agony for him that he both despises and craves? How can he tell her that being alone in his trailer, waiting for news of his son, is a worse kind of horror?

He takes the bills from her fingers. The transaction makes him feel weak. He puts the money into his pocket as she stands and wishes him goodnight, then moves down the hallway, carrying her tea before her like a chalice. Amador leaves the house feeling a humiliation that is no different than if he had just come from a whore's bed.

That night, lying on his mattress, he tries to ignore the paint-and-sweat smell of his sleeping roommate and imagines Caroline's throat. With one hand crooked overhead, the other beneath his blanket, he pictures her neck, her hands, the way her lips part in the center, revealing a small opening that makes him think she is always just about to tell him what she wants.

After he finishes, he lies with his arms over his eyes in order to block the beam from the outdoor safety light filling the curtainless window.

All these years his family has waited for him. Now he knows how waiting leaves your body restless with unrelieved wanting. He understands why Rogelio ran.

15.

*The girl calls again* the next afternoon. Will races to the phone before his grandfather can get to it.

"Is it you?" he says.

"Yeah," Marlene says. Her voice is more childish than he remembers from the first call. "How did you know?"

"I just knew."

"Smart kid."

He smiles. "Where do you sleep?"

"I met this girl at a record store. She lets me sleep on her floor. *Skanky* floor. She does tattoos."

"Did you get a tattoo?"

"No way!" Marlene exclaims. "You know what those things look like when you get old? My mother has one on her hip that used to be a butterfly, but now it looks like a drawing you left out in the rain. You got to think about the future, Will."

"Okay," he says. He feels she has said something important and that she has other necessary things to tell him.

"What do you look like?" he says.

"If I told you, would it make a difference?"

"What do you mean?"

"Would you be able to picture me if I said blond and kind of short, kind of tall and kind of skinny but a big fat ass?"

"Well, yeah," he says, laughing. "I mean, not really."

"What do you look like?"

"Blond hair and kind of tall but not really and pretty thin, and I wear glasses."

"So we must be twins," she says. "Except for the glasses."

"And the big ass," he says.

"Hey!" she says, but he can tell she is joking.

They are both quiet for a moment. He tries to think of something to ask her so that she won't hang up.

"You're a nice person," she says finally.

"Want to come over?" he says.

"To your house?"

"Yeah."

"No," she says. "Not your house. I can't do that yet."

Her voice is distant, as if she is looking away from the phone, searching for someone else to talk to.

"I could meet you," he says.

"What? You drive a car? How old are you?"

"Ten," he says, embarrassed.

"I thought about ten."

"I mean if you could take a bus or something over here. I'm allowed to take a walk."

"Where?"

"There's a river," he begins. And as he tells her what streets she should be looking for so that she will find the river his grandmother insists lies just beyond where their walks end, he sees everything in his mind, the sidewalks that sparkle, the street sign that is bent at a right angle, and he describes it all for her. He feels wonderful.

*A few hours later* he waits impatiently for his grandfather to bring his grandmother into the kitchen so she and Will can take a walk. Luckily his mother is still at her job, and Ethan is in his bedroom doing or not doing homework. So no one notices when he puts two peanut butter sandwiches in his backpack along with an apple, a juice box, and half a tube of Pringles. He finds a thin blanket in the linen closet and stuffs it in the backpack along with the food.

"Here she is," his grandfather says, escorting Eleanor out of her bedroom. "All ready for her big trip."

Will takes his grandmother's arm. His grandfather stares at him, making him uncomfortable.

"What?" Will asks.

"I think she likes these walks with you," his grandfather says. "She got excited when I told her."

"I like it too," Will says. He is anxious to leave, not wanting to miss Marlene.

He and his grandmother walk arm in arm down the

street. The afternoon is windy, and he has to hold her tightly so that she does not veer off course or blow over. He wishes she would move faster. "Will you show me the river, Grandma?" he asks, shouting to be heard over the *swoosh* of the trees.

"The river," she says, without commitment.

"The one you always talk about." His heart races. What if there is no river? What if she has been making this up the way she makes up those stories about olive trees and rain? "Is it over there? Should we cross the street?" he asks. He knows he is disobeying his mother, traveling too far from the house. But it is still light out, and he won't get lost, and he has to meet Marlene.

"Wait, Grandma," he says, holding an arm out to stop her from moving into traffic. When the cars clear, they cross. She gently pulls him toward a side street.

"It's a dead end," he says, hanging back. "It doesn't go anywhere."

"I remember," she says.

"Maybe this is the wrong street," he says, worried. It's been hours since his phone call with Marlene. Surely she is here by now, looking for him.

His grandmother grips Will's arm, and reluctantly he walks her down to the end of the street where a metal barrier stands, separating the street from bushes and a chicken-wire fence beyond.

"The river," Eleanor says.

Will's heart sinks. He feels sick. Marlene will think he is a stupid, useless boy. She will never call him again. "It's not a river, Grandma. It's just a dead end."

"I like to walk by the river all alone, but Daddy says it's too dangerous," she says.

"Grandma, you're not making any sense," Will says, upset. They have walked farther from the house than they are supposed to go, and she is getting strange. He tries to remember what Amador has told him to do when his Grandmother goes crazy like this. *Tell her the truth.* "There is no river," Will says. The wind blows dust into his eyes.

"We can hunt for fossils, but it's too cold to swim."

"Grandma! You're talking about the wrong river," he says, desperate to bring her back from wherever she is. "You're here. In Los Angeles. There is no river."

"But I jumped in. And it was so cold! And underneath the river was so quiet. I could hear the inside of my body hum."

"I don't know what you're talking about." His frustration about missing Marlene is replaced by fear. He must get his grandmother home before she gets more lost in her mind and something bad happens. Quickly he unloads the contents of his backpack and leaves them on the far side of the metal barrier. Maybe Marlene will see them as she searches for a river that isn't there. Maybe then she won't hate him so much and she will call again and give him one more chance. Or maybe, he thinks, with a sick feeling in his gut, he's lost her, too, and whatever she has to tell him he will never know. He slings the empty sack over his shoulder and leads his grandmother home.

*Amador enters Mrs. Eleanor's kitchen* with the wind. The calm of the morning has been replaced by an afternoon of flying newspapers and women holding down their hair with their hands as they wait for buses or drag children in and out of stores. The weather makes Amador as crazy as the neighborhood dogs, who bark and squeal as if they sense an imminent earthquake or fire.

Caroline sits at the kitchen table, wearing a bathrobe. Her hair is wet; the curls pressed close to her head. Her hands lie on the tabletop and she stares at them as if she is unsure what they might do next. It is disconcerting to see the object of his recent fantasies in the flesh. He feels as if she knows his darkness. He nods a greeting and heads toward the hallway.

"Here, I'll move," Caroline says. "You don't have to leave." She sounds tired out.

"I check Mrs. Eleanor."

"She's listening to the radio with Will."

"The radio," he says.

"No TV," she says. Her smile vanishes nearly as soon as it appears.

He opens the cupboard below the sink where the cleaning supplies are stored. He will make sure the bathroom is clean and dry before Mrs. Eleanor's bath. He is sure the toilet seat is dotted with the boys' urine.

"You don't have to do that," Caroline says, standing. "I'll take care of it."

"It's not your job."

"But I don't mind."

"It's my job," he says, more sharply than he intends. She looks hurt.

"I don't know what I'm doing here," she says.

Her eyes search his face for a response. The smell of disinfectant and damp rags rises up from the cleaning bucket by his side.

"I miss my mother," she says. "Isn't that strange? To miss the person who's with you?"

"Not strange," he says.

"My husband left me," she says.

"You mother, she told me."

"She did?" Her face brightens. "I didn't think she understood."

"You mother, she talk about you a lot," he says. It is a lie, but her relief is justification. "She never forget you."

She rakes her fingers through her hair, then pulls her robe close around her neck.

"He never calls anymore," she says. "To talk to the boys, I mean. It's finished between us. But I don't understand how a person can do that to children. Just disappear."

He wants to tell her there are reasons, real reasons she has never had to consider in her life. But he knows this is not what she means. She brings her hands to her cheeks as if to feel their coolness or their warmth. He wonders which sensation she wants.

"It's hard to understand someone else's sadness," she says. "To really know what it feels like. I tried."

He doesn't understand her, exactly. But his need to continue this conversation is so strong. "My son is coming." There. He said it. He has told her a piece of who he is.

"You have a son?" she says.

"Two sons. And a daughter. In my country."

"Oh," she says, with sad understanding. "That's hard."

He pushes back a swell of feeling in his throat.

"But you must be so excited about your son," she says.

How can he tell her the truth? She imagines reunions at the airport with balloons and flowers. What will she think of him if she knows his son is lost in a desert, and that Amador is doing nothing to save him?

"I have to——" he says, gesturing with his bucket.

"Oh," she says, surprised, her face coloring. "Please don't. I . . . please," she says. "I want to hear more about your son."

He tells her everything. As he speaks, he stops periodically, certain that she must be bored or irritated that he is presuming her interest in his life. But she sits at the table, her hands folded before her, listening and, he thinks, understanding.

"My wife say he is alive. She say he comes to me. She has a dream."

"I'm sure he'll be okay," Caroline says, although he hears the hesitation in her voice.

"You don't believe in dreams."

She shakes her head, smiling at herself. "I'd like to. I would."

"In this country no one trust his dream."

She looks away. He feels he has insulted her. Will she fire him? Will she stop talking to him forever? He lifts his bucket. "I go now," he says.


*Caroline hears the familiar coaxing* and low laughter as Amador leads Eleanor into the bathroom. She realizes that Amador doesn't feel foreign to her because he is from Mexico or because he speaks with a heavy accent, but because he is that truly strange thing: a person who is patient with life. He waits patiently with an old woman while she washes her unlovely body. He listens without distraction as Eleanor spins fractured tales out of memories.

That's all it takes, Caroline thinks: a willingness to be filled by the life of another. How odd that this quality in a man makes her so uncomfortable, almost embarrassed. Yesterday, at the park next to the boys' school, she saw a young man draw his lover to him and rest his head on her shoulder. She was taken aback by his frank need. She has never been with a man who needed her, not her father, not her husband. She wonders if she would know how to love such a man and be loved by him. Her love has always been a desperate, defeated thing. The men in her life have taught her nothing about men.

*Will lies in his bed.* Ethan sleeps silently in the trundle next to him. The room is absolutely dark. He raises a hand in front of his face but cannot make out its shape. He waves his fingers. Nothing. He has no idea where the door is. Where is he?

He thinks about Marlene. She didn't call. He has forced himself to stay awake in his bed, hoping that if she does call he'll hear the phone and be able to run for it before anyone else gets to it. He doesn't even care if he knocks into walls and furniture, if only he can talk to her again and apologize.

Suddenly he is overwhelmed by the sensation that his father is in the room, sitting on the end of his bed. The air seems charged with warmth and an energy. His father used to come into his room at night when he thought Will and Ethan were asleep. Will never said anything during these nighttime visits, sure that if his father knew he was awake, he would not stay. Instead he lay on his bed, his eyes closed, listening to the sound of his father's breath and once, he thinks, tears.

Now he wishes he were sitting on his father's bony lap at the observatory, listening to the tap-tap of Frank's fingers on the computer keyboard, watching as the great arched ceiling splits in two and the machine glides into place. He wants to shoot his vision through those elegant telescope tunnels until he sees what his father sees: a black world so full of light.

*Dad.* He hears the word inside his chest. It is a rubbery word. He wants to feel it in his mouth, to chew on it. "Dad!" he says, out loud, but the person on the end of the bed does not respond. How loud must he shout in order for his father to hear him?

*Amador cleans the bathtub* with disinfectant when he hears the boy cry out. He grows hot. His stomach turns over. Has he heard his own boy? Is Rogelio crying out for him to come save him? He stands in the doorway and listens, his heart beating rapidly.

"Is everything okay?" It is Caroline. She stands in the doorway of the living room. She wears only her nightgown. The neckline falls in a wide arc across her shoulders revealing the long muscles of her throat.

"A noise," he says. "The boys."

"I didn't hear," she says worriedly, moving toward the extra bedroom.

"They quiet now," he says, seeing her alarm. "Maybe they ... *están soñando* ... dream? My middle boy, he talk in the night."

Standing only an arm's length from him now, she becomes aware of her outfit. She crosses one arm over her chest and grips the opposite shoulder. Her attempt at modesty only succeeds in drawing the material of her nightgown closer to her body so that Amador can see the gentle swell of her belly and breasts.

"You must miss your children so much," she says.

He reaches out and touches her arm. She stares at his hand but does not move away. He lifts his fingers to her face and runs his thumb across her lips. He closes his eyes. The skin of her lips feels like the foot of a newborn, like something that has not yet touched earth. He needs for her to lay a hand on his chest and stop this jagged feeling in his body. He kisses her. His hand traces her clavicle, falling into the gully below her throat. He wants to be *there*, in that shallow. It is the only place on earth he wants to be.


*The shock of his weight* on top of her. The sweet smell of him. The sound of his moist breath in her ear and the guttural groans of his effort. His hands move across her body, hungry to fill themselves with the flesh of her ass and her breasts. His body moves around her and inside her, not because he loves her, but because he is willing, *demanding*, to occupy this moment in time, this place in the world, *with her*. She has given him this right and he has taken it, grabbed it with his fists and his legs and his mouth.

They lie outside in the backyard. The grass scratches her skin. She is cold, but she doesn't mind because whenever he moves a part of his body over hers, she relishes the sense of being newly covered. And his body is warm even in the night air. She touches the sweat at the base of his spine and paints it downward, over the solid curve of him, a planet under her palm. Looking up, past his shoulder, she sees the night sky splattered with stars. The day's wind has cleared the air as if drawing back the curtain of brown haze. She feels, for an instant, the simultaneity of being bigger than the whole world and being smaller than one of those grains of light. And she is certain she exists wholly in both forms. She gently pushes at his shoulder until he rolls underneath her. Bending over him, her hair dusting his chest and face, she is thrilled to feel his hands on her hips as he repositions her, places her where he needs her to be, where she matters.

*Afterward*, as she sleeps in her bed, he sits at the kitchen table, waiting for Mr. Vincent to return. He opens his vocabulary builder and looks up the word: *Miss*. Noun: a young woman. Noun: failing to hit. Verb: to be without. Verb: to feel the lack of. Verb: to be absent.

16.


*One of the boys* from the tunnel is apprehended in a police raid. Rogelio, Tonio, and a boy named Alfonso meet outside a tile factory after escaping. They laugh at the stupidity of the police. Even if the kid's family still lives in his village, they might not be happy to have one more mouth to feed. The boys take guesses as to how long before they see that same boy back in the tunnels again.

"It's like throwing a fish back after you catch him," Rogelio says. Roof tiles are draped over poles. The smell of wet clay hangs in the air. "Put him back in the water so you can catch him again."

"*Está de la chingada*," Tonio snarls bitterly.

In recent days Tonio has become testy. In the tunnels he is keyed up, listening for sounds that signal danger. He inhales more than usual, but the drugs only agitate him. Now he lies back on the dirt, a reed jiggling in his mouth like a frantic television antenna.

"You ever gone fishing?" Alfonso asks no one in particular.

"I did, one time," Rogelio says. "I caught a big fucking fish. Fucking trout."

The boys murmur their approval.

"As big as my arm!" Rogelio says. He exaggerates, but he knows the boys appreciate the lie. Some hope has been squeezed out of the group by today's raid and capture.

"Fuck that," Alfonso says, admiringly.

"Cooked it up and ate it right there by the river." The boys are silenced by the memory. The part about cooking the fish is a lie, too. Rogelio remembers the day. He was seven years old. Amador promised him a day at the river. His mother begged them not to go. "*¡Es un río malvado!*" she cried. Amador tried to soothe her. "It's only a river," he said, rubbing her cheek. But when Erlinda would not relent, Amador became angry. "You don't trust me," he said sharply. Amador grabbed Rogelio's hand roughly and pulled him toward the road. Rogelio looked back at his mother. She was holding baby Miguel in her arms. Rogelio knew about the baby named Rubén who was killed by the river. He'd climbed to the cross at the butterfly sanctuary with his mother. They'd brought sweets to Rubén's grave and sung songs with their neighbors on *el día de los muertos*. "I'll catch a fish for you!" he called back to his mother, trying to make her smile.

He and his father caught two fish that day. The fish were

small, and Amador wanted to throw them back. But Rogelio pleaded with his father to take the fish home. He wanted
to show his mother that he had succeeded, that he was not
like that dead baby who made his mother and father so sad,
that the river had not eaten him up too.

"I would like to be fishing right now," Tonio says. He
takes the weed out of his mouth and pretends to cast it into
the air. "On a beach," he adds. "Where the sand is so hot you
burn your feet. I would like to be burned by the sun."

Inside the tunnel, the boys become argumentative.
Nightly, fights break out over drugs or food, over insults,
real and imagined. Tonio does nothing to stop the fights but
crouches down against the wall, lost in his high. Rogelio no
longer feels safe sleeping. He lies awake, and his heart beats
so hard he can hear it. He does not feel like the king of the
*barrio* anymore. He feels like a rodent, living unseen and
unwanted underneath the earth. No one knows where he is.
No one is looking for him. No one is going to rescue him
from this life. Ever.

He becomes more and more terrified of his fear. It lurks
inside him like a parasite and it will destroy him if he does
not kill it first. To convince himself that his fear is no threat,
he becomes recklessly brave. On a dare, he stands outside a
police station and yells obscenities before running away. He
steals a carton of crackers from under the nose of a *bodega*
owner.

When the boys convene inside the tunnel, they give
Rogelio a wide berth. He is offered the spray can second
after Tonio. Rogelio knows the boys' admiration is laced

with fear of his impulsive, dangerous behavior. And he is afraid of himself, too, afraid of what he might do, now that he cares about nothing.

*A new boy* arrives in the tunnels. He is older, and his chest is wide as a table. His arms hang from his torso like two thick sausages, as if the muscles prevent them from hugging his sides.

"Where are you from?" Tonio asks.

The boy crouches against the side of the tunnel, keeping a distance between himself and the group. His arms rest on his thighs. His head hangs low between his clenched fists.

"I asked you a question," Tonio says with something less than his usual courage. When the boy still refuses to answer, the other boys shuffle and look at Tonio. "Must be deaf," Tonio says. He tries a short laugh. A few boys join in, and Tonio nods his head, regaining his footing. "Deaf as a rock," he says.

The boy stands and walks even farther from the group. Once he establishes a new distance, he crouches again, turning his back to everyone.

Alfonso arrives with a nearly empty can. The boys gather around eagerly. Tonio stands outside the cluster, assured of his first turn at the drug. But then the new boy rises from his crouch, approaches Alfonso and holds out his hand.

"We do things here a certain way," Tonio says, moving next to Alfonso. His eyes dart from the new boy to the ground and back again, unable to hold the older, bigger boy's gaze for more than a few seconds. Rogelio feels a knot of fear in his stomach.

"I do things my way," the new boy says.

"Not here," Tonio says. His adam's apple pushes at the skin of his throat.

The boy does not lower his outstretched arm.

"Don't do it, Alfonso," Tonio orders.

Alfonso looks miserable. There is no gain in being at the unfortunate center of this tug-of-war. Tonio reaches for the can, and a cry pierces the tunnel. Tonio doubles over screaming and clutches his stomach. Rogelio sees the knife in the new boy's hand. It glistens with blood.

As if he is holding a bomb, Alfonso throws the can to the boy, who catches it, wipes his knife on his pants leg, and casually drifts down the tunnel, shaking the can slowly so that its rattle echoes.

Rogelio rolls Tonio onto his back.

"*Ay, Dios mío,*" someone whispers.

Despite Tonio's screams, Rogelio pries his friend's hands from the wound. The slash is wide and deep. Blood runs over Tonio's stomach and down his sides. Rogelio feels sick. He has never felt another person's blood. A chorus of astonished curses flutter against the tunnel walls like birds' wings.

"You have to go to the hospital," Rogelio says.

"No." Tonio rocks his head from side to side. "It's not so bad." His voice strains against his pain.

"You're going to bleed to death," Rogelio says. He turns to the boys. "We have to get him out of here."

"The police are at the hospital," one boy says. Others mumble in agreement. A few back away.

"He's bleeding, you fuckers!" Rogelio cries. But his words don't provoke anyone to action. "Fuck you!" Rogelio screams as he struggles to help Tonio to his feet. He slings Tonio's arm around his neck, grabs him around the waist, and slowly drags him to the tunnel entrance. Tonio screams in pain, begging Rogelio to stop as Rogelio hoists him onto the street.

"*¡Mamá!*" Tonio cries into the night.

"If somebody sees you, they'll get help," Rogelio says, pulling himself out of the tunnel. He turns Tonio over on his back.

"Nobody—gives a fuck—about me," Tonio says, his words interrupted by long rasping breaths.

"Fuck all of you!" Rogelio screams into the mouth of the tunnel. He wedges his arms underneath Tonio's body.

"No!" Tonio begs.

"Fuck you, too," Rogelio says, without conviction. He maneuvers Tonio so the boy's back is to his own. Then, linking his arms through Tonio's, he lifts him the way the women in El Rosario lift baskets of wood on their bent backs, and carries him to a street he knows will be more heavily trafficked during the day. Once there, Rogelio falls to his knees and shrugs Tonio onto the ground.

"Someone will come," Rogelio says, arranging Tonio's body. "Someone will take you to the hospital."

Tonio whispers something. Rogelio has to lean over to hear. "Don't leave me," Tonio says. Rogelio lets his head drop onto his friend's shoulder.

He sits with Tonio throughout the rest of the night. Tonio shivers like he has ice for blood. Rogelio takes off his shirt to cover Tonio's chest, but the shirt is soon soaked red. He lies next to his friend, hoping that his own body heat will warm Tonio. As the hours pass and Tonio's breathing becomes shallower, Rogelio begins to shake. He draws his legs toward his chest and wraps his arms around his knees. He knows the shaking is his fear that has come to invade him now that he is weak.

Hours later, a faint light begins to insinuate itself on the darkness. Tonio's chest barely rises with each breath. Rogelio crouches beside his friend. "I have to go," he whispers. Nothing registers on Tonio's face. He looks so young, Rogelio thinks. This boy who he thought knew everything—he can't be older than Miguel. "How old are you?" Rogelio whispers. He doesn't expect an answer. Tonio is as old as he will ever be. Rogelio puts his hand underneath Tonio's nose and feels a trace of wind on his fingers. He says a prayer, crosses himself, and runs.

He spends the morning sitting against the wall of a shack, clutching a sharp stone in his hand for protection in case he should cross paths with Tonio's murderer. For the first time in many days, he thinks of his father. He pictures Amador against a backdrop of palm trees. He imagines his father wearing a clean shirt and new trousers. But, no matter how hard he tries, he cannot summon his father's smell. Suddenly he needs to know what his father smells like. It is a requirement of his survival, as important as breathing and eating. *5436 Tyrone Avenue.* He sees the address as it was written on one of the packages his father sent. He whispers the words over and over to himself so that he will not forget.

Later that day he watches as a *pollero* leads a group into the tunnel. He feels his pocket for his sharp stone. Making sure no one is watching, he slips down the hole and follows the bounce of the *pollero's* flashlight. The group stops at the underground fence, repaired since Rogelio and Tonio's trip. The *pollero* produces a wire cutter from a bag and begins to work.

Rogelio takes a deep breath. "*¡Es la policía!*" he cries out, deepening his voice. "*¡Policía! Corran!*"

Women scream. The guide, holding the flashlight, streaks past Rogelio, heading toward the tunnel entrance. A knot of people stand frozen by the fence. Rogelio counts five or six adults in the darkness. He hears the whimper of children. He sucks in his breath and begins to yell.

"*¡Su dinero!*" he demands. "*¡Sus joyas. Te voy a matar!*" He has to roar this last threat to kill in order to get the words out of his mouth. He pulls bags off shoulders and shoves bodies against the walls. He reaches into pockets. Children scream. Women cry and beg him not to hurt their babies.

The group is made up entirely of women and children. Women and children on their way to reunite with husbands and fathers. Rogelio stops for a moment, weakened by his discovery. One of these women could be his mother; these crying children, Berta and Miguel. His fear sounds in his ears. *Here I am*, it whispers. *I am going to destroy you.*

"Fuck you!" Rogelio screams to his fear. He pushes another woman against the fence and orders her to give him her valuables. She holds her hand against her throat, hiding a necklace. Her eyes shine in the darkness.

"*Te conozco*," she says.

Rogelio freezes. Is she telling the truth? Does she know him? He leans forward to see her more clearly. She is from his town. She cooks at a food stand near the church. Mirelia. That is her name.

"Give it to me!" he demands. She shakes her head, defying him. He pulls her hands down and yanks her necklace off her throat. It falls to the ground. He reaches down to retrieve it and when he stands, a hock of spit hits his face.

"Shame," she whispers.

That night he follows a group across the border and into the desert. He has water and food, and if he keeps a safe distance the *pollero* will not see him. But, a few hours later, when a truck appears out of the night and the guide pushes his charges into its open doors, Rogelio runs as fast as he can, waving his arms and crying out.

"*¡Espérame. Por favor espérame!*"

A hand grabs him by the shoulder and spins him around. The tip of a knife blade stings his neck. Rogelio looks into the dark eyes of the guide and fishes the money and jewels from his pockets. "*Por favor*," he says, offering up his bounty. "*¡Ayúdame!*"

17.

*She calls.*

"You stood me up," Marlene says.

"I couldn't find you," Will says, too pleased to admit his mistake.

"Well, I found you. Or your stuff. I'm not crazy about peanut butter, by the way. It makes me thirsty, and you only gave me one juice box."

"Where did you sleep?"

"Camping out. Like a good Girl Scout, which I never was, by the way. I might have to find that tattoo chick again."

"Are you lonely?"

"No," she says. "A little. Hey! I've been meaning to ask

you," she says, suddenly energized. "What happened to the stars?"

He is amazed that she has "been meaning" to ask him anything, that she has held him in her mind as a possible future. "Smog. And too many lights. That's what my dad says about cities. He says the best would be to live in a place with no electricity at all. Then you could see the stars. He taught us about the stars."

She is quiet.

"Are you still there?" he says, his heart quickening.

"What else did he teach you?" she asks. Her voice hitches in that way he has memorized.

"Well," he says, thinking. "He taught us how to cross the street. You know, look both ways. He had these buttons from a car rental place. They all said 'We Try Harder' in different languages. In French and Italian and even Chinese, I think."

"He gave you those buttons?" she says.

"Whenever we crossed right, he gave us one. We were five," he adds, feeling foolish.

"Do you still have them?"

"Yeah."

They are both silent. It feels good to talk about his father, but it also makes him feel like there is a hot wind blowing in his chest.

"Meet me?" she asks.

"Now?"

"You have other plans?"

It's Saturday. His mother is at her job. Ethan is outside,

trying to ollie on and off the curb with his skateboard. Will tells her he will meet her and hangs up the phone.

"I'm going for a walk," he says to his grandfather, who sits in the living room with his grandmother, watching television.

"It will take me a while to get her ready," his grandfather says.

"I want to go alone," Will says. "Just for a little bit."

His grandfather seems surprised. "Well, don't get lost."

Will's hand instinctively rises to his glasses. "Why would I get lost?"

His grandfather smiles in a way Will has never seen. It is a forgiving smile, as if Will has just done some mischief his grandfather has decided to keep a secret from the others. "It's harder in the dark, isn't it?"

Will cannot make himself speak. He nods.

"Then you better go before it gets too late," his grandfather says.

"Grandpa?" Will says. "She doesn't know."

"I was an actor once," his grandfather says. "I'm a great liar."


*Marlene sits on the bench* Will described to her. It stands in the center of a small triangular park at the intersection of three streets. A woman walking two French poodles stands by a street sign planted in the grass, waiting for her dogs to lower their legs.

Marlene stands. She is taller than he is but thin, just as

she said. She wears a faded pink leather jacket and jeans. A bag is slung across her chest and hangs low at her side.

"You look different than I thought," she says, when he stops, a few feet away.

"I don't really look like anything," he says.

"Everyone looks like something. Or somebody."

"Who do you look like?"

"My mother, only less."

They sit down next to each other on the bench.

"I can't stay very long," he says. "I'm not supposed to go past my block." He stares at her for a long time. Green eyes. Not-quite-blond hair. Her light purple nail polish is chipped, and her natural, pearly nail color shows where the nails are growing out.

"What are you looking at?" she says, sliding her hands under her thighs.

"I'm trying to memorize you," he says.

She laughs. "Waste of time."

"I'm gonna be blind one day," he says. It is the first time he has ever said this to anyone, but his conversation with his grandfather has started something inside him.

She touches the side of his glasses.

"Already I can't see at night," he admits.

"Are you scared?" she asks.

"What I worry about most is that I won't be able to recognize my dad when I see him."

"You think he's coming back?" she asks.

"He doesn't call anymore," Will admits. "My mother says some people aren't supposed to be parents. They just wait until it's too late to find out."

"It's a good thing he figured it out late," she says. "'Cause then you wouldn't be here."

"I can't remember what he looks like," he says. "Not really. And if he comes back and I'm already blind—"

She says nothing, and he wonders if he's frightened her away.

"He's tall," she says. "He's got this really long face, like almost longer than a person's face is supposed to be. And his nose is very straight. Mine is kind of roundish on the end, which I hate," she feels the tip of her nose. "And he has eyebrows that you almost can't see, they're so blond. And pale, pale skin. Almost white. Just like yours."

Will shuts his eyes as she speaks. The face of his father appears on the screen of his mind, so real he thinks if he reaches out, he might touch it.

"And he frowns when he smiles," she says. "My mother says, Never trust a man who frowns when he smiles."

Will opens his eyes and looks at Marlene. He understands something about her at the same time that he does not understand it at all. "He's your dad too," he says.

She shrugs. "Whatever that means."

And then it comes clearly to him, like an answer to a math problem that just appears as if it is written on the brain: "He's not coming back," he says.

Marlene's eyes fill. "I know," she says. Then she smiles and laughs. "You know this guy came up to me at the bus station and asked me if I was a runaway. I told him I was a run-to. I thought I was going to be with this whole other family. I'm an idiot," she sighs.

"What are you going to do now?" he asks.

"I guess I'm gonna run *back*," she says.

"Here," he says, pulling a handful of buttons out of his jacket pocket. He opens his palm so she can inspect them. She fingers the buttons as if they are as breakable as glass.

" 'We try harder,' " she says, reading one in English.

They investigate the buttons in French and Spanish and Italian, trying to sound out the words and laughing at their mispronunciations.

"Here's one in Egyptian, I think," he says.

She leans her head close to his in order to study the strange curls of writing. A warmth spreads through his body. He feels so *good*.

"Arabic," she corrects gently. "That's what they speak in Egypt."

"You know a lot," Will says.

Marlene sighs and wipes her eyes.

"Did I say something bad?" Will says.

She shakes her head. "It's just that everything is so good and so shitty at the same time. How can that be?"


*At first Caroline* doesn't even focus on the girl Will has brought home. Her rage is a confusion of feelings toward the obvious manipulations of a runaway and retroactive terror that her own child has been wandering the streets with a stranger. He could have been hurt, or worse.

"You may *never, never* go out alone, do you understand me?" she says, shaking Will by the shoulders.

"Mom, you're hurting me."

"*Do you understand me?*" She glances angrily at the girl.

The girl looks as if she wants to disappear, Caroline thinks, and then her body shudders with recognition. The girl looks like . . . him.

"Let me go!" Will says.

She drops her arms, unbalanced by his sudden authority. Her anger transforms itself into a dumbfounded wonder, as though she is watching a magician perform an impenetrable sleight-of-hand. She stares at the girl and does the calculations in her head. The girl is six years older than Ethan and Will. So she was born a year before Caroline's own marriage to Frank? But Frank didn't know about the baby at first. That's what Marlene said in her wide-open accent, as she twisted her hair around and around her finger until it threatened to cut off her blood supply. But then he found out, and for all those years of Caroline's marriage he existed in a different universe than she did, one in which there was a woman and this child.

No, the girl is not his child, Caroline tries to convince herself. She looks nothing like him. Her features are so bold, her lips' fullness almost unseemly, her nose like a remark. She is so plainspoken, so palpable, so resolutely *here*—her jeans hug her narrow thighs, her cheeks are still soft and round, like a child's. She is *nothing* like him.

"You don't have to believe me," Marlene says, as if reading her mind. "But you should."

"Listen," Caroline says carefully. "I know you think he's your father—"

"He *is*," Will says. "It's true." He stands next to Marlene, fidgeting excitedly, as though he has found a puppy on the street and is hoping Caroline will let him keep it. "Mom, you have to believe her," he pleads, his eyes wide behind his thick, distorting lenses.

When Will places his hand in the girl's palm, Caroline understands that he needs the girl's story to be true because it makes his own story less singular. If Marlene tells the truth, then Will is not the only one Frank has abandoned. "Oh, honey," she says. She moves to him but he steps back, his jaw set with determination. For the first time, she glimpses a man in her boy.

"It was Will's idea for me to come here," Marlene says. "But I'll go. I mean, Frank didn't even tell me he was moving, so it's not like he wanted me around, or anything." She turns to leave.

"Wait." Caroline says.

The girl turns back, but her face is void of expectation.

"Don't you think you should call someone? Your mother?" Caroline says. "Someone who can come and get you?"

Marlene narrows her eyes, as if she suspects a trap. "It's long distance," she says.

"It's okay," Caroline says.

Marlene stands in the kitchen, the phone in one hand, the cord twisted around her fingers. "Answering machine," she says to Caroline and Will, holding up a finger as if instructing them to wait. "Mom, it's me," she says into the phone. "I'm in L.A. and I'm—" She stops abruptly. She lets the cord fall to her side and turns to face the wall.

"Yeah," she says softly. "I'm fine. . . . Yeah, I know. . . . I'm sorry." Her shoulders begin to shake. "He's not here,"

Marlene says, her voice strangled. "He's like, gone. I don't know . . ."

Caroline wants to grab the phone from the girl and speak to this woman in order to lay bare this ridiculous lie.

"He's gone, Mom," Marlene says. "He just disappeared."

And suddenly Caroline is heartbroken by this girl's fragile shoulder blades, those delicate wings that poke out at the material of her shirt, by the inelegant sound of her sobs. And she finally, fully admits to herself that Marlene is telling the truth. Frank left a trail of fragments in the wake of his unpredictable orbit, and Caroline and her boys are just some of those random, lost particles. And so is this girl.

As Marlene continues to talk to her mother, Caroline has an unmooring thought that she has been living the wrong history. Her life has been something completely other than she thought, something that both included and excluded her. She does not feel spurned or cheated on, or any of those self-righteous feelings articulated in self-help books. It's too late for jealous rage. She feels as if she was chasing her life down the street, thinking she recognized it, but that when it turned to face her, it wasn't her life at all.

She walks to the girl and whispers. "Let me talk to your mother, Marlene."

"She wants to talk to you," Marlene says, and hands over the phone.

Caroline holds the phone to her ear but the obvious salutations feel inadequate to the situation. Hello? Hi? How are you? "My name is Caroline," she says finally. "But I guess you know that."

"I always have," the woman says. "I'm Diane."

"Diane," Caroline repeats.

"This is pretty strange, I guess," Diane says.

"Yes."

"I'm sorry about Marlene bothering you. She gets big ideas into her head."

"It's not a bother," Caroline says. "I understand."

"I just want you to know I didn't put her up to it or anything."

"No," Caroline agrees. The woman's voice is blunt and raw. Caroline tries to imagine what she looks like and immediately pictures someone as rough and unadorned as this voice. But of course this woman could look like anything.

"I never wanted to get in your way," Diane says.

"Okay." Caroline looks at Marlene sitting at the kitchen table with Will. Her head is in her hands; she pushes the skin of her cheeks up to her eyes so her face looks like a mask. Will giggles and imitates her.

"Marlene just always wanted things from him, you know?" Diane continues. "Things he never promised her."

"I don't have any money," Caroline says.

"Not money. I don't mean money."

"I'm sorry. I don't know what you mean," Caroline says.

"She wanted him to be around. Like a dad, I guess," Diane says. "Even though that was never his intention."

Caroline feels her chest cave in. In an instant she is herself at fourteen, refusing to join her father for a lunch or a movie, then watching from the living room window as his station wagon pulls away from the curb.

Caroline and Diane discuss various ways of getting Marlene home. Diane will investigate cheap airfares, or she might wire money for a bus trip back to Ohio.

As Caroline watches Will and Marlene whisper and laugh with each other, she finds herself resisting the plans she is making. "Maybe she can stay for a little while," she says to Diane. "A week or two?"

"She's got school and all," Diane says.

"Sure," Caroline says. "Of course."

"She wants to try for college. She could do it, too. She's a smart one, that Marlene."

Diane talks about her daughter with a kind of amazed detachment that Caroline imagines must come as your children age, when their abilities and inclinations finally and fully dispel any notion you have held that your kids are just like you.

"But I guess what's a week or two, right?" Diane says. "I mean, she's been waiting for this her entire life."

"Do you want to talk to her again?"

"No," Diane says. "We're on your dime. But tell her I love her, even if she doesn't believe it."

"I'll tell her," Caroline says.

"Listen," Diane says quickly, as if she wants to say this before she second-guesses herself. "If it had been up to me, you never would have known we existed."

Caroline says good-bye and hangs up. That is the problem, she thinks, as she watches Will and Marlene engage in a thumb war: Diane does exist. And so does Marlene, and so do Will and Ethan and so does she. Frank made them all feel as though they didn't, but they do. Caroline knows how hard it is to claim your existence once it has been denied, and she admires this girl for trying. She wonders if any of them will ever be able to succeed.

Ethan enters the kitchen door, his skateboard under his arm. He stops when he sees Marlene and looks to his mother for an answer.

"Ethan, this is your sister," she says. "This is Marlene."


*Vincent is surprisingly* unruffled by Marlene's presence. When Caroline corners him alone in the backyard and explains the situation, his only comment is that the girl has come a long way on her own. Perhaps, Caroline thinks, he does not feel entitled to make any remarks about her marriage's failures and deceptions. Or maybe he understands, as she does now, that opinions and judgments are only pointless and narcissistic inhibitions to the necessary forward movement of life. What does it matter what any of us thinks, his reaction seems to say. The girl is here. She has come to this place like an unexpected weather system, and Caroline and Vincent must simply accept, make appropriate rearrangements, fold all this newness into the rough-edged thing that is life.

That night, the entire family, including Marlene, sits down to dinner together. Eleanor is calm. When Caroline introduces her to Marlene, she smiles and compliments the girl's hair. Marlene returns the compliment by praising Eleanor's eyes. "Like if you tried to explain blue, that's what you'd say," she says. She doesn't seem taken aback when, midmeal, Eleanor points her knife at her and says, suspiciously, "Who is that girl?" Marlene simply introduces herself again. She even refers to herself as a "friend" of the boys, instinctively sensing that the truth would be too confusing.

Later Caroline cannot sleep. Everyone else in the house went to bed long ago, but she cannot relax now that everything has shifted. The girl sleeps on the floor between the boys' beds, taking up no meaningful amount of space, but her presence feels as unsettling as it would if she were another entire family, straining at the walls of this small house. Caroline wanders from the living room to the kitchen, opens the refrigerator, closes it without taking anything from it, then finally goes outside and sits on the front porch steps. She wishes Amador were here. They have only been together three times, but already she craves his touch, his smell, his quiet assurance that he wants her. And now, confused as she is by Marlene's revelation, she would like Amador by her more than ever, simply to reassure her that what she thinks is happening with him *is* actually happening. She would like to be certain of at least this one thing. But she doesn't even have his phone number.

The following day is Sunday, and Caroline takes the children to the beach. As soon as she parks the car, Ethan bursts out the door and races to the water's edge, throwing himself headlong into the oncoming waves. Will negotiates his way across the sand, clutching a towel over his narrow shoulders to protect himself from the chill of the fall day. Caroline opens the trunk and begins to unload an umbrella and plastic grocery bags of food when she sees that Marlene is still sitting in the car.

"Everything okay?" Caroline asks, coming around to the open door.

"Yeah, sure," Marlene says quickly, and slides out of the car.

"Give me a hand," Caroline says, holding out two grocery bags. Marlene takes them and Caroline hoists the umbrella onto her shoulder and slams the trunk lid. Will is now splashing in the shallows, jumping the small waves that lap the shore. He turns back toward the car and waves his arm. Caroline can tell he's calling to them, but she can't hear his voice through the wind. She walks toward him, stopping to kick off her sandals and squatting down to pick them up with her free hand. When she stands she notices that Marlene is not following her.

"What's wrong?" Caroline says.

"I feel kind of funny . . . in my stomach."

Caroline lays the umbrella and her shoes in the sand and walks back to Marlene.

"Are you sick?"

"I don't think so," Marlene says.

Caroline takes Marlene's face in her hands and lays her lips on her forehead. "No temperature," she says, pulling back. Marlene's eyes are full. "What's wrong?" she asks, dropping her hands.

"I just . . . I don't know if I'm allowed to be here," Marlene says.

"Allowed?"

"I mean this is just . . ." she stops, looking out helplessly at the ocean.

"It's beautiful," Caroline agrees. "Living in the city, you

forget that you're this close to something so . . ." she stops, at a loss for a word that doesn't trivialize this place.

"Strong," Marlene says, finishing the sentence. "My whole life, I've felt something in my body like that," she says, gesturing with her chin at the succession of waves, pushed to shore by the wind. "All jaggedy and like *moving* but not getting anywhere, really."

"Well, you're here now," Caroline says. "You got somewhere."

"Me being here makes everything harder, doesn't it?" Marlene says. She looks at Caroline and then drops her eyes to the sand as if she's not sure she wants the answer.

Will runs toward them, his lower legs kicking out to the sides as he runs, his arms pumping to help him through the sand.

"Look at him," Caroline says, with a sudden swell of love for his effervescence in the face of such awkwardness.

"He's the most honorable person I've ever met," Marlene says.

"Marlene!" Will calls, his voice finally reaching them.

"Is it okay?" Marlene asks again. She seems to be asking for much more than permission to join Will.

"It's right that you are here," Caroline says.

Marlene's smile reveals herself at six, at eight, at an age when this moment was only an impossible fantasy.

"Leave the bags," Caroline says.

Marlene sets the bags down, kicks off her shoes, and races down to the shore to join the boys. Her run turns into a joyous skip that leaves Caroline's chest tight with feeling.

—

*That evening Marlene*, Ethan, and Will sit on the porch outside the front door. Ethan is surprisingly shy around Marlene. He seems unable to comprehend the fact of her. For
the first time he looks to Will for an indication of how to
behave toward the girl. He follows Will's lead.

"It's kind of ugly here," Marlene says, gazing out at the
street. "I mean for a place that's supposed to be so, you know,
*all that*."

"All what?" Will asks.

"You know, like in the magazines."

"You mean like movie stars and—"

"And mansions," Will chimes in on top of Ethan.

"Yeah!" Ethan says, "We've never seen a mansion, right,
Will?"

"They must be somewhere else," Will says thoughtfully.

Marlene looks at the boys affectionately. "I always knew
about you two," she says.

"What did you know?" Will says, eagerly.

"Well, that you existed, for one," she says.

"What else?" Ethan says.

"I knew that Frank chose you over me."

They turn to watch a lowrider sputter noisily down the
street.

"That's cool," Ethan says of the car.

"You like cars?" Marlene says.

"I guess," Ethan says.

"Most boys do," she says. "I don't know why. And, like,

the order of songs on a CD. I mean, who cares about the order of songs on CDs?"

"I don't," Will says.

"You will," she says, smiling, giving him a nudge with her shoulder. "And fart jokes," Marlene says, giggling. "I bet you guys make fart jokes all the time."

"Not me!" Will says. But Ethan is already laughing, and Will can't help but give in and accept that she is right.

"Like everything that comes out of your body is so hysterical," she says.

Ethan produces a magnificent raspberry.

"See?" Marlene says, through her laughter. "I know you better than you think."

Will is so happy to have an older sister who can tease him and tell him who he is, he feels like he will burst. "Shooting star!" he says, pointing up at the sky.

"Airplane, probably," Ethan says.

The three contemplate the sky.

"Sometimes he took us to the observatory," Will says. "And he let us look through the telescope."

"But he didn't like us to touch things," Ethan says. "The knobs and stuff. He got angry one time when I pressed the wrong button. He acted like I'd almost blown up the world or something."

"I bet he got mad a lot," Marlene says, almost hopefully. "I mean the way dads do."

"It wasn't like that," Ethan says. "It was more like he didn't say anything. Like you weren't there."

"He didn't like us to bother him," Will says. "My mom says he was sad a lot and that's why he had to leave us. She said some people have a hard time with regular stuff, like having conversations and playing and stuff. And they feel bad everyday, even when things are good, even if you are nice to them and you don't bother them."

"My mom and him used to fight about it," Ethan says.

"How do you know?" Will says.

"I heard them," Ethan says. "I *heard* them." His voice shakes. Marlene reaches over and puts her hand on his shoulder.

"I thought he would be like a real dad," she says softly.

Ethan shakes his head. "He wasn't."

"That's not your fault," she says.

"Or yours," Will says.

"Right," she says. "He never even knew who I was."

18.

*Monday afternoon Amador* waits at the bus stop. The sickness in his gut occurs daily now. It is the sickness of despising his longing. He has become a meaningless man. He has no meaning in a country that ignores the necessary fact of him. He is meaningless to a wife he failed so long ago when he did not listen to her about the river and his baby died. And now he fails her again by taking Caroline in his arms, and hoping to do it again and again. Sitting on the bus as it roars onto the freeway, his self-reproach pounds at his skull. He tries to pry open one of the windows so he can breathe, but the side of the bus is painted to advertise a television show, and the windows are permanently shut.

When he arrives at Mrs. Eleanor's, he finds the atmosphere tense and dangerous. The boys sit at the kitchen table, not eating the food in front of them. A strange girl sits with them. She twists her hair around her finger nervously. All three look up when Amador enters the room. They are terrified.

"Enough!" It is Mr. Vincent's voice, rising in unbridled frustration from the direction of Mrs. Eleanor's bedroom. "This is what happens!" he yells.

"Dad!" It is Caroline.

"Get away from me!" Mrs. Eleanor's voice breaks through, louder than Amador has ever heard it.

Mr. Vincent enters the kitchen, moving back and forth like a rat in a cage, as he looks for his wallet and keys on the countertops.

"She thinks she's helping her," he says. "Taking her on outings, for God's sake. Showing her pictures of how things used to be. She's frightening her, is what she's doing. My wife is goddamn terrified in there, Amador. You have to do something." He finds his keys and leaves through the kitchen door muttering about missing his class. The three children at the table look down to avoid his fury.

In Mrs. Eleanor's bedroom Amador finds Caroline sitting on the bed. At first he thinks she is embracing her mother. But then he realizes she is trying to pin the old woman down.

"What are you doing?" he says, pulling Caroline away. Mrs. Eleanor has a scratch down her cheek. Her braid is frayed. Hair springs from the plaits like saw grass. The room is too hot, and Mrs. Eleanor is sweating.

"I don't know what's happening," Caroline says. She is frantic. Tears stain her cheeks. "She's scratching her face, hurting herself."

"Open the window," he orders.

"We should call a doctor," she says, as she lifts a window sash.

He strokes Mrs. Eleanor across the forehead and down each arm.

"*Cálmate*," he whispers again and again as she thrashes and moans.

"I don't know what happened," Caroline says weakly. "She just started yelling and hitting herself. Why is she trying to hurt herself?"

"Leave us," he says, for once not worrying about his commanding tone.

"Amador—"

"Go *now*!" he says.

He waits until he hears the door.

"What happen, *mi amor*?" he says to Mrs. Eleanor. "What make you sad?"

"Stop!" Mrs. Eleanor says sharply.

"You want your bath?" he says. "A nice warm bath?"

"Go away!"

"Some food? Maybe you no eat your dinner?"

With tremendous force, she pushes him off her body. Amador steps back from the bed. An object grazes his shoulder. She has thrown a book at him. It lies on the floor by his feet, its pages ruffled and bent. He crouches down to retrieve it just as she throws a pill bottle. It falls, bursting open, and the blue pellets scatter across the carpet.

"Shoo!" she yells. "Shoo!"

He straightens up. Anger seizes his body. She has spoken to him as she would a dog. She holds her water glass in both hands. "Don't do it," Amador says. His voice is low and dangerous. Every muscle in his body tenses; he knows he will attack her if she throws the glass.

She throws it. It falls weakly on the end of the bed, then rolls onto the carpet without breaking. "I hate you," she growls fiercely.

He grabs her under her arms and lifts her roughly from the bed. "It is time for your bath now, Mrs.," he says, avoiding her kicks. It is not a question. He is tired of asking for approval for everything he does, tired of waiting for someone to tell him he has the right to exist. Mrs. Eleanor is right. He acts like a dog that has been beaten so often it ducks its head even when offered a gentle hand.

He untangles Mrs. Eleanor from the sheets and carries her to the bathroom. She sees her disheveled self in the mirror and gasps, bringing her hands to her face in alarm. He sets her down on the bathroom stool and stands back, waiting for her to undress. When she does not move, he yanks the gown over her head. She cries out that he is hurting her, but he doesn't stop. Now she sits naked before him, and he does not turn away. Once she is in the tub, he scrubs her back, her breasts, and between her legs. He works quickly, handling her like any random body. His head is filled with noise, and he can barely hear her protests. He reaches around and loosens the clip that holds her braid. He fills the plastic Tupperware container with water and pours a heavy stream over her hair. She gulps air and coughs out water. He rubs shampoo into her scalp. She screams when the shampoo stings her eyes.

"No, Vincent! Please, no!" She is crying now, not as a

child cries, overwhelmed by all-encompassing but momentary sadness, but as a woman cries, deeply, sorrowfully, for the past.

He sits back on the floor, exhausted. Water has splashed over the lip of the tub during their fight and it now soaks through his pants. He hangs his head.

"I'm sorry," he says. "I'm sorry."

"Vincent," she whimpers.

"No, Mrs. I am not your husband. I have a wife. Her name is Erlinda. I have a wife."

When he finally dares to look at her, he notices beads of water trapped in her eyelashes, refracting the blue of her eyes. Her gaze is desperate, as though she is trying to read a lover's feelings.

Once she is dry and dressed, he sits her at her small vanity table and summons Caroline. "You do it," he says, holding Mrs. Eleanor's wooden hairbrush toward the beautiful daughter.

Tentatively Caroline takes the brush and moves behind her mother. Amador watches her for a moment, mesmerized by the way her fingers follow the brush through Mrs. Eleanor's hair, imagining the feeling of them sliding down his own skin. She looks at him gratefully. It is so easy to cross this line, he thinks. She is the other side, and the border is nothing but a thought. It is nothing but air.


*When he returns home* late that evening, the trailer is dark and bodies fill the main room, sleeping side by side. Silently Amador curses the owner of the trailer. Amador and his roommates pay their rent on time. The man has no right to offer the rooms to his relatives. Amador stumbles over the bodies into his own darkened room. He crouches down, ready to fall onto his mattress and drown this awful night in sleep, when he feels a body. He curses out loud at the stranger who has the nerve to take over his bed and lie beneath his covers.

"*Amigo*," he says darkly. "You are in the wrong bed."

The person, a man by his voice, moves, grunts, falls back to sleep.

"Get out," Amador says more forcefully, prodding the man's shoulder.

The man screams like a wounded cat and bolts up. He throws his hands around Amador's neck and tightens his grip. Amador begins to choke. Finally he manages to break the man's hold and wrestle him off the mattress and onto the floor. Now Amador's hands encircle the man's thin neck. His anger and humiliation well up as he squeezes harder. "This is my room. This is my bed," he roars between gritted teeth. He shakes the body. The man's head bangs against the floor.

"*¡Papá!*"

The voice pierces him. He knows it as surely as he knows the exact timber of his children's laughter, as surely as he can identify their brown heads from all the others in a crowd. He loosens his grip. "Rogelio?"

"*¡No me mates! No me mates!*" the boy cries, covering his face with his arms. He crawls into the corner of the room and curls into a ball.

"No, no," Amador whispers, shaking. "*No te voy hacer*

*nada.*" He crawls cautiously toward his boy, as though approaching a wild animal. He holds out a hand to convince Rogelio of his harmlessness. Slowly Rogelio lowers his arms from around his head.

In the spray of outdoor light, Amador sees his boy. Rogelio's face is caked with dirt. His lips look like the cracked earth of the desert. His clothes are only rags hanging on his impossibly thin body.

"*Aquí estoy,*" Amador whispers, taking his son to his chest. Rogelio sobs as Amador rocks him back and forth. The boy's body feels bigger than Amador remembers, but when was the last time Rogelio cried in his arms? How many years has it been? "*Mi hijo,*" he says over and over, as he kisses Rogelio's head and face. "*Mi hijo.*"

*The next day* Amador purchases a phone card and he and his son place a call home. They stand near the booth as they wait the necessary minutes for the message to be relayed from the telephone office in El Rosario to Erlinda. Amador has given Rogelio one of his T-shirts to wear. His slacks could not be made to fit the boy's narrow hips, so the over-size shirt hangs low over Rogelio's torn pants. Rogelio does not offer much conversation, and to fill up the awkward silence Amador tries to describe what he knows of the city—Hollywood Boulevard, the beaches, Beverly Hills, where the movie stars live—places, Amador realizes as he speaks, he has never seen. A glut of teenage boys passes, wearing pants that fall in elephantine folds around their fat sneakers, and T-shirts to their knees. Amador watches as

Rogelio takes in the group, turning himself away from them as if he is embarrassed to be seen.

"You are braver than any of those boys," Amador says. "You traveled across the world to me." Amador has asked Rogelio a few questions about his journey, but Rogelio is reluctant to offer more than single-word answers, and Amador does not want to demand more and push his son away.

"Everyone speaks Spanish," Rogelio says, when a pair of mothers pushing baby strollers passes.

"Yes," Amador says. "It is a country of a million strangers."

The phone rings. Rogelio looks at Amador fearfully. Amador smiles and puts a hand on his son's shoulder. "Take the phone," he urges. "Let her hear your voice."

"*Mamá?*" Rogelio says into the receiver, and immediately begins to cry so much that he cannot speak.

Amador gently takes the receiver from him. "He is here," he says to his wife.

"Oh, Amador!" Her voice sounds young through her tears, as it did when they first made love and she said his name over and over again, and in his name he heard relief, and salvation, and pure pleasure.

"I want you to come here," Amador says, knowing now that this is exactly what he wants. "All of you. I want my family."

They speak briefly. He tells her he will call her soon to plan her crossing. He hears the fear in her voice, and he reassures her: The border is a thought. It is air. When he hangs up, he takes Rogelio in his arms and holds him close.

He smells his head. It smells of the morning's shampoo, but beneath that smell is the earthy, bodily smell of his child, of all his children. All four of them.

Amador takes Rogelio to a store on the boulevard and buys him new clothes. Rogelio is tentative about picking out what he likes, and Amador has to encourage him to choose more than one shirt, more than one pair of pants. Rogelio follows his father's suggestions and is careful to thank him for each purchase, as if Amador is a distant relative who has come to visit bearing unnecessary gifts. Amador worries about Rogelio's uncharacteristic submissiveness. Has the journey leached some essential fight from Rogelio's nature? Once again he feels that he cannot have a conversation with his son, but it is not Rogelio's anger that stands in the way anymore, but something darker and more disturbing. He cannot allow himself to think of who or what has hurt his son in ways unimaginable while he was lost. Walking out of the shop, Rogelio clutches his shopping bag to his chest. He stares at the other shoppers warily. He startles when a passing store clerk accidentally brushes against him.

Amador buys hamburgers and leads Rogelio to a park. They sit at a picnic table, watching young children stumble up and down a field, chasing a soccer ball. A few men run after them, calling out directions, cheering wildly when someone's foot connects with the ball and heads it in the right direction. Rogelio watches everything as if he is taking in the customs of a place where he is not meant to stay. Amador knows he must speak or risk losing his son again.

"I'm sorry," he says, knowing no other way to begin. Rogelio does not look at him. Amador knows he is owed no help from his son and continues. "Because I have made it difficult for you."

Rogelio does not respond. "It's good that you are here," Amador says, then chides himself for missing the point. "I'm so happy you are here," he says.

Still Rogelio is silent, and Amador wonders whether he can ever say what the boy needs to hear. "I know that you hate me," he says.

"I don't hate you," Rogelio mumbles. "You are my father."

"You can say anything to me," Amador says encouragingly.

Words play silently on Rogelio's lips, words he is unwilling or unable to say. He slams his fist down onto the picnic table in frustration.

"Say it," Amador says.

"I just——" Rogelio stops. "I can't," he says, defeated, cradling his head in his hands.

"Please," Amador says. He pleads with his son the way he wished he had that afternoon at the butterfly sanctuary when they were both too proud and too frightened of each other.

"When I was coming here," Rogelio says, "even when I was with other people, I was alone. Like when you left. I don't want to be alone anymore, *Papá*."

Amador reaches across the table and folds his hand around Rogelio's clenched fist. He tightens his grip so that Rogelio will feel him. "Look at my eyes," he says. "I will never again leave you alone."

19.

*During the bus ride* to Mrs. Eleanor's home, Rogelio begins to tell the story of his journey. Amador says nothing, deciding that reacting to the terrible, terrifying situations his son endured will only appear as judgment. But he cannot stop from thinking how many times and in how many ways his son might have been killed, and the thoughts nearly make him gasp out loud.

They get off the bus. Night has fallen, and Amador leads Rogelio toward Mrs. Eleanor's house. Rogelio has finished his story. He seems exhausted, as though the memories caused him nearly the same terror as the actual events.

"*Papá*," he says so softly that Amador almost doesn't hear him.

"Yes?"

"There is something I didn't tell you."

"No. You don't have to say anything more," Amador says, not wanting to hear that even worse things have befallen his son.

"I have to. It's something I did. Something bad. I have to tell you."

Amador faces his son. "All right," he says.

Rogelio reaches into his pocket and brings out an object in his fist. When he opens his palm, a necklace with a large stone at the center glitters in the streetlights.

"I stole it," Rogelio says. "Right off the neck of a woman. We know her. Mirelia Cortez."

"Mirelia Cortez?"

"She wasn't the only one," Rogelio says. "I told them that I would kill them, and then I robbed them all. They were screaming." His whole body begins to shake. "I can still hear them. Little kids. Babies. *Papá*. They thought I would kill them. And I would have. If they didn't give me what I wanted, I was going to kill them."

Amador puts his hands on his son's shoulders. "No," he says, firmly. "You were not going to kill them. Do you understand me? You were not going to hurt anyone."

Rogelio looks up at him, his watery eyes asking for reassurance.

"I know you," Amador says. "I know who you are. You are a good, strong boy. You will never hurt anyone in your life." He takes the necklace from Rogelio's hand. "We'll send it back to her," he says calmly.

—

*Amador and Rogelio* stand outside the front door of Mrs. Eleanor's house. When he presses the doorbell, Amador feels his stomach drop.

"You don't have to ring the bell," Caroline says, laughing lightly as she opens the door. She still wears her black waitress uniform. Her hair is caught up in a bun. Loose tendrils trail down her cheeks. Her smile quickly turns to confusion as she takes in the boy by Amador's side.

"This is my son," he says. "This is Rogelio."

"But that's wonderful!" she exclaims, smiling at Rogelio. Her smile is so generous, so filled with appreciation of his joy. Her kindness weakens Amador. He thinks of her legs wrapped around his back, the smooth stretch of her throat when she leans her head back in pleasure, the gratitude in her eyes.

"Come in," she says, widening the door, and he can see now that she is working hard to bury her feelings. "The boys will be so excited. And Marlene."

The desire to walk into that house and resume everything as it was overwhelms him. He resists entering.

"Come," Caroline says, looking at Rogelio. "*Por favor.*"

She introduces Rogelio to the boys and Marlene. The boys say "Hi" and wave shyly. Marlene bursts forth with an unexpected greeting in Spanish.

"School," she says, by way of an explanation. "*Me llamo Marlene,*" she says to Rogelio.

Rogelio looks to his father, who nods encouragingly. "*Me llamo Rogelio.*"

"*¿Dónde está el discoteca?*"

Rogelio and Amador look at each other in confusion. Then everyone laughs.

"That's pretty much all I remember," Marlene says. "I mostly suck at school."

Caroline and Amador leave the children together in the bedroom and walk to the kitchen. Caroline opens a cupboard and takes the hot cocoa mix from a shelf. She hands it to Amador.

"I cannot work no more for you family," he says when she holds out the teapot.

"I don't understand," she says. The color disappears from her cheeks. Her features seem to float apart from one another, as if they have lost their way on her face.

"I don't belong here with you," he says.

Her eyes fill. She nods. He knows she cannot speak. "My family is coming. My children. My wife."

"What will you do?" she asks weakly.

"I get another job."

She nods, attempts a smile. "Your kids will learn English."

"They can teach me," he says, smiling.

"And your wife?" she ventures.

He smiles at her. How brave she is to ask this question, the answer to which she must know will cause her pain. And what about his wife? Will it be any better in this country? Will they be able to put aside the past they got lost in and find each other again? "She tell me she have a dream of two butterflies together," he says.

"A dream," she says, smiling.

"A dream," he repeats.

She puts the pot on the counter, then picks it up again. She puts her hand over her mouth and nods.


*He walks into* Mrs. Eleanor's bedroom, and stands by her bed for a few minutes, watching her untroubled sleep. Perhaps it would be better to leave without speaking to her. What will she remember, anyway? Won't this visit only cause her needless pain?

"Mrs.," he says.

Her eyes open. "Amor," she says, dreamily.

He smiles. "Amador."

"Is it time?" she says.

"Time for what, Mrs.?"

She doesn't answer.

He sits down on the side of her bed. "I leave you now," he says, taking her hand in his. "I am not coming back. You understand me, Mrs.?"

She looks at him steadily. Her eyes are clear like the water of a fast-moving river. He sees the light burning behind those eyes. She understands him.

"You're going away?"

"Yes, Mrs."

"Forever?"

"Yes."

"You won't go away."

His heart sinks. She does not understand. He must make her know this truth so that one day, when she looks for him and he is not there, she will not be frightened. "No, Mrs.," he says. "I am going. I am not coming back."

"You won't go away. I'll remember you," she says.

"Oh, Mrs.," he says. How will she remember him when she can't remember that Tuesday follows Monday, or that those two boys in her house are her own dear grandsons? He is too new to her life for her to remember him the way she remembers her childhood on a farm of olives or dances in barns where young men smiled at her. Won't he evaporate from her memory the minute he walks out the door?

He wonders where her memories go when she loses them. Is the life they represent erased as casually as a child wipes out sums on a blackboard with his fist? Is it gone? He is overwhelmed by the finality of this choice to remove himself from this house, this old lady, the lonely, lovely woman standing in the kitchen in her uniform. But there are Rogelio and his brother and sister, and Erlinda. And there is Rubén, too, whose memory he must never again, *never again*, run from.

"I am sorry," he says, bending his head. She puts her hand on his hair.

"Don't be sad," she says.


*Later, after Amador* has gone and Caroline has absorbed the full fact of his departure, she checks on the three children. The boys are asleep. Marlene lies on the floor in the sleeping bag. She clutches her pillow to her chest. Caroline gently tries to remove the pillow in order to put it under Marlene's head, but Marlene's hands close around the pillow more tightly. Caroline wonders if Marlene's physical response has become tangled with her unconscious, and whether she dreams that someone is taking something from her. Caroline silently vows that she will never take anything from these children again. But as soon as she makes this commitment, she knows, inevitably, that she will break it. Marlene will leave in two weeks. How will she not understand this as some fresh rejection? And the boys will have to suffer that loss too. They will blame Caroline for "sending" the girl away, as if Caroline had any right to keep her.

She stays awake in the living room until her father returns from work. She expects Vincent to be furious at the news of Amador's departure, but he only nods his head as if he has been expecting as much. It is nearly midnight. Vincent stands in the living room doorway. She sits on her bed. It is the first time she has unfolded the couch while he is still awake. Once the opened bed felt too intimate, too exposed. But there is nothing to hide.

"I don't blame Amador," Vincent says. "It's a burnout job. I burned out, didn't I?" His eyes skip around the room, avoiding hers.

"Oh, Dad," she says sadly.

"I'll have to finish out the week of classes," he says. "Maybe you can cover until then. I hate to ask you."

"Why?" she says. "Why do you hate to ask me?"

"That's not why you came here," he says.

"Why *did* I come here?"

He looks at her the way he used to when she was sixteen, when he was scared of what she might do or say next to hurt him.

"I'm asking you because I need to know," she says.

"I don't think I can help you," he says, beginning to leave the room.

"Dad, sit by me." She pats the bed. "Please?"

Awkwardly he sits next to her.

"Why do people leave?" she says.

"Oh, Carrie," he says warily. "I can't do this now. It was so long ago."

She puts a gentle hand on his knee. "I need your help, Dad. To do this next part. I just have to understand why he left us."

He shakes his head. "I don't know," he says. "Maybe people leave to try to get rid of themselves. To get lost in the world."

She nods. "I just can't imagine leaving them," she says. "Ever. It terrifies me to think about it."

"They're lucky boys."

"Not lucky," she says, shaking her head. "No one's lucky."

They sit together in silence.

"Let's take care of Mom together," she says.

His shoulders rise and fall with a deep, unburdening sigh. His body seems suddenly smaller, as though he has finally let go the weight of his buried grief.

20.

*It is twilight.* Erlinda, Miguel, and Berta walk through the square for the last time. They pass faces they've seen for years, faces they have relied on as familiar markers just as they rely on the rise of a certain hill, the cant of a particular tree. These people are features of the landscape they are leaving now, forever. They pass a group of young men who talk and laugh, and Erlinda notices how Miguel is mesmerized by the swagger and low laughter, the rich scent of men's bodies. He is getting ready for his father.

The next day, she leaves the children with her sister and climbs the mountain to see the butterflies one last time. The insects fly—a thousand, a million sparks of fire. Rubén's cross is cocked at an angle like one of Berta's loose teeth. She kneels before it and straightens the weather-beaten wood, patting the earth around it so it will continue to stand at attention, at least for a while longer. She tries to remember Rubén's small face, but the faces of her other children crowd out his image. His smell is their smell, his laughter, theirs.

She's sold everything she owns—her house, her furniture, her pots and pans. She is surprised by how easy it is to let go of the things of her life. But this cross, this child . . .

Rogelio once told her angrily that Rubén was not in this place anymore. Perhaps he needed Rubén to be gone in order to find room for himself. But she knows Rubén is here. He will always be on this mountainside among the butterflies that travel so many thousands of miles south each year so that their babies can travel those same thousands of miles back north. Rubén will be here, looking over a dusty, forsaken, beautiful town. He began and ended here. He is dirt. He is air. He is food for new life.

"You are with me always," she says. She leans forward and kisses the cross.

Three nights later, she stands by the bank of a shallow river, holding Berta in her arms and clutching Miguel by one hand. They watch as others walk across, holding bags and water jugs and children. She thinks that her life up to this point has been a gathering. She collected the past in her arms and held it close, hoping it would provide the necessary ballast to weight her family to this earth. Now she feels like a stone about to be released from a slingshot.

"When will we see *Papá* and Rogelio?" Berta asks.

"Soon," Erlinda says. "Very soon."

The *pollero* signals her. Together she and her children wade into the water.

—

*Caroline, Will, and Ethan* accompany Marlene to the airport. The three are not allowed to go past the security checkpoint so they say their good-byes there. Marlene hugs each of them. The girl's body feels fragile in Caroline's arms. She wants to reassure Marlene that she will be all right, that life will be full of good things that will fill the hole in her heart. But all she can do with assurance is reiterate her plan to have Marlene visit the following summer.

"Promise?" Marlene asks.

"Promise," Caroline says.

She watches as Marlene hikes her little bag onto her shoulder and lifts her small suitcase filled with the clothes Caroline bought her to wear during her stay. Marlene throws out a jaunty wave. Will keeps his hand raised long after Marlene has disappeared through the metal detector. Caroline thinks that if he could, he would keep his hand raised forever, so that Marlene would always be able to find her way back to him. She touches his hair. How does he already know that everyone needs a beacon to help find their way home? Generous, knowing boy.

That night, after sending the boys to bed, Caroline steps into the scalding bath. Her body stiffens as it withstands the shock of heat. The sting is almost unbearable, a necessary kind of pain. She lowers herself bit by bit. When her skin and blood finally find their equilibrium, she is able to sit.

She has lost Amador. Well, they never belonged to each other, she thinks, gently splashing water over her breasts and shoulders. Even making love, their mutual sorrows formed a wall that separated them. But she will always be grateful to him for being there. *Being there.* It occurs to her that it is not given to us to occupy the life we live, that we must choose each day to be present.

She is overcome by a need to see her sons in their beds, to be sure of them. She steps out of the tub, quickly dries herself, and dresses in her robe. The boys' room is warm and smells of food and the insides of old sneakers—a good, safe smell. Ethan snores lightly, lying on his back. How she loves to see him running at full speed, jumping over five steps at a time on his skateboard, confounding her with his physical knowingness. She has come to rely on his assurance. It reminds her that there are reasons to be confident, to look forward with certain faith that you can run and not fall. She sits at the end of Will's bed and leans back against the wall. He looks older to her now. Maybe the time of running and leaping is coming to an end. Maybe her sons' lives will turn inward, away from her, and she will have to bear that departure. Will's hand hangs off the side of the bed, as if he is dipping his fingers into the calm waters of a dream whose contents she will never know. She stands up from the bed, leans over each boy, and feels the smooth cool of their cheeks on her lips. The smell of Marlene's cheap perfume still lingers in the room. It reminds Caroline warmly of uncomplicated things.

Vincent dozes in front of the television in the living room. She will let him rest. There will be so much to do tomorrow, and the day after and after that. She checks on her mother. The spill of light from the hallway illuminates the smooth covers of the bed. She thinks it amazing that her mother can be so motionless in her sleep. Perhaps Eleanor does not flee her dreams the way Caroline does, fighting her sheets and blankets into a twist each night for reasons she can never remember in the morning. Lucky, Caroline thinks, approaching her mother.

Then, a sudden sickening knowledge spreads through her chest. She snaps on the bedroom light. Her mother is gone.

*Will sits in the kitchen* next to his sleepy-eyed brother, both of them having been woken by their mother's frantic cries. He listens while Vincent calls the police. At first his grandfather seems purposeful, dictating his wife's description and address. But then his voice falters, and he puts his hand to his face. "I'll go look for her," Vincent says as he hangs up the phone and heads out the kitchen door. A half hour later he returns without her. "I drove everywhere," he says.

"Where does she go?" Caroline says, alarmed.

"Amador was always the one who found her," Vincent says.

"What is she looking for?" Caroline says.

"I don't know," Vincent says.

"I know where she is," Will says.

"And the police haven't even come yet," Caroline says, ignoring Will. "It's been thirty minutes."

"I know where she is," Will repeats.

His grandfather and mother look at him.

"Honey, we'll find her. Don't worry," Caroline says, laying a hand on his back.

But his grandfather continues to stare at him. "Where?"

"I can't explain it," Will says. "I have to show you."

"Will," his mother says warningly.

"No," Vincent says, putting out a hand to stop Caroline. He turns back to Will. "Show me," he says.

Will leads the family away from the house. The night is starless and moonless. Light from the streetlamps hovers gauzily above the ground. Will tries to mask his tentative steps. Without much light, he has to remember everything.

"Go to the corner and turn right at the house with the stone rabbits in the garden," he says, as they reach that exact house. "Cross the street at the crosswalk that was just repainted."

"There?" Ethan says, pointing.

"To the house with the fairy-tale roof that looks like melted chocolate. There is a sidewalk that shines."

"I see it," Vincent says.

His grandfather's attention gives Will confidence. "It's down this street," he says, turning a corner.

"It's a dead end," Caroline says, her voice rising with worry. "She's not here. Dad, we should go back to the house and wait for the police."

"It's not a dead end," Will says.

"Will, honey," Caroline says tensely. "I know you're trying to help."

"I *am* helping," he says.

"It's not a game!" she says angrily.

Will walks down the street alone. His heart beats quickly. It is dark. He can barely make out the porch lights of the houses along the street. He wants to stop, to call out for

Ethan to come and be the leader. But Will is the only one who knows the way. At the end of the street he climbs over the metal barrier.

"Will!" his mother calls from behind him. "Will. Come back here!"

He clears the barrier and begins to move down the brushy slope toward the fence. Beyond is an embankment lit fully by a string of safety lights leading down to what he knew would be there, what his grandmother always said was there: the river.

The river is a concrete causeway that stands nearly empty except for a ribbon of shallow water moving desultorily through it. Swirling letters of graffiti decorate the sides—fat, colorful names and spiky, crudely drawn declarations of love and existence. Ethan reaches Will first and climbs nimbly up and over the fence, deftly avoiding the spikes that poke out at the top. Once he is on the other side, he tries to walk down the slanted sidewall, but falls and slides the rest of the way. At the bottom, he looks up and down the corridor and then suddenly runs. "Grandma!" he calls out, splashing through the shallow water.

Will looks in the direction Ethan is running and sees a vague shape standing on an overpass. A car drives by and lights up the ghostly figure. "Grandma!" he cries.

Caroline reaches Will. "Mom!" she calls, seeing what he sees. "Don't move!"

Vincent is already rushing along the perimeter of the fence toward Eleanor. Will wishes he could be like his brother and run in the darkness. He reaches out and grabs his mother's arm.

"I'll help you, Mom," he says, hoping she will not notice his need. Together they make their way along the uneven ground alongside the fence. Caroline shakes her arm from Will's and begins to run but turns back when she senses he is not with her. "Grandma's there," she says. "Come on!"

He takes a step, then stops. "I can't," he says.

"Will," she says impatiently.

"I can't see."

She says nothing for a moment. Then she walks back to him and holds him by the shoulders, staring into his face. "Will?" she says.

"I can't see, Mommy. I can't see." He wants to say it again and again, to confirm its truth, to free himself of his secret. Will she be mad at him? Will she leave him too?

She takes his hand. "Come on, baby. I won't let you go."

By the time Will and his mother arrive on the overpass, Vincent and Ethan are already there. Vincent stands behind Eleanor, cloaking her with his arms.

"Mom!" Caroline says breathlessly. "What are you doing here?"

Eleanor looks at Caroline and smiles. "It's beautiful by the river," she says.

Vincent lifts his hand to her hair and pats down the strands that fly loose in the night wind. "It is," he says. "Beautiful."

"Once the river overflowed," Eleanor says.

"There's no water in the river, Mom," Caroline says gently.

"No," Vincent corrects her. "She's right. It happened. A long time ago."

"The things that got carried away in that river!" Eleanor

exclaims. "They found dogs and a cow! And a stove! Remember, Vince?"

"You could catch a fish in the river back then," Vincent says. His eyes shine.

Will stares into the nearly empty corridor. He imagines water rising up until it overflows the sidewalls, soaking the ground where he and his family stand. He can almost hear the powerful sound of the river rushing toward the sea. He imagines the dogs and cows spinning in the current, their feet twirling, marking out the pattern of a dance.

He closes his eyes. He can see it all.